White Sheets

White Sheets

MAE BASHA'

Library of Congress Control Number: 2021913904

PAPERBACK: 978-1-955955-32-4
EBOOK: 978-1-955955-33-1

Ordering Information:

For orders and inquiries, please contact:
1-888-404-1388
www.goldtouchpress.com
book.orders@goldtouchpress.com

Printed in the United States of America

Thank you; to My God for all my blessing and for those to come.

This book is dedicated to my late mother Mary Jackson (who I miss every hour). To my two sons Demetrius and Sedrick, stick to your dreams, and to my sister Geraldine.

Chapter 1

She squints as tears run from her eyes because of the pain generated in her body when she moves. It has been a very difficult birth for her small frame. Her heart is racing. Soon she will have to move to sit upright in a straight back chair. It has been eight days, and she is still in pain and bleeding to the point of weakness. The local doctor will make a house visit to check the baby and her mother, who will pose as the birth mother to keep the secret—no, to keep the lie about the baby from others. Lucille, her mother, is a big-boned heavy woman who can hide a pregnancy well. Netta is a large girl for her age of twelve. Lucille made her wear large dresses and bind her belly to keep the growth of her womb from showing.

Netta matured early as a child. By the time she was eight and a half, she had a menstrual cycle and breasts. It was about that time that her mother met Walter, her live-in boyfriend.

Lucille works late at night. Netta gets to go to school and cook for the family most of the time during the week. Walter works at the lumberyard part time, so he would be with Netta majority of the time. Netta has to go to bed early; she has to wake in the predawn hours to prepare for the long distance to school. She only sees her mother in the early morning and in some weekends when work allows.

From time to time, the men who work with Walter will come over in the evening and sit under the big sweet gum tree in the yard. The men talk of their dreams and the adventures that have brought them to this place in time. Often Walter calls for Netta to bring a pail of water out to the tree to help chase down the homemade whiskey that they drink from glass jars and discarded handy bean cans.

One day, most of the men leave to go home except Levy, who is a drifter. He has been in town only a few weeks. Levy secured himself work at the lumberyard and befriended Walter because other men look up to him. On that night, Walter is very tired and falls asleep while leaning in a chair against the sweet gum tree. Levy taps Walter on the knee to say good night. Realizing Walter is completely asleep, Levy makes his way to the house.

He stands in the doorway that leads to the kitchen. He can see Netta washing her body by the light of the oil lamp. Levy watches the young girl, who is still a child but with a woman's form. He watches her like an animal watches its prey. As Netta completed her nightly wash, Levy knocks on the door. This frightens Netta.

"Walter is under the tree in the yard,"

Netta says.

"I know," Levy replies.

"You want something?" Netta asks. Levy's eyes scan the room.

"Walter says I can have some bread to take with me. I will sleep in the shack down by the lumberyard."

"I guess it's okay then," Netta answers. Levy starts into the room.

"Can I have a cold glass of water? With that, would you give me a glass?"

Netta walks with a pail of water in her hand. She passes it to Levy. He manages to press up against her as she passes by. She empties the water out at the edge of the back porch. She can see Walter by the tree. She calls for him, but he does not answer.

"He's just fell asleep," Levy answers in a hurry.

"Excuse me," she says. Netta has to cross his path again in order to reach the glass for the water.

Levy waits until Netta steps up on a chair to reach a glass. Then he grabs her around her waist with one hand and around the throat with the other.

"Don't say a word. I just want to kiss you." Netta is paralyzed with fear. "Show me where you sleep." As they leave the kitchen, Levy glances back at the sweet gum tree to make sure Walter is still asleep. They enter a small bedroom. Levy starts to stroke Netta's hair and shoulders.

"You are real pretty, you know? Turn around here." By now, Levy's breathing has changed.

"All I want is a little kiss. Have you ever kissed a boy before?" Netta rapidly shakes her head to answer *no* in mute fashion. Placing his hands on both sides of her face, he forces a whiskey-smelling kiss and steals her innocence.

"Don't you scream! If you do, I will stab you with my blade." Netta never knows this type of horror. There is no bogeyman in her life; her favorite book is *Mother Goose.* The pain and ripping of her body causes her to pass out even though her eyes are fixed. Soon she can feel her body being shaken in a jerking manner.

"You hear me, and hear me good. If you tell anybody about this I will push Walter into the standing saw at the lumberyard and come back and kill you and your mother living out here alone." As he pulls up his pants, he runs out the door.

Netta lies shaking in shock all night until she hears the rooster crowing, preparing for the day.

Netta can hear her mother in the kitchen. "Netta, come on in here, I hear you in there," she says.

"Yes, ma'am." Netta slowly turns and starts to put on her panties. She puts her dress on in a hurry for fear her mother may come into the room. She balls her gown up in a small ball and places it under the bed. She hopes that she can clean it before her mother notices.

"I love you. Here is some milk," Lucille says, smiling. "I figured you would want some since you left the glass down."

"I getta go. I need to be early for the spelling test," Netta mutters.

"Okay, be careful. Love you. Bye."

On the long walk to school, her longtime friend, Connie, joins Netta. "Why you so quiet and looking all mad, Netta?" Connie says as she bends her head to look at Netta's bowed face. "Why are you mad at me, Netta?" Connie begs. Netta can see the school in the distance. She runs off; Connie comes running behind her.

For the next few days, Netta is caught up in a dream world of bad nightmares and unexplained emotions. She tries so hard to sort things out in her head. She starts staying in her room more. A chair is placed up against the door even in the daylight.

Two weeks later, Lucille loses one of her jobs. It is bittersweet, but this way, Lucille is able to spend more time with Netta and Walter. This is the first in a long time that the three of them can eat supper together almost every night. It makes Netta feel a little safer to know that her mother will be with her in the evenings.

On Thursday night at supper, Walter says, "Some of the fellows are coming by after work tomorrow if it does not rain, okay?" Netta panics and chokes on her food; she stops eating at once.

"Slow down. Lately, you have been eating up everything in the house," her mother tells her. Netta leaves the table and goes into her room.

Later that night, Netta begins to scream out in her sleep, "Don't let him hurt me, don't let him hurt me!" Lucille has to push her way into Netta's room.

"What is the matter with you, baby? You are having a bad dream." Lucille comforts her child as a mother would. Netta never says why.

On Friday morning, Lucille calls for Netta to come and eat before she goes to school. Netta runs out of her room, goes straight to the back porch, and throws up.

"Netta, are you feeling bad?" Lucille places a cool wet rag on Netta's forehead. "Maybe you should stay at home today."

"No, Mama, please don't make me stay here alone. Can I go over to Aunt Dean's to stay? It is on my way to school," Netta manages to say in between the panting.

"Okay, I will send her a note."

Dean is Lucille's eldest sister. She has two sets of twins that are nine months apart. Netta is now eleven. Dean will be happy to have the help.

"Aunt Dean, Aunt Dean, it's me," Netta says as she opens the back door. "Here is a note from Mama. She says I can stay with you today."

"Sure, baby, me and the twins are always glad to have you here with us. Now let me see what your mother has written here. Hum, she says you might be getting close to your period. You are sick this morning?" Dean asks while placing her hand on Netta's forehead. "Okay, better safe than sorry. Go get a pad out of the top dresser drawer in my bedroom. Put it on just in case you start during the day."

Netta goes into the bathroom. While placing the white cloth pad in her panties, it reminds her of the horror of that day. Her body was still hurting. It feels like she has been stabbed between the thighs. Netta slowly walks back into the kitchen.

"You want to help me feed the boys before the girls wake up. They are always hungry when they first wake up," Dean says with a smile. "When your Mama comes to pick you up this evening, I am going to tell her about the Johnson's house. They are leaving town, and the house next door will be vacant. I want to see us closer together, and besides, the electric company will not put poles out your way for another year or so. This way, you can come over all the time and stay with the twins and me. Would you like that?"

"Netta, Netta, did you hear what I say? Oh, poor baby, are you in pain? I will put some tea on for you."

"Thank you, Aunt Dean, it doesn't hurt much now," Netta replies slowly and withdrawn.

"Oh, remind me to tell your mother they need someone to bake at the new bakery."

Netta walks around in a trance all day once the sun has come out. Sunshine is not what she had hopes for that day. The fear starts to build inside her; today, she wishes for rain. If it rains, the men will not be able to come to sit under the sweet gum tree after work.

Looking out of the kitchen, Dean finds her staring at the movement of the leaves in the tree from the blowing breeze.

"We need to get the washing done. Do you feel like helping me?" Dean asks Netta. "We can let the boys play close to the porch, and the girls can stay on the porch in the play box Walter built for us." Dean and Netta go to the backyard; they start the fire under the big black pot sitting upside down in the yard.

"We are going to need a lot of hot water today. The girls are cutting teeth," Dean says.

The time passes fast on this day. Soon the water is boiling. "Okay, ready to slang the first load, Netta. Get the paddle from the porch, please."

"Do you want to wring or scrub? We can take turns, okay?" Netta starts to scrub the white diapers on the scrub board. A strange feeling comes over her as she begins to scrub the diapers up and down. With all her might, she forcefully pushes the diaper downward; she can feel the force rubbing up against her knuckles. Downward and downward, she pushes until she scrubs the skin loose on her fingers.

"Honey, you will scrub the white out of those diapers if you keep that up.

Why don't you wring and hang for a little while?"

Dean watches Netta and notices she is not really there in her spirit. But in the same thought, she blames it on Netta's monthly period. Washing and cleaning the babies consumes most of the day.

It is getting late. The sun has shifted farther west, and the shade is over the freshly washed clothes. It is time to take in the wash and fold it for another day's wear. Once the clothes are taken into the house, Dean suggests feeding and giving the twins a bath before folding the clothes. That way, they will not be interrupted.

For the first time, Netta really examines the difference between the twin boys and the twin girls. It is still so confusing to her; she has helped with the twin's bath before but never noticed. Once the twins are fed and cleaned, they are ready to sleep. Once the twins are on their beds, Netta and Dean are free to fold the clothes on the kitchen table.

"Netta, you have been distant today. Are you feeling any better now?"

"I am okay, Auntie. Don't forget to tell Mama about the house and the job when she comes. I don't like living out on the edge of town."

Dean starts to sing church songs. "Sing with me, Netta." Netta just obeys.

"Hello, anybody home?" It is Lucille. Lucille goes to Netta, hugs her, and asks if she is feeling better.

"Lucille, the Johnsons are moving. I know the owner of the house. Maybe you would like to move. I would like to have the family closer rather than strangers with a lot of children to deal with," Dean says. "Oh yeah, the new bakery needs bakers, and nobody can bake like my little sister. I hear the pay is good."

"Mama, can we please move up here?" Netta says, begging.

"I will see. We can ask Walter. The lumberyard will be sending people away soon. It's getting close to the slow months."

"But Walter always manages to work. He is a very resourceful man," Dean interjects.

"Netta, did you have a good time with the twins? I need to see them even if they are asleep," Lucille says as she leaves the room. "Girl, you get your hands full, but they look so peaceful."

"Yeah, sometimes when Paul comes home, the boys will wake up to see their daddy. Paul thinks it is cute. It is work for me!" Dean says.

"Okay, Netta, you get everything, let's get on our way. Thank you," Lucille says as she kisses her sister on the forehead. Netta starts to shake and cry.

"Honey, what is it? What is the matter? Answer me, Netta," Lucille says anxiously.

Netta jumps up from the table, runs out the door, and throws up. Lucille chases after her, and Dean stands just inside the back door.

"Mama, Mama, please don't make me go home."

"Why not ... why not?" Lucille now turns Netta's face into the light. She wants to see Netta's eyes when she answers.

"Tell me why." Dean is now standing next to her sister in support.

"Honey, tell us why." Both Lucille and Dean are now very concerned.

"That man is going to be under the tree with Walter," Netta says, shaking.

"What man?" Lucille and Dean say at the exact same time. Lucille's heart is racing now. She kneels to Netta.

"Did he do something to you?"

"Yes, ma'am. He hurt me and told me he would kill Walter at the lumberyard and come back and kill you and me if I told."

"How did he hurt you?" Netta slowly presses her hand between her legs.

Without speaking a word, Lucille runs into the kitchen and takes the large knife off the cutting board. Lucille pushes past Dean and Netta with a look of murder in her eyes.

"Lucille, wait, please wait! Paul will be here soon. Please wait!" Dean shouts with tears in her eyes.

Nothing or no one can stop Lucille's rage. All she needs is the full moon of that October night to find the man that hurt her baby. Lucille runs and stumbles along the road. She is being driven by a mother's hurt and her daughter's shame.

Meanwhile, Netta is crying for her mother. She is afraid this man will hurt or kill her mother. She tries to run after her mother, but Dean stops her, hugging Netta tightly to control her. Dean urges, "We have to go into the house to get a look at you. Come with me, Netta".

Dean walks Netta into the bedroom. "Baby, you need to take off your panties and lie down on the bed for me, okay?" Netta slowly moves to obey her aunt.

"Now open your legs. Tell me if I hurt you, okay?" Dean positions Netta's body toward the light. She covers her mouth and fights back the tears when she sees how Netta's young body has been torn and ripped. Netta goes into a trance with tears running down her face. Dean picks up Netta limp body and rocks her back and forth to comfort her.

"Where is everybody?" A voice calls from the kitchen. It is Paul, Dean's husband.

"In here, Paul," Dean answers.

"Hi, what's the problem?" Paul asks. Sobbing, Dean answers, "Some man raped Netta." Paul rushes to the bed and sits down on the edge. In disillusion, he looks at the floor.

"Paul, please see if you can catch up with Lucille. She took a knife to kill this man. He should be at Lucille's house with Walter now," Dean explains.

"At Lucille's house with Walter?" Paul asks in surprise.

"He is one of the men who sit under the sweet gum tree. Netta does not know his name." Paul gets into his truck and starts driving toward Lucille's house.

By the time Paul drives away from his house, Lucille arrives at hers. Lucille bypasses the front porch and goes to the back of her house where the sweet gum tree is located. When Lucille reaches the sweet gum tree, she sees only empty seats. Unknown to her, Walter is watching her from the kitchen window.

"Lucille," he calls to her. She turns. He sees she has a knife in her hand and rage in her eyes. Lucille runs to the kitchen.

"Where is he, where is he?" she screams.

"Where is who?" Walter answers.

"The man who raped my baby," she says as she tries to catch her breath.

Lucille just collapses to her knees on the floor, screaming and crying. Walter grabs her by both arms, gently lifts her from the floor, and places her in a chair. He asks her to start from the beginning and tell him everything. Lucille can hardly explain; she cannot tell him who the man is. Walter slowly takes the knife away from Lucille.

Walter wants to talk with Netta. He needs her to describe what the rapist looks like. He explains to Lucille why the men are not under the sweet gum tree. "Tom Johnson, who works with me at the lumberyard, will have a barbecue tomorrow. Johnson and his family are moving away, and everybody is invited," Walter explains.

"Lucille, Walter, where are you?" They can hear someone calling from the back porch. It is Paul. "Dean asks me to find Lucille. She told me what happened."

"We need to get to Netta right away. I need to find out what son of a bitch raped her," Walter says to Paul.

"Okay, I have my truck outside. Let's go." Lucille and Paul climb into the truck; Walter hops on the back. It seems like a painful eternity to Lucille driving back to Dean's house, but in reality, it takes only minutes.

Before Paul can come to a complete stop, Walter jumps off the truck and runs to the kitchen in back of the house. Netta and Dean are frightened by his sudden entry. Walter bends down on his knees in front of Netta, who is sitting in a chair and drinking water.

"Baby girl, I am so sorry. Who did this to you? Tell me, and I will make it right. I promise," Walter says to her as he holds both her hands in his. Netta holds her head down in sadness and shame. She cannot find the words to say it again. Netta hears Lucille enter the room.

"Baby, go ahead and tell Walter what you said to me and your aunt Dean." Lucille kneels and tilts Netta's face up toward the light with her hand.

Netta feels tightness in her chest. She places her hand over her heart. She takes a deep breath and begins to retell the story to Walter with all her might. Walter listens in disbelief as this child tells him how someone he brought into their life had done her wrong and threatened to kill them all.

"What is his name?"

"I don't know," Netta says.

"What clothes did he wear?"

"A blue and white shirt and a pair of overalls," Netta says as she wrings her hands together.

"Netta, I know this is hard, but you have to tell me more, okay?" Walter says, trying to hide the madness that is raging inside. "Does he have a wife and children around here anywhere?"

"I don't know," Netta replies.

"Do you know where he lives?"

Netta says slowly, "In a shack by the lumberyard."

"Levy," Walter says, grinding his teeth. Walter turns and runs out of the kitchen without speaking. Paul runs after him.

"Wait a minute, Walter, let's think about this."

"There is nothing to think about! I brought this man into my yard and let him drink with me, and he goes and hurt my family like that! You would not stop to think if this was one of the twins!" Walter yells.

"What about the law?" Paul yells.

"What law?" Walter yells back.

Walter bends down, touching his knees and swaying his head right and left, saying, "Lucille and Netta are the only real family I have. I love that woman and that little girl in there, and now, I have allowed someone to hurt them. I will kill anyone who would do that. I know you don't understand, but don't try to stand in my way. I need to make this thing right!"

"Okay, if I can't stop you, I will drive you there. Do you know where he is?" Paul asks.

"I've got a good idea," Walter replies. Walter and Paul climb into the truck.

"Go down toward the river," Walter directs. Dean and Lucille are listening while standing on the back porch. They are both worried as they watch their men drive away.

"Do you know what you are going to do when you get there? How do you know this is the right man?" Paul asks.

"Levy is the only one that lives in the shack down in the cove by the lumberyard. What am I going to do? I am going to beat his ass like he stole something from me. Then we can turn him over to the law," Walter says with vengeance in his voice.

After another half a mile, Walter has Paul turn off the road onto a path with a gate across it. The sign says, "Private Property." Paul hesitates. Walter assures him it is okay. The men use this road to go back and forth from the lumberyard. The property belongs to the lumber company.

"Well, I will feel safer if I take my shotgun. The road looks kind of dark.

There can be wild animals down there," Paul says.

Paul tears off a piece of canvas that was lying on the bed of the truck. He wraps the canvas around a stick to make a torch.

The fence is down on one side of the gate. Access is easy. A few yards down the path, they can see the small shack. There is a light coming from the window in the front of the shack.

"Oh yeah, he is in there," Walter says with satisfaction. Walter rushes off running and kicks the front door open. He never gives Levy the opportunity to get up.

"You son of a bitch!" Walter yells while pounding Levy in the face with his fist. Walter grabs Levy by the same blue and white shirt Netta has described. Walter throws Levy to the dirt floor and kicks him in the ribs.

"You raped my girl," he says as he hits Levy in back of the neck with his fist.

"Wait a minute, wait a minute," Levy begs. "I don't know what you're talking about, man. I do not know your daughter," Levy says as he tries to pull himself up onto the bed.

Paul can see the fight. He hears the conversation from the distance. He is invisible to Levy in the dark where he stands. He can see the lamp on the table next to the bed. There is a potbelly stove and one chair. He listens as Levy tries to tell Walter he just went home when Walter fell asleep that day under the sweet gum tree.

Suddenly, everything changes. Walter jumps up and hits Levy in his bloody mouth. At this point, Walter remembers what Netta says—*It was the day you fell asleep under the sweet gum tree.*

Levy reaches under his mattress and pulls out his knife. Levy stabs Walter in the fleshy muscle of his arm. Walter stands back and reaches for the chair. Walter swings it at Levy. Levy dodges and knocks over the small table and oil lamp. The lamp spills onto the mattress, bursting into flames.

Both men continue to fight. Levy manages to push Walter down. Walter lands half in and half out of the doorway of the shack. Levy jumps over Walter.

Levy reaches for the woodpile where an axe is resting. Levy raises the axe to hit Walter in the head. Walter closes his eyes and prepares himself for the end. At that very moment, Walter hears one shot.

He opens his eyes just in time to see Levy fall backward onto the ground with the axe still in his hand. Walter stands up and goes to where Paul was standing. When he reaches him, Paul is in a state of shock. Shooting another human being is the last thing on his mind that morning.

"Paul, Paul, snap out of it. We have to leave this place!" Walter says while shaking Paul.

Paul helped Walter put Levy back in the shack. They can see the flames as they run back up the same path that brought them there. Paul runs around to the driver's side and throws up.

"You okay, man?" Walter asks.

"I will be all right. Get in. Let's go," Paul says, wiping his arm across his mouth. "What have we done? I cannot go to prison! I have a wife and four children. They need me," Paul says in a panicked voice.

"Okay, calm down and watch the road. We will figure this out," Walter says. "There is no way out. A man is dead or dying back there, and we are responsible. We have to tell somebody!" Paul says.

"No, no. Pull over, pull over now!" Walter says, grabbing the wheel. "Listen to me. Nobody has to know. We must never tell anybody. Levy was an evil person. We have to swear here and now that we will never mention this to anyone—not Dean, not Lucille ... no one!

"Paul, I am forever in your debt, you saved my life. If you have not been there, that would be me back there in that burning shack. I owe you, and from this moment on, you have my loyalty," Walter says, wiping the sweat from his brow. Paul turns back onto the road to continue his drive home. Walter tears his shirt to make a tourniquet for his arm to stop the bleeding.

Once they arrive at Paul's house, the men walk directly to the washtub of water that is left from the wash earlier in the day. Paul splashes water over his face and dries it with his shirt. Walter takes off his shirt. He soaks the shirt and applies it to the wound. He expresses his pain by groaning. They look at each other and know the bond must be stronger than blood and more loyal than a brother's trust.

"Let me do the talking, okay?" Paul nods yes.

Dean and Lucille are standing on the porch. "Is everything okay?"

"Everything is fine. Just get the bandages, please," Paul says. Walter sits down on the edge of the porch. Lucille joins him and gives a kiss on the lips.

"Did you find him?" Walter will not say anything. He is stalling until Dean and Paul comes back with bandages. He can hear the spring on the door as it opens.

"Yes, we found him. I beat him, and he leaves town. I told him if he ever comes back, I would have him put in jail for stabbing me and raping Netta—"

"Walter, you need to come into the light. I can see how to bandage your arm better," Dean interrupts. Everybody moves into the kitchen.

"Tell me what happened. I need to know!" Lucille begs. Walter is speaking with his head cast down, trying hard to convince Lucille that she and Netta had been vindicated. Lucille becomes hysterical with frustration over Walter's answer.

"Come with me, come with me now," Dean says with authority. Dean escorts Lucille from the table. They go outside. Dean places both hands on Lucille's shoulders.

"Can't you see something went bad out there? Your man has been stabbed, and my man looked shaken and upset. If this is all they are telling us now, this is all we need to know now." Looking into her sister's eyes, Lucille knows her sister is right.

"I will make some mint tea with paregoric. Everybody will sleep here tonight," Dean says as she hugs her sister.

Walter and Paul are in the same positions. Dean finishes cleaning and dressing Walter's wound. By now, Paul has gotten the whiskey and two small glasses. He sets one glass in front of Walter and fills it to the rim. He then leans back against the countertop and drinks two full glasses.

Dean starts the mint tea. Lucille gets the blankets from the hope chest at the foot of the bed.

"Walter, I would like for us to stay here tonight. Is this okay with you?" Lucille asks. Netta has drunk the mint tea. She is fast asleep.

"It will be okay. One thing more, about tonight, no one must ever know about tonight—not Netta, not nobody …" Walter says with a fading voice.

The combination of mint tea and paregoric works well as a sleeping potion, but the potion cannot stop the dreams. Walter relives the fight, surrounded by a green smoke haze cast by a green fire. Paul jumps in his sleep from the resounding echo of a single gunshot.

Chapter 2

Soon the rooster is crowing, preparing for the day. Dean gets up to make coffee, joined by Lucille. Lucille thanks her sister for being there for her last night. Both look out at the sunrise and exhale. The moment is disturbed by the comical sight of Tom Johnson. He is chasing chickens for his barbecue.

Soon they are around the table. Netta is scared, coming out of the bathroom. She does not know how to react, sitting at the table. Netta gets to the kitchen. Dean is the first to see Netta enter the room. She can see the fear in her quiet child's eyes. "Come on in, Netta, and eat."

As soon as Netta takes her seat, Lucille asks everybody to hold hands and pray. "Lord, bless this family. Guide us, protect us, and forgive us for our transgressions on others. Please bless my baby, Netta, that she may someday understand. We know she did nothing wrong and that we love her very much. Amen." Netta feels serene, but she is still feeling confused at the same time. Dean smiles as she watches her family feed one another. This is the first morning she can eat without feeding her twins. She thinks that alone is a miracle.

The noise coming from the Johnson's house is the sound of chaos. Now Tom Johnson has his children chasing chickens.

"Walter, Dean knows the owner of the Johnson's house. We must speak to them before someone else does," Lucille says.

"The owner is Ms. Helen. She lives on the west side of town. You know, the lady Martha works for."

"You mean our cousin Martha?' Lucille asks.

"Yeah, she is the one," Dean replies.

Paul is preparing to leave to open his corner store, where he sells fresh produce, honey, occasionally fish, and fresh meats of the season. Paul was once a teacher, but he says he is not free enough to soar to his heights, so he starts selling in the small structure he made on the side of the house.

"Paul, would you take us back to the house? Netta can stay with Dean until we return." Walter and Lucille know they must make an appearance at the barbecue or questions will be asked.

Once at home, Walter takes Lucille in his arms. He tells her how sorry he is for everything. He reassures her everything will be okay. He goes on to tell her he loves her. She and Netta mean everything to him. Lucille cries and smiles at the same time. Lucille and Walter change their clothes. Lucille gathers a change of clothes for Netta. Walter and Lucille mount their horse. They head due west to find the house of Ms. Helen. There they will try and secure the Johnson's rental house.

Meanwhile, back at Dean's house, Netta sits on the back step, watching all the activity going on at the Johnson house. Connie sees Netta and calls to her.

"Can you come over Netta?" Connie asks.

"Not now. My Mama is not here."

"Go ahead, Netta," a voice from behind says. It is Dean. "Tell Ms. Johnson we will be over later." Netta goes around the house and enters the gate of the Johnson's home. She runs up the back step of the house and yells out, "Hello, Ms. Johnson! My Mama and aunt Dean will be over later."

"Okay, Netta. Thank you," a soft voice answers from the kitchen.

"Come and jump rope with us, Netta." The Johnsons have six children. There is always something to do there. Netta's mind is free from all the problems of her world as she returns to her innocence.

Paul comes home for lunch. Dean is surprised. He explains to her that he has made all his deliveries for the day. There is no need to stay at the store today since most people on this side of town are going to the barbecue.

Walter and Lucille soon return to Dean and Paul's house. "Good news— Martha talked to Ms. Helen, and she will rent the house to us. Did you know what type of business Ms. Helen runs?" Dean just nods yes, raising her eyebrow.

"Okay, everybody grab a baby, and let's go," Dean says. They all file out of the house carrying one of the twins. The barbecue allows them to get a small piece of normal life back for a few hours.

Walter, Lucille, and Netta stay at Dean and Paul's again. Early Sunday morning, Dean and Lucille go to church.

After church, Dean is in a hurry to get home to the twins. Once they reach the house, no one is there. Dean can hear her baby crying in the distance. There they are at the Johnson's. Dean suggests that Lucille goes and gets enough clothes to stay until the move on Wednesday night. While the men and children are occupied, they leave to get their personal items and their clothes.

On Monday morning, Walter woke up early, anxious.

"You want some coffee?" Dean asks.

"No, thank you. I will just go now. Tell Lucille I will see her and Netta tonight." Walter says sadly as he leaves the kitchen. On his way to work there is a small movie replaying in his head of the last time he came down this road. Soon he will come to the path that leads to the cove. He has used it many times before. On this day, he opts to go the long way.

Once Walter reaches work, he tries his best to act normally. The men are still talking about Johnson's barbecue. They laugh and talk as they work until lunch time.

Pete, the foreman, comes over to the tree where the men eat lunch. "Has anybody seen Levy today?" Pete asks. Someone says no, and the other men just shake their heads.

"I told him if he was late one more time from being drunk, I would let him go," Pete says. "Okay, you guys finish eating. I will take a walk over to the shack and see if he is sleeping one off."

"Come to think of it. Levy was not at the barbecue," someone says.

"I heard he had some young girl in town. He says she acted like she did not like having him, but he knows she wants him,"

"I told him if her people found out, he would be dead meat," someone says laughingly.

Walter starts back toward the controls to start up the saw that stood in the center of the yard.

"'Walter, are you finished?" someone asks.

He keeps walking as though he does not hear them. Walter is taking deep breaths to try to hide his anxiety. Time is passing. Walter works on while glancing up the hill at the payroll shack where Pete's office is located. Hours pass.

The door to the payroll shack is opened. Pete steps out and looks up at the sun. He mounts a horse. There is no doubt in Walter's mind where he is going. Walter notices Pete returning in a hurry. Pete goes into the office and comes back out. Pete goes over to the lumber truck. Sweat has start to bead on Walter's face. His mind is racing. He walks over to the well and draws a pail of water. Walter takes the ladle from the pail and drinks from it. Wanting to run, he comfort himself long enough to go back to his position at the saw.

Soon Pete returns alone. Walter is puzzled. Pete is walking and waving the men together. Once all the men are gathered, he begins to tell them his grotesque findings. Pete is under the impression Levy got drunk, knocked the lamp over, and burned up in the flames. He goes to town to get the sheriff. Pete is more concerned about the shack than about Levy. This was Pete's fishing shack, and he hates to lose it. While the men are standing around, the sheriff drives up.

"Good, I am glad you are all here. By now, Pete has told you about Levy. Do you fellows know if someone wants to hurt Levy?" the sheriff asks.

"Levy was always getting drunk and falling down," Pete interjects.

"That is all okay, but I found blood outside the shack," the sheriff says.

Walter holds his eyes down so his guilt will not show in his eyes.

"Levy was a drifter. No one around knows much about him," Pete says.

"He says he had a girlfriend in town," someone says.

"Do any of you know who?" They all shake their heads no.

"Okay, if I need any more information from you all, I will come back," the sheriff says as he walks away with Pete.

"I wonder, did Levy mess with someone's daughter and they stopped him for good?" someone says. Walter tried to be invisible.

The talk for the remainder of the workday is centered on Levy's death.

Walter is quiet, hoping no one would single him out to ask him his theory about what happened to Levy.

Walter mounts his horse. He heads straight to town. Most of the men take the path leading to the shack. The sheriff's deputy is there with the wagon taking the body away.

"You men, go on. Leave here now!" the deputy yells.

Walter stops at the store where Paul is. He wants to tell Paul that the body has been discovered. It is too late. The sheriff has announced, and it has spread through town like wildfire. Paul closes the store.

"Let's get to the house," Paul urges. When they reach the house, Lucille and Dean are at the table. Everybody looks into one another's eyes, but no one says a word. Paul grabs the bottle of whiskey and two glasses. Without a word, he goes to the back porch. Walter follows. Dean stops Lucille from following.

"Let them go. We can't say a word—not a word," Dean says, grabbing her sister's arm.

The two men stay outside most of the night talking and reinforcing their bond and promise.

"Come and eat," Lucille says. Dean and Netta are in the bathroom with the twins.

As Lucille prepares each plate, she wants so badly to question Walter, but the sound of her sister's voice singing reinforces the secrecy. Lucille leaves the men and joins Netta and Dean in the bedroom.

Soon they can hear the rain falling outside. "The weather is changing," Lucille says. In saying that, she knows that their lives have changed forever.

"Morning came so soon," Walter says as he drinks his coffee. Dean gives him a brown bag that contains his lunch. "Tell Lucille and Netta I will see them this evening at our house so we can start the moving tonight."

"Okay," Dean replies.

When Walter arrives at work, he is distressed to learn the sheriff has had dogs sniff around the burned-out shack where Levy died. Pete has spent most of the day down in the cove. He is just being nosey.

When Pete comes back, Walter yells for him. He wants Pete to come and see if he thinks the saw needs greasing.

In fact, Walter wants to know what is going on in the cove. He waits for Pete to turn and walk over.

"Hey, what happened down in the cove today?" Walter asks.

"The sheriff thought he can get the dogs to sniff the blood outside the shack and maybe find out if another person was there when Levy died, but the rain washed everything away." Walter takes a silent breath of relief. Somebody from behind says, "I told Levy about messing with the girls in town." There is laughter.

Chapter 3

"Walter, do you need help moving tonight?"

"Yeah, I will take all the help I can." After work, Walter goes home. Netta and Lucille are there already. In a matter of hours, the house is completely empty.

"Thank you, guys, for all your help," Walter says.

"No, Lucille has get to have a fish fry for us," Adley tells Walter.

"Okay, this Saturday is Halloween. We can have a party for the children and a fish fry," Lucille says. She is thinking ahead. She wants Netta never to walk the street at night alone again.

After everybody leaves, Lucille and Netta go next door to Dean's house.

"Can Netta stay the night here? The Johnsons took all the firewood with them. We only have firewood for one room tonight," Lucille says.

"Sure, she can," Dean answers.

"Paul, can you take me to the fish market early Saturday morning? I promised the men who helped us move to have a fish fry for them and for the children for Halloween."

Lucille retreats to her new house. For the first time, she has electric lights and indoor plumbing. This minute and this second of the day, everything seems so right.

Halloween comes and goes. The pattern of their new life is changing. Lucille starts working at the new bakery. Netta spends every evening with Dean and the twins. Walter finds himself spending more and more time with Paul. Paul tells Walter he should make some small chairs to sell at the store. He had made chairs before for the twins. They can split the profit.

Lucille and Dean are preparing for Thanksgiving dinner. Thanksgiving is in two weeks. Paul will travel to the country to get Lilly and Uncle Boe; they will stay for the weekend.

Lilly—or "Mama" as they call her—is Lucille and Dean's mother. Uncle Boe is Lilly's brother who lives with her. Most of the products from the store comes from the farm they live in. Both Lilly and Boe are old in age; Boe is seventy-five, while Lilly is seventy-two.

"Hello, how are my babies doing?" Lilly asks.

"Dean and Lucille are fine."

"Not those babies. I was talking about the twins," Lilly replies. "Paul, will you go out to the yard and tell Boe we need to get going before it turns dark?"

Paul goes to the backyard and calls for Uncle Boe. He suddenly appears from the cornfield with a bushel of corn.

"Hello, Paul. I get us some good corn, greens, and beans. I want those girls to cook everything fresh from the garden for turkey day."

"That's good, Uncle Boe, but we need to get started," Paul says as he lifts the bushel from Boe's hands.

"Tell Mama to bring something for you to sit on in the back of the truck."

"You need to get in the truck, son. As soon as she is settled in the truck, I will turn the dogs loose while we are gone," Uncle Boe says.

On the way to town, Lilly questions Paul about what has been going on. Unknown to Paul, Lilly has always been clairvoyant, especially when it is about her bloodline. Paul is not sure how to answer Lilly. He tells her he has to concentrate on the road in order to stop her questioning.

They arrive just as the sun is setting. Netta and the twins are in the front of the house, playing games. Dean is in the kitchen. She is chopping up vegetables for the Thanksgiving feast.

"Netta, go get your Mama. Tell her Mama is here with Uncle Boe." Netta runs next door for Lucille and Walter. Lucille is busy baking pies. "Mama, Grandma's here with Uncle Boe."

"Okay, we are coming," Lucille says.

Lilly manages to get up the stairs leading into the kitchen. Dean is waiting with open arms. When Lilly hugs Dean, she sees flashes of light and scenes in her mind's eye she cannot understand. Nevertheless, she hugs her daughter with great cheer.

"What do we have here? Are these my babies? Look how you have grown.

Let Granny give you a kiss."

"Granny, Granny," Netta says in happiness. When Lilly hugs Netta, she can feel and see flashes of red light, the smell of smoke, and the pain of shame.

"How are you, Mama Lilly?" a deep voice says. It is Walter. When Lilly hugs Walter she can feel the pain of his stabbing. She has to push herself away.

"I am good, son. How is your arm?"

There was silence in the room except for Uncle Boe, laughing at the twins. At that very moment, Lucille comes in the door. "What's the matter? Why is everybody sitting like they have seen a ghost?" Dean and Paul move to pick up the twins to get them ready for bed.

Lucille moves toward Lilly to hug her. When Lilly hugs Lucille she feels a sadness that makes her cry.

"What is it, Mama?"

Lilly knows it is too soon to say what she is feeling, so she answers, "I am happy to see all of you together."

Lilly sets to work cleaning vegetables and preparing the large bird the family will eat. Lucille leaves the kitchen to see if Dean needs help with the twins. Dean motions for Lucille to close the door.

"Mama knows something."

"What are you saying, Dean?"

"Remember how she would always know when we are sick and when we would lie to her? I tell you, Mama knows something."

"Okay, do not panic."

"Let's go back in the kitchen and just act normally," Dean says.

Once the twins are asleep, Dean and Lucille go back into the kitchen. Once they get to the doorway of the kitchen, they can hear Lilly talking to Netta.

"What has happened to you? Something you want to tell Granny?' Lucille rushes into the room.

"Netta, go see what Walter needs."

"Mama, why don't you sit and drink some cider. Dean and I can cook the dinner."

"You know I have been cooking Thanksgiving dinner since before you are born," Lilly answers. "When are you two going to learn you cannot hide anything from me?"

"What are you talking about, Mama?"

"Okay, misses, I won't push. But before I go, I will know."

Lucille and Dean start singing church songs. They know that is one way to change the conversations. Lilly loves church songs. On the other hand, Uncle Boe is happy. He is drinking whiskey with Paul and Walter, chasing it with cider. Uncle Boe tells the two men how Lilly has dreamed they are in trouble. Paul looks at Walter. Walter shakes his head and places his finger to his lips as a sign of silence. Soon Uncle Boe is asleep, holding a glass in his hand.

Walter and Paul walk into the kitchen. "Uncle Boe is out for the count," Paul says. "Honey, will you get the blankets from the hope chest?"

"Mama, are you sleepy? We can finish up here," Dean says.

"No, I am just getting started," Lilly replies.

Walter leaves to go home. Paul goes to his bedroom. Netta is asleep with her head on the table.

"Do you need me to stay?" Lucille asks.

"No, take Netta home and get some rest," Dean says. "Mama, come over to the house for breakfast. The twins can be a handful in the morning."

"No, everybody comes back here for breakfast, I want to cook," Lilly says. "I will see your new house tomorrow."

"Okay, good night. Come on Netta, you get to walk now. I can't carry you."

The next morning, Lilly cooks ham, grits, eggs, sausages, onions with potatoes, and biscuits. Milk and cold apple cider are waiting when Dean gets up.

"Mama, you really should not have cooked." Lilly puts the ham and the turkey with the dressing in the oven.

"Mama, Lucille must have smelled your biscuits. Here she comes," Dean says looking out of the window.

"Happy Thanksgiving, everybody."

"Good morning, everyone" is said simultaneously. The twins are sitting at a miniature table in the chairs Walter had made for them.

Everyone is seated. "Let's pray," Lilly says. "Thank you, Heavenly Father, for this day. Oh, Heavenly Father, bless this house and all that dwell in it. Bless each person here. We give thanks and honor for all you have done. Amen."

"Let's eat."

"Mama, Martha and her friend Adley are coming over today to have Thanksgiving with us." Dean says.

"Who is Adley?"

"He works with Walter at the lumberyard," Lucille says.

"He is a good guy," Walter adds.

After breakfast, Lilly goes with Walter and Lucille. They walk down the sidewalk to Lucille's house. Lilly looks around the house and gives her decorating suggestions. Shortly everyone returns to Dean's house carrying the pies Lucille has prepared for Thanksgiving.

They met up with Martha and Adley at the gate.

"Hello, Aunt Lilly. Meet my friend Adley," Martha says. "Aunt Lilly, when I heard you were coming, I said I had to come and visit just to eat your cooking."

The miniature table set is moved to the large dining room. The table is full of food. The menu consists of turkey and dressing, green beans, rice, ham, gravy, candies yams, cranberry sauce, okra, corn, tomatoes, green onions, and an assortment of pies and cakes.

After the prayer is over, conversation shifts. Martha asks Dean if she wants to wash sheets for Ms. Helen. She has increased Martha's workload. Ms. Helen has told Martha she will pay twenty-five cents a sheet if she has to send out her wash. Dean looks toward Paul to give an answer. Lucille suggests that Dean and Netta can wash the sheets when Netta comes home from school and split the money. Paul says that might work.

Dean asks Netta, "Do you want to help me with the wash and get paid?" Netta says yes.

Martha adds, "There are always ten to twelve sheets every evening to wash." Martha and Adley laugh.

Martha says, "Ms. Helen runs a home for wayward girls." Dean and Lucille look at each other and grin.

"As a matter of fact, she is in Paris now, bringing more girls back with her.

Because she is in Paris, I can have the whole day off."

The conversation is joyful, and everybody has plenty to eat. Martha and Adley have to leave early. The men retire to the front porch to watch the children play as they drink whiskey and cider. The women clean the table and start washing dishes. Netta comes into the kitchen to get a glass of water.

Lilly asks everybody to form a circle and hold hands. Without question Dean, Lucille, and Netta obey. Lilly closes her eyes and tilts her head back. She opens her eyes in horror. Lilly breaks the circle and grabs Netta.

"My poor baby! Sit down. Everybody, sit down! What this family is hiding will never come to light. The sins of the unborn child's father will travel for four generations."

As soon as Lilly says "unborn child," Lucille begins to cry. Up to this point, it has never crossed Lucille or Dean's mind that Netta can be pregnant.

Netta sits at the table, confused. Walter walks into the room. He notices the tears in Lucille's eyes.

"What is wrong?" he asks.

"Netta is going to have a baby."

"How do you know this?"

"Mama just told us so."

"That's no reason to think it is true."

"You don't understand. Mama always knows when a child is coming," Lucille says, crying.

"What you and Paul did will never come back to hurt you, but you must pray for forgiveness, you had no choice. No one must ever know this family's shame. Netta will not be able to bear children again. This is the price to be paid. Her child will carry its father's ways."

Walter cannot believe what he is hearing. He becomes angry. "Lilly, stop it."

"No, Walter, you must believe me. This is my blood. I am here to protect and guide them, no matter what. We need to decide now how this will play out in May, or someone will remember the day under the sweet gum tree."

When Lilly says that, everybody's face turns white. Netta becomes very afraid and starts to cry without knowing why. Walter's legs goes limp. He leans on the countertop to compose himself. Paul has come into the kitchen to see what is taking Walter so long. When he enters the room, he knows something is wrong.

"What is it?" Nobody speaks. "Dean, what's going on?"

"Netta is going to have a baby. It will be born in May." Paul is shocked.

"How can she be having a baby? She is just a baby herself. She still plays with dolls and jumps rope. Netta does not have any boyfriend." Lilly stands up and moves toward Paul. She can see that he is in a state of denial. He has pushed the rape completely to the back of his mind, mainly because he is trying so hard to suppress the shooting. Lilly holds his hand and closes her eyes. She can see the bridge that causes the division in his thoughts.

"One day you will understand," she says. "We are strong. We can do this." "It is late. Please, can we just rest now?" Dean says.

Walter, Lucille, and Netta go home. Lucille stays in the room with Netta until she goes to sleep. Lucille goes to the kitchen to make some mint tea. Walter joins her.

"We need to get married," Walter says.

"What makes you say that now?" Lucille asks.

"When the baby comes, I can give it my name."

"How can marrying you give that baby your name?"

"You will have to act as the mother. We need to hide Netta's pregnancy. We can send her home with Mama Lilly. No one will ever know," Walter proposes.

"No, I will not send her away. This is not her fault!" Lucille shouts.

In the meanwhile, Dean and Paul are arguing about what Lilly had said.

"You know your mother is getting old, and sometimes older folks will ramble on without making sense," Paul says.

"She is not rambling. If you think hard enough, you will see how everything she has said is true." That night, Dean cries herself to sleep.

Chapter 4

That Friday morning, Walter goes to work. Paul proceeds to the store. Uncle Boe goes with Paul to keep him company for the day.

Lucille has to go to work, but she is afraid to leave Netta alone with her mother and Dean. Lucille knows Lilly will make Netta confused. Before going to work Lucille and Netta go to Dean's house.

"Good morning, everybody." Lucille says. "Mama, can I talk to you outside for a few minutes. Mama, please don't push all of this on Netta. She is still a child. She thinks like a child. Until there is a change in her body, she won't know something is wrong."

"Okay, Lucille. Go and have a good day at work. Don't worry, I will not hurt Netta in any way," Lilly says.

In the middle of the day when the twins are taking a nap, Dean, Netta and Lilly are sitting around the table. Netta asks, "Granny, will I have a baby? How can I have a baby like the twins?" Lilly reaches for Netta to sit on her knee.

"Baby, one day you will understand. This thing that has happened to you is not your fault. We love you. If you ever need Granny, I will come for you as long as I am on this earth. Okay?" Lilly holds Netta in her arms and rocks back and forth with a broken heart.

By lunch time, Paul and Uncle Boe return home from deliveries. Uncle Boe says to Paul, "Son, you need to listen to the women on this matter. Lilly knows what she is talking about."

"How can she know? She was not here," Paul answers.

"Because she told me about the dream—the dream about the path that leads to the small shack."

At that instant, Paul hears a single gunshot in his ear. By this time, Paul and Uncle Boe reach Paul's house. Paul is in deep thought; it shows on his face.

"Uncle Boe, you go on in, I forgot something. Tell Dean I will be home later." The truth is Paul needs to go somewhere to be alone.

Uncle Boe enters the kitchen. He is hungry. Boe and Lilly eat lunch at the same time every day.

"Sit down, Boe," Lilly says. Dean asks Uncle Boe about his day at the store. "All the pretty ladies love our vegetables," Boe says. The day moved along slowly.

"Hello, Mama. How was your day?" Lucille says as she enters the kitchen. Netta gets up to greet her mother. "How was your day, baby?" Lucille hears Paul, Walter, and Boe in the front of the house.

Lilly stops Lucille from leaving the room. "Listen to me. I know I have stirred things up here, and for that, I am sorry. I must tell the things I see or I will go crazy," Lilly says. Soon everybody retires.

Early on Saturday morning, Netta is excited. Today Lucille, Lilly, and Netta are going into the center of town to the five and dime. Netta has twenty-five cents. She wants a doll and some hard candy. Lilly and Lucille shop for cloths. Dean is a dressmaker. Dean asks the ladies to buy cloth. She will sew new dresses for them by Christmas.

Lucille, Netta, and Lily return from a long day's shopping. "Thank you, Mama," Dean says. "The colors are beautiful. I will measure everybody after supper."

The weeks pass. Christmas is fast approaching. Lucille and Dean watch Netta closely to monitor her period, but it never comes.

Walter comes home one day, he asks Lucille again to get married. This time, Lucille agrees to marry him. Christmas night will be the perfect time. This way, Lilly and Boe will be in town for the holidays. Walter asks Paul to be his best man. The wedding will take place at Dean and Paul's house. Martha and Adley want to host a party for Walter and Lucille. Walter and Lucille allow them to decorate their house. The men from the lumber mill and others are invited to share their reception.

After the ceremony, they go to Lucille's house, where everyone is waiting. When Lucille and Walter enter the house, everyone yells congratulations. Lucille blushes as a bride should. Walter has his best suit on and is very proud.

While preparing another tray of food for the wedding guests. Lucille, Netta, Dean, and Martha are alone in the kitchen. "Martha, I guess I can tell you now. I am going to have a baby," Lucille says. Dean is in shock. She asks Lucille to help her for a minute in the other room.

"What are you doing?" she asks.

"I am doing the right thing. Once Martha finishes telling everybody, it will be all over town." Lucille says, leaving the room to go back to the kitchen.

"Well, well, well. I thought you'd said you never want another child," Martha says laughing. To everybody's surprise, Netta says, "I am going to have a baby too."

Martha smiles. "I guess we are all going to have a baby now?" Martha leans toward Netta and pats her on the head, saying, "Yes, you will have a new baby sister or brother to care for soon."

Before Netta can answer, Lucille says in a hurry, "Netta, go get some of the dirty glasses up front for me, please."

Lucille leaves the kitchen. She calls for Netta to follow her into the bedroom. "Netta, never—never—say that again. Please, honey, do not say that to anyone ever. It must be a secret. Do you understand?"

At this point, Lucille realizes Netta has the mind of a child. She will be twelve in March. She holds Netta close, hugging her child. Tears start to well up in her eyes. The thought of October rushes into her head, followed by the thought of what Netta will have to go through in May.

Netta sees her mother crying. Netta thinks she has said something wrong. In a soft, frightened voice she says, "Mama, I won't tell." Netta can see the pain of her mother from the reflection in the mirror across the room.

"You get a book and a blanket and stay in here.' Lucille says as she wipes the tears from her eyes. Lucille reenters the party. Everyone is waiting. Martha has worked her magic. The women crowd around Lucille to ask her about the baby news. Walter is trying his best to make eye contact. He wants a hint from Lucille about what to say. The men are joking with him.

Dean is watching the whole room. She walks over to Walter to say, "Have a drink, brother-in-law. You are going to be a father in May." Walter looks into Dean's face. He understands.

Later, Dean, Lilly, and Martha clean up. Walter and Lucille retreat to their bedroom. "Why didn't you tell me about this baby idea?" Walter says.

"If this baby is to carry your name, I have to be the mother," Lucille replies. Walter kisses Lucille. He says to her, "I love you, Mrs. Lucille Jones." She smiles, and they melt into passion.

Early the next morning, Lucille is in the kitchen. Netta comes into the room. "Mama, there is blood in my panties." Lucille is excited. "Come into the bathroom and let me see." Lucille gives Netta a wet towel.

"Wipe between your legs with this, honey. Here is a pad. Put it on." Lucille is so happy. She runs next door to Dean's house. "Dean, Mama, Netta got her period." Lucille says. Dean is happy.

"Be sure before you speak," Lilly says.

"Mama, please," Lucille says infuriated.

"Just listen to me, Lucille. A spot of blood in the first few months is not unheard of," Lilly says. Lucille loses all her energy. She pulls a chair from the table to sit on. With her head in her hands, she moves her head from side to side.

Dean asks, "Do you want you something to drink?"

"Last night, you made up your mind to accept this. You told everybody you are going to have a baby. Not because you are, but because you know what I know. Netta is pregnant! Nothing can change that now. Soon Netta will be showing. You will need to decide how you will dress her. Will she continue to go to school? Can she play the same way? How can you explain to a child about what is taking place in her body?"

The door to the kitchen opens. It is Netta.

"Come over here, baby," Lilly says. "Close the door to the hallway, Dean." Lilly starts to lift Netta's dress. She resists. "It will be okay. Let Granny see something." Lilly pulls up Netta's dress. She presses the bottom of Netta's stomach. "Come over here, Lucille. I want you to feel. Feel the bottom of her! What do you feel?" Lucille takes Netta to the bathroom. She asks Netta to remove the pad from her panties. The pad is clean. Lucille comes out of the bathroom. "I have to go to work before I am late. Can Netta come over today and stay?"

"You know Netta can stay," Dean replies. Lucille leaves the house.

The weather is cold and gloomy. Walter is outside, cutting wood for the fireplace. Paul and Uncle Boe walk over to help. "Need some help?" Paul asks.

"No, I am about to finish. Thanks anyway," Walter replies.

"Let's go into the house. I have some warm cider on the stove." Uncle Boe wants to know if there is any whiskey left from last night. The men play dominoes and talk about the party. Uncle Boe wants to know about every woman at the party.

"Paul, will you pick up Lucille today? I will ride along with you. I do not want her walking in this weather. It looks like it will rain," Walter says. Uncle Boe remains at the house.

On their way to pick up Lucille, Paul tells Walter it will be good if he can learn to drive the truck. This way, he can help with delivery from time to time. He can also go with him to Lilly and Boe's farm to pick up vegetables.

Paul and Walter discuss how to enlarge the tiny store. Walter is a very talented carpenter. Walter explains how he can collect discarded lumber from the lumber mill. For now it seems the men have a plan for the future.

Lucille starts on her walk home. To her surprise, she sees Paul and Walter in the truck. "Hey, baby, want a ride?" Walter says as he steps out of the truck.

"Sure, but I am married, so no funny stuff," Lucille says with a smile.

"Oh please, you two have only been married one day. Wait until you have been married five years," Paul adds. "Now let's go. It's cold."

By the time the threesome reaches home, the rain starts. Lucille can see Dean and Netta removing diapers from the back porch railing. Walter and Paul go to Walter's house. Uncle Boe is asleep with his head on the table.

"Hi, Mama," Netta says. "I helped Aunt Dean sew today."

"That's good. Did you have to change your pad today?" Lucille asks Netta.

"No, ma'am. There is no more blood," Netta answers. Lucille opens the door. The setback can be seen in her face. "Hi, Mama." Lucille says.

"Lucille, come with me?" Lilly answers. Lucille and Lilly walk to the front of the house. "Listen to me, I know this is hard. But, this too will pass. I know it is hard to accept things not of our making or when other people place problems in our lives. Netta is your baby—the only baby you have. You need to make life for her as good as you can. You know in a few short months, her whole world will be changed forever.

"In a few weeks let her come and stay with me. Boe and I will be happy to have her there with us. Paul can give her lessons and check them when he comes. Tell the school she has the measles. The time is coming when she will start to show. We can only hide so much," Lilly suggests.

"Mama, Netta has to be with me. She cannot go through this without me there," Lucille argues.

"She can come home when her time is near. I will come up to help with the delivery. We cannot let her go out in public. If she is on the farm with me, very few people will see her," Lilly says.

"I will talk with Walter. I am so confused. I don't know what is best anymore," Lucille says.

That night while Netta is asleep, Lucille and Walter are sitting in the front room of their house. Walter knows the lumberyard will be closing until the snow leaves. He shares his thoughts about the plans he and Paul had talked about earlier in the day. Walter is building a cabinet for Ms. Helen; the money will help them until the spring.

"Walter, Mama wants Netta to come and stay with her for a little while," Lucille says, with sadness in her voice.

"What do you think?" Walter asks.

"I don't know. I just don't know," Lucille answers.

"We don't have to decide tonight, so let's go to bed," he says.

Chapter 5

Days pass. The town cannon is marking the start of something new. Nineteen hundred and twenty is the year. New Year's Eve is sounded in. The holidays are over. Walter is out of work until the spring. Lucille is happy that he will be home. This will delay Netta in leaving the city. Walter is in the middle of building a cabinet; this will help with money. Netta is still in school. She goes over to Dean's after school.

"Hi, Aunt Dean," Netta says. "Pauline, Paulette, Paul, and Dean, what did you do today?" Netta asks the twins.

"They all have colds," Dean answers for the twins.

"Aunt Dean, can I show you something?"

"Sure, Netta. What is it?"

Netta pulls her dress up slowly. "Look at my stomach, it is hard. Something keeps moving inside. I told my teacher," Netta says innocently.

"You told your teacher? What did she say?"

"She asked me, 'Did it hurt?' I told her no. She says it must be gas. It happens at night too," Netta answers. Dean looks under Netta's dress. She can see the oval pear-shaped belly.

"It will be okay. We will let your mother know when she comes in from work," Dean says.

Netta says, "Okay."

She begins playing with the twins. Dean anxiously waits for Lucille.

The evening moves slowly. Dean rushes through her day so she can have some extra time. She knows Lucille will be upset. Netta is starting to show.

She knows it will be hard to keep the secret if Lucille does not act now.

"Hello," Lucille says, "where are the twins and Paul?"

"Paul is over at your house. The twins are asleep."

"Lucille, we need to talk," Dean says.

"Okay, what is it?" Lucille acknowledges.

"Netta is showing. The baby is moving," Dean says.

"What are you talking about?" Lucille raises her voice.

"Netta, come over here. Tell your Mama what you told me," Dean says. Netta explains. "Now show her," Dean continues.

Netta raises her dress. Lucille tries hard not to cry. She is so tired of crying over this madness. Lucille gently places her hand on Netta's stomach. Lucille can feel the jelly-like movement in Netta's stomach. She is hurting so much inside; she feels ill.

"Dean, can I have some water please?" Lucille asks. Dean can see the color has changed in her sister's face.

"Netta told the teacher her stomach is moving. It is time to let her go to Mama. I can make bands for her stomach, but we can't stop what she is feeling. Somebody will become suspicious," Dean adds.

"I just don't know. I need to be with her. I don't know what to do. How can this be happening? My poor baby," Lucille says.

Lucille and Netta walk home. They can hear Walter and Paul in the workshop Walter has built behind the house.

"Good, the house is warm. Netta, come to my room when you get ready for bed." Lucille says.

"Yes, ma'am," Netta answers. Lucille goes to the bathroom. She begins to pray. "Oh, Lord, please guide me in this. I don't know what to do. I know this is not about me. How do I know all the answers? Please show me the way. Help me, oh, Heavenly Father." When she returns to the bedroom, Netta is waiting.

"Netta, I need to tell you something. You will go and stay with Mama and Uncle Boe. Your uncle Paul will bring your lessons when he comes to the farm."

"Mama, why do I have to go? I don't want to go out there to stay. There are no children out there … just Uncle Boe and Granny," Netta says.

"Netta, listen to me. Do you know what is happening to you? I need to make you understand you are going to have a baby. That is what's moving inside you."

"Mama, how can I have a baby?" Netta questions. "Where will the baby come from? Who will give it to me?"

"Netta, I cannot tell you all the answers now. When the time comes for the baby to be born, it will come from between your legs." Lucille touches Netta between her legs.

Netta is confused. She decides not to ask any more questions. She is afraid; her heart is racing. She does not want to think anyone or anything will ever touch her there again. Netta slowly gets up and tells her mother she needs to go to the bathroom.

When Netta leaves the room, Lucille realizes Netta needs to go to the farm.

Netta sits on the bathroom floor, trying so hard to understand. She manages to get up off the floor.

"Mama, I am sleepy. Good night," she says, walking toward her room.

When Walter comes into the house. Lucille is sitting at the kitchen table. She is drinking cider. The whiskey bottle is down on the table.

"Are you drinking?" Walter asks in surprise.

"I tried to talk to Netta about going to the farm. She doesn't understand. She does not understand any of it. I don't know what to do." Lucille is holding her face down. "Walter, the baby is moving inside of her and I don't know how to make her understand. This is so hard for me. I want to wake up and tell everybody about this bad dream. Maybe we will laugh about it. Maybe we will keep our baby closer. I just don't know if I can do this."

Walter just holds her. He knows he does not have the answer either.

That night, Lucille is restless. She gets up and down, stirring the fire in the fireplace in the front of the house. She reads her Bible until she gets sleepy. Walter is aware that Lucille is up. He knows there are no words to express his sorrow and the sadness.

When the morning comes, Lucille is up early, cooking breakfast. She goes down the hallway to Netta's room. "Netta, today you stay home. Go over to your aunt Dean. I will talk to her on my way to work." Walter is puzzled. He knows Lucille has made a decision.

"I will see you tonight. I have to go get a ride with Paul," Lucille says, leaving the house.

Walter drinks his coffee before going out to his workshop. He stands on the back porch looking toward the field behind the house. He says, "Lord, I am not a praying man, but please help us. Everything has gotten so tangled up. We do not know how to untie the knot. Thank you."

"Walter, I am going over to Aunt Dean!" Netta yells.

"Okay," Walter answers from the workshop.

"Hi, Aunt Dean. What can I help you with?" Netta greets her.

Dean says, "Netta, sit down, I want to talk with you. You know we love you, don't you? Don't ever let anybody tell you different. Your mother is really trying to figure things out—"

"Aunt Dean, is Mama going to make me go to Granny?" Netta interrupts.

"Netta, your mother doesn't want to send you away. It is necessary to keep you safe," Dean continues.

Netta is more confused than ever. Now her small brain is trying to understand. She only knows one horror in her small life. The horror of a strange man hurting her. Was she going to be hurt again? No one seems to give her the answers she needs to feel safe. All she knows is her Mama doesn't want her around anymore.

Netta plays and talks with the twins all day. Occasionally she tells her aunt Dean to feel the movement in her stomach. Dean is upset each time Netta lights up about the movement. Dean knows the joy of feeling a baby in her womb. Netta just thinks it is funny. She is too young to know she is carrying a life inside her body.

The next morning is Saturday; Lucille goes over to Dean before Netta awakes. She asks Paul to take her and Netta to Lilly's house.

"Walter, I am going out to Mama with Netta. I will return by myself on Sunday night," Lucille says.

"Are you sure?" Walter asks.

"Yes, I will be all right," she answers. Lucille has spent most of the night packing clothes while Walter and Netta are asleep. Netta is not aware of the trip.

"Netta, go get dressed. We are going to go to Mama's," Lucille says. Netta knows deep inside that she will not be coming back.

The ride is long and silent. Paul asks Lucille if she wants him to wait for her.

To his surprise, she tells him, "I will be staying the night."

"How is Granny's baby?" Lilly greets them with open arms.

"Hi, Granny and Uncle Boe," Netta says. Paul and Uncle Boe go to the barn.

Lilly, Netta, and Lucille go and sit by the fireplace.

"Netta, I made you a new quilt. Go to my room, and get it out of the hope chest." Netta obeys.

"Mama, I did not know what to do. Everything is caving in on me. You are right. Netta will need to stay out here with you for a while. This is tearing me apart. My heart is breaking. What did I do to deserve this?" Lucille says.

"This is not about you, Lucille. What you feel is a fallout from a bad situation. This is about Netta. We need to plan how she can recover her life.

We have no idea what this birth will be like for her. When I was a girl, I saw young girls who could not bear the pain of giving birth. We need to pray hard. Do not look for answers about what happened. Look for solutions to get past it," Lilly advises.

Paul loads the truck with fresh eggs and winter vegetables. "Mama, Uncle Paul is leaving," Netta says.

"I know," Lucille replies.

"I have fixed up the back bedroom for you, and Netta, I knew you were coming," Lilly says. "Come, let's eat. I baked cookies. You can have one if you eat all your food."

"Feel, feel, feel," Netta says. She wants her grandmother to feel the movement in her stomach. Lucille leaves the room. She does not want Netta to see her cry.

"There will be more in the coming days. It means life. There is something growing in there," Lilly tells Netta.

"Really, Granny?"

"Yes, really."

Netta and Uncle Boe go out to the barn after dinner. This gives Lucille and Lilly a chance to talk. "Mama, I did not know how to tell Netta I was bringing her here today," Lucille says, cleaning off the table.

"Remember, what doesn't kill you will make you strong. I have gathered some roots and herbs for you and your sister. I want you to fast once a week for strength."

"This is February. Next month, Netta will be twelve. You make sure everybody comes here for her birthday. This will be the last time she can enjoy her birthday as a child."

Lucille gets down on her knees. She lays her head in her mother's lap. She says, "If only I was at home that day. This would not be happening," Lucille cries.

"This had to happen. I don't know the reason just yet. What I do know is that only two people can create this new life. Those two people are Netta and the man who raped her. No matter how much confusion and pain, something has been set in motion. And no one can stop it now, no one but God. Now wash your tears away. Netta needs to see strength, not weakness," Lilly advises.

The sound of a rooster in the barn, preparing for the day, is the clock Uncle Boe and Lilly need to begin their day. It is Sunday. It is time for everyone to get ready for church.

"Lucille, I will ask Sister Smith to give you a ride back to town. Her daughter brings her out here every Sunday for church. So pack your stuff, and take it with you." Lilly knows she needs to make the goodbye as public as possible. This way, Lucille and Netta will not cry as much with other people around.

The church service is long as usual. Lunch is served afterward in the church kitchen. Soon Sister Smith and her daughter are ready to go. Lilly tells Lucille to kiss Netta.

"Try not to cry. Reassure her you will send her a letter every time Paul comes. Let her know you will see her every weekend you can. Above all, tell her you love her." Lucille takes Netta aside to say goodbye. Lilly is watching; she can see the anguish in her children's eyes.

Uncle Boe, Lilly, and Netta ride back home in the buggy without Lucille. Netta cries all the way home. Lilly goes into the house to reheat the supper she had made early that morning. Netta goes to the barn with Uncle Boe.

Lucille has a silent ride back to town. "Thank you. Here take this money for bringing me back to town." Lucille hands her the money and walks away. She is a few yards from her turn off. She walks slowly, wondering if she has done the right thing. Soon Lucille can see the light from her house.

"Hello, anybody here?" No one answers. Walter is in the workshop. Lucille goes to her bedroom and unpacks her clothes.

Her thoughts turn to Netta. She feels she has not done her duty as a mother. Every feeling of guilt, deception, and emptiness wells up inside her. She sits down on the edge of the bed. She cries into the clothes that are in her hand. "Lord, why? Why me, Lord?" Lucille prays." As clear as a bell she can hear Lilly saying to her, *You are strong.*

When Lucille looks up, Walter is standing by the door. He does not know if he should hold her or keep his distance.

"You okay?" he asks. "Come see. Come with me." Walter leads Lucille to the kitchen. There are wild flowers in a mason jar. He continues on out of the back door and down the stairs to his workshop. In the workshop, there is a beautiful cabinet. The cabinet is three feet wide and six feet tall. Hand carvings top the freshly stained wood.

"Ms. Helen will pay well for this. You did good," Lucille says hugging Walter around the neck.

"Look behind the cabinet," he says. Lucille slowly passes by Walter. There stands a dark brown rocking chair. The name, Lucille, is carved into it. "We can do this," Walter said.

Chapter 6

The first week is hard for Netta. She misses her mother and the twins. Her days are supervised by Lilly. In the morning, she does her school lesson. In the afternoon, Lilly teaches Netta how to cook canned foods, to sew, and other life skills. At night, Lilly tries to explain the changes that are taking place in her body.

Each week, Lucille comes to see Netta. She can see the changes in Netta's body. Walter finds it hard to deal with. Lilly explains to Lucille, "Netta is having a hard time. Her back is hurting. She is having a hard time sleeping."

It is March. Netta's birthday is bittersweet. Everyone comes out to celebrate. The focus of the day keeps shifting to the reality that is facing them. Lilly, Dean, and Lucille gather on the porch. Lilly asks if supplies are being gathered.

"Mama, Netta needs to come home with me now. She may deliver early. I need to be there when that time comes," Lucille begs.

"I know. Next week, Netta will return home. I am coming with her," Lilly answers.

In the evening, Lucille spends time swinging on the porch with Netta. Humming, they hug together like Siamese twins. "Honey, you cannot go home tonight. Uncle Paul will be back to get you and Granny next week," Lucille says.

"Promise, Mama?" Netta asked.

"I promise, baby." Lucille promises.

Lucille rushes her coffee that morning. She goes to Dean's house. She needs to ask Paul if he is going to the farm that morning. She can see Paul walking toward his truck.

"Paul, Paul, I am glad I got to you before you left. Will you go to the farm today?" she said, breathing hard.

"Yes, do you want a ride to work?" Paul says smiling at her excitement.

This morning, Lilly and Netta are waiting when Paul arrives at the farm. Lilly has cooked enough food for Uncle Boe until next week. Netta is anxious. As they get close to town. Netta starts naming people she knows. She is waving with delight. "Mama worked down there," Netta says. Soon they are approaching home.

"Just stay seated, Netta, until I come around to help you out," Paul orders. Paul goes back to help Lilly and take down the supplies. Lilly goes to help Netta. Paul opens the gate. Netta is in a hurry to see Dean and the twins.

"Careful, Netta," Lilly commands.

"Aunt Dean, Pauline, Paulette, Paul, and Dean … it's me, Netta. Mama, I am so glad you are here. Now I can start washing. Can I help Aunt Dean?" Before she can answer, Dean can see Lilly in the background, shaking her head no.

"Not this time. Help Mama cook," Dean answers. It is hard keeping Netta inside the house. She wants to help with everything.

Lucille is in a hurry to get home. "Where are you going in such a hurry?" a voice calls to her. It is Martha.

"Oh, I did not see you. I am in a hurry. Mama is in town for the night," Lucille answers.

"Tell her I said hello," says Martha. "Ms. Helen is talking about leaving town. She goes where the money is, or should I say … where the men are? Someone told her about a gold mining town somewhere out west—"

"I really get to go," Lucille interrupts.

"Okay, I am telling you because of the house!" Martha yells as Lucille walks swiftly away.

Netta runs to meet her mother before she can open the door. "Mama, Mama, let's go home. I brought my new quilt. We made little tops and pants. Granny says they are for me and the baby," Netta says.

"Let me speak to Aunt Dean and Granny for a little while." After a short visit. Lucille and Netta walk next door. Paul has joined Walter in the kitchen. Netta hugs Walter and goes to her room. Now there is a small bed in Netta's room. Lucille put all of Netta's dolls on the pillows. She also has a small hope chest Walter has made.

"Thank you, Walter." Netta returns to her room. Lucille is sitting on the bed.

"How do you feel? Do you want some milk?" Lucille asks.

"I feel fine, Mama. Can I have some milk?" Netta answers.

"Fine, you get ready for bed. I will be back," Lucille says.

Lucille can see Netta through the crack on the door. This is the first time she can see the growth in Netta's body. She pauses. She watches Netta talking to her dolls. *How innocent,* she thought.

"Be strong," Lucille says to herself as she enters the room.

"Mama, don't make me leave again, please." Lucille just hugs Netta and lies there with her long into the night.

The next morning, Lilly comes over early. "Good morning, Walter. I hope you don't mind me starting to cook? Is this your first day back at work?"

"Yeah, Lucille will be out soon. You have a good day," Walter says, going out of the back door.

"Hi, Mama. I hear Netta stirring in there. I will just take a piece of bread and drink a cup of coffee. Just cook breakfast for you and Netta," Lucille says. Lilly watches Lucille. She seems so nervous as she moves toward the door to leave.

"Morning, Granny. I hope you cooked grits and eggs," Netta says, standing in the doorway.

"Come over here. Let me look at you this morning." Lilly places her hand between Netta's breasts and her stomach. She is measuring the space between the two. She knows the lower the stomach, the sooner the birth. Lilly kisses Netta on the head and prepares her plate of grits and eggs.

Lilly cooks and cleans while Netta plays with her toys. Lilly can see Dean coming down the walk. She has one baby on her arm and one baby by the hand. The twin boys are holding hands in front of her. They walk and explore at the same time. Lilly goes to greet and help her on her long walk next door.

"Thank you, Mama," Dean says, exhaling.

"I was watching out of the window," Lilly says laughingly.

"Hi, Aunt Dean," Netta says.

"Netta, do not carry the twins around today. They are getting too big for you to carry," Lilly advises.

"Pauline, Paulette, come to my room and play with my dolls."

"Mama, can I leave the twins over here while I wash? Martha has brought some sheets today."

"Aunt Dean, can I help you?"

"Mama, can she?" Dean asks.

"No! Wash over here," Lilly says.

"Okay, I have diapers and other things to wash as well," Dean adds.

"I guess we can all help if you do. I can wash for Lucille today." Lilly volunteers. Dean walks next door to get the clothes for washing.

Soon the fire is blazing under the wash pot. Netta wants to be helpful.

Several times, Lilly tells her to go back to the porch. Once the scrubbing begins, Netta is anxious to scrub. She finds herself hindered by her arm's reach.

"Netta, why don't you wring and hang?" Lilly says. Netta notices the whiteness of the sheets.

"These sheets look new," Netta notes. "They are so pretty and white." Netta sniffs the wet sheets while she hangs them and smoothens the wrinkles out of the sheets. The sweet smell of perfume lingers in the fiber of the fabric. She enjoys watching the sunrays as they seem to flash off the sheets when the wind blows. They make the popping sound of wet clothes as they move. Netta stands between the two rows of sheets. To her it is like a white hallway dancing to the unheard song of the wind.

Soon the sight of the boys standing at the other end breaks her concentration. "Don't touch the sheets!" she yells. Netta leads the twins back to the steps. Netta tries to continue her meditation, but the girls demand her attention.

After lunch, Netta and the twins are soon fast asleep. Netta and the girls are asleep. The boys are on the small bed with dolls at their heads.

It is a little past lunch. Paul comes over. Dean gathers the freshly folded sheets for Paul to deliver to Martha at Ms. Helen's. Dean enlists Paul to help carry all of the clean clothes. They take the twins so Dean can complete her daily chores at home. Lilly checks on Netta, who sleeps long into the evening.

Chapter 7

The weeks pass quickly. Soon it is Easter. Netta wants to go to church for the annual Easter egg hunt. Lucille proposes they have a private Easter egg hunt just for Netta and the twins as church on Easter day is the last thing they need. Lilly notices Netta is overly active this Sunday.

In the predawn hours, Netta wakes up, going back and forth to the bathroom. Lilly goes to Netta's room.

"Are you okay?" Lilly asks.

"I am wetting the bed, Granny. Don't tell Mama, please," Netta begs. Lilly turns on the light to get a good look.

"Are you in pain?" Lilly asks.

"No, ma'am." Lilly leaves Netta and goes to the kitchen.

As she moves about the kitchen, she prays for what she senses is about to happen. Lilly goes outside to the backyard and looks up to the sky with tears in her eyes. "Lord, please be with us this day. Please let this child bear her offspring without death. Please guide us through this." A strange sense of urgency wakes Lucille. She moves through the house to the back door.

"Mama, what are you doing out there?" Lilly returns to the back porch.

"You need to get ready. Soon it will be time." Lucille can feel her heart start to race.

"Lucille, you have get to be strong now. You need to help me start the fire under the wash pot. We will need lots of hot water. Gather all the supplies. Place them to be put in Netta's room."

They start all the preparation. Walter soon wakes. He can see there is more activity than usual.

"Walter, Mama says it will be soon," Lucille greets him.

"What will be soon?" Walter asks.

"The baby," Lucille answers. Walter sits down looking as in a trance.

"What can we do?" he asks.

"Walter, you need to go to work as usual. I will have Paul come for you later." Lucille says. Lucille walks over to Dean. She gives a note for Paul to drop off at her work. The note says, "I am feeling sick. I will not be able to work today. Signed, Lucille Jones."

Dean and Lucille carry the twins over to Lucille's house. Everybody needs to be in place if anything happens. Lilly suggests that Dean will make mint tea with paregoric. Give some to the twins so that they will be sleepy. Make some stronger when Netta needs it.

The hours pass. Netta comes out of her room. She holds her stomach as she goes into the bathroom.

"Mama, Granny, it hurts!" Netta yells. They slowly move Netta to the bed.

"Mama, Mama, I am scared. Oh, it hurts. It hurts so bad."

"Lie down." Dean lines the bed with newspaper and brown paper bags.

"Get water!" Lilly orders. "Okay, Netta I want you to open your legs wide, push them up. Just like that." Lilly puts her finger inside Netta to see if she can feel the head of the baby. Netta's pain causes her to scream. This is the same pain she has felt once before in October. Netta calls on her mother and grandmother to help stop the pain. Between pains, Dean is massaging and slowly pushing downward on Netta's stomach.

"Oh, oh, please, it hurts!" Netta is panting hard and passes out. Lucille panics.

"Mama, what to do?"

"Get the camphor oil." Netta slowly opens her eyes. Her mouth is dry. All the energy has drained from her body. She fades out.

"I can feel the head," Lilly said. "Netta, you get to push down like you do when you use the bathroom. Okay?" Netta starts to scream again. "Push, push, push!"

"I can't, I can't." Lilly takes a straight razor in her hand.

"Mama, no!" Lucille screams. Netta screams. Lilly makes a small cut. The baby's head is through.

"Push, Netta!"

Netta fades in and out. Dean is massaging and pushing. Lucille is wiping and blowing into Netta's face.

"Netta, push now!"

Lucille props Netta almost in a sitting position. Dean is pressing on Netta's stomach. Lilly is slowly pulling the baby from Netta's body. A wooden clothespin is placed on the umbilical cord. A small thin piece of leather is tied around the cord. Lilly cuts the cord with sewing scissors that are standing in alcohol. She burns the end of the cord on the baby. The afterbirth is wrapped in paper and burned on the fire out back.

Lilly sews Netta's cut up with a thread. She knots the thread. Netta is unconscious. The baby is placed in a tub of warm water to be cleaned. The baby's cry is healthy and strong; The baby is perfect.

"Mama, will Netta be all right?" Lucille asks with concern.

"As long as the bleeding stops and there is no long fever, she will be all right." Lilly answers.

Lucille leaves Netta's side. She goes over to the hope chest where Dean has the baby. She looks like Netta when she was born. Lucille just stands there in shock. Motionless she looks at this small baby sucking on her finger.

"Go ahead, pick her up. You have got to touch her," Lilly says. "Lucille, snap out of it. Pick the baby up." Dean hands the baby to Lucille. Slowly Lucille reaches her hands out. She has no emotions. Her thoughts are fresh with the pain she has just witnessed Netta go through.

From the window, Dean can see Paul and Walter in her backyard. They are looking toward the house.

"Mama, I am going outside for a minute," Dean says. Paul and Walter can see her from the back porch. They walk over.

"It's all over. Netta has a little girl."

"How is she?" Walter inquires.

"Okay."

"Where is Lucille?"

"She is inside," Dean answers.

Walter enters the kitchen. Lilly washes her hands.

"Can I see them?"

"Go ahead. Lucille is in there," Lilly answers. Walter opens the door. Lucille sits at the foot of the bed. She has tears in her eyes and is holding the baby.

"How is Netta?" Walter asks.

"We don't know. She is sleeping now," Lucille says.

"Can I see the baby? She looks like Netta," Walter says.

"Walter, what are we going to do?" Lucille asks.

"We can figure that out later," he says.

Dean returns with baby bottles and clothes. Lilly sits on the back porch reading her Bible.

"Ask Paul to take me home tomorrow, please."

"Mama, why are you leaving so soon?" Dean asks.

"I need to go home now. Boe is out there alone." Lilly knows the rest is up to Lucille and Walter. If she stays, Lucille will depend on her. No one can cover this up. The baby is there for everybody to see. From this moment on, everything Lucille and Walter do will include this child.

$$Chapter\ 8$$

Lilly and Dean enter the house. Walter sits on the table. Lucille comes out of Netta's room. Everyone takes a seat at the table.

"I am leaving tomorrow," Lilly says.

"Mama, don't go. Why?" Lucille begs.

"You two need to get your life in order now. You know how to take care of a baby. Dean will be next door to help if you need anything," Lilly says.

"Walter, when you go to work tomorrow, you should be the happy father. Lucille, you need to send a letter to your job to let them know you have given birth. Let Martha know. People will want to see the baby. You must delay this until after you have a doctor come. He needs to check you and the baby. Do you know what you are going to name her?" Lilly asks.

"Her name is Anna Belle. That is what Netta calls her favorite doll," Lucille says.

"Lucille, you need to be checked by a doctor within the next ten days. If you have your period, it will be good. If you don't have your period, you need to take a piece of feed sack, cut it into a square, and place rock salt in it. Tie the square with a cord. Wet the square. Rub the square up and down between your legs until you are sore down there. Do this the day before the doctor comes. It will look irritated, puffy, and red. Sit Netta up to be seen. Bind her breasts so they will not leak. Ask the doctor for medicine for an infection. Give this to Netta to help her heal. Do you understand?" Lilly asks.

The night is busy and restless. Lucille's role as new mother is in full force. Netta is too weak to care for the baby. Lucille squeezes Netta's breasts to fill bottles with milk to give to the baby. Netta's little breasts are not making enough milk for Anna Belle. Lucille opens up a can of evaporated milk to add to the breast milk she has collected. Taking care of the baby and helping Netta to the bathroom consume most of Lucille's night.

The next morning, Walter wakes to find Lucille in the small bed with the baby. She is asleep. He prepares something to eat.

"Lucille, Lucille," Walter says softly, trying hard not to wake the baby and Netta. "I am leaving now. You need to write a note to send to your work." Lucille slowly moves her arm from under the baby's head. She tiptoes out of the room.

"I am so tired. I forget what it is like to have a new baby. Give this note to Paul, please. Ask him to take the note to the bakery for me," Lucille says, wiping the sleep from her eyes. "Please tell Mama to come see me before she goes home."

Walter kisses her on her forehead and walks out the door. Lucille sits, staring out of the window, thinking about her past and wondering about her future.

"Mama," Netta calls.

"What is it, Netta?" Lucille answers opening the door.

"Can I see the baby now?" Netta says. In all the excitement, Lucille realizes Netta has never really looked at Anna Belle. Netta looks at the baby in amazement.

"She is so little," Netta says.

"Netta, you know this is your baby, and I know this is your baby. You can never tell. This has to be our secret, never tell. If you do, someone will ask you who the father is. Do you remember the man that hurt you?" Netta nods yes. "He is the father. We can never let anyone know. Remember what happened and never tell. This is your sister, not your baby. I am the Mama," Lucille stresses. Netta sinks back into the pillow in fear and confusion.

"Her name is Anna Belle like your baby doll. In a few days, a doctor will come to see the baby and me. You will have to act as if nothing has happened to you. Do you understand?" Lucille leaves the room.

"How is Netta?" Lilly asks. "I am getting ready to leave. I want to see Netta before I go." Lilly says.

"Mama, are you mad at me?" Lucille asks.

"I don't know. I think I am mad at the world because of what happened here yesterday. I feel bad for Netta. She is so young. I always kept you girls so close to me when you were small. I am not blaming you for what happened. The problem is I can't blame anyone now for what happened," Lilly explains. Lilly walks past Lucille to see Netta.

"Oh, Granny," Netta says with hands held out. "Mama, says the baby's name is Anna Belle like my baby doll."

"Netta, if you want to come and stay with me some time, you can. I am leaving and going home today." Lilly says.

"Granny, don't go. I want you to stay. Please don't leave. I am sick," Netta begs.

"No, you are not sick. This is what happens when a woman has a baby." Lilly explains.

"Mama says I cannot tell about the baby," Netta adds.

"She is right. Netta, you can never tell. It will make people ask questions— questions we cannot answer. It is something you will have to take to the grave. I am sorry you have to know this so early in life. Give me a hug," Lilly says as she leaves the room.

"Lucille, you get a good kid in there. She has been through a lot. Be careful, the stitches will be ready to come out in a few days. Check them every day. Make sure there is no infection. Wash them with warm salt water. I will pray for you and Walter. This is not going to be easy. Don't push Netta to the side. It was not her fault." Lilly kisses Lucille and left the house.

As Lilly gets in the truck to leave, she feels very sad as if a death has occurred. She knows Netta is no longer a child. The sad part about it is Netta does not know she is not a child. Lilly fears Lucille and Walter will get so caught up with the new baby, they will forget that Netta needs to be loved too. The ride home is long. Lilly wonders if she should have stayed longer, but for some strange reason she is being pulled back home. When Paul pulls up to the house, Uncle Boe is not in sight. "Boe must be in the barn," Lilly says.

"I will check," Paul answers. Lilly makes her way up the stairs. She enters her house. Things are in disarray. *Just like a man*, she thought to herself. She can hear groans coming from Boe's room.

"Boe, you in there?" Lilly opens the door. Boe is lying in his bed.

"What are you doing in bed this time of the morning?" Lilly asks.

"Last night, while I was sitting on the porch, I had a pain in my left arm. All morning I have been having heartburn. I am glad you came back home. I was hoping Paul came out today. I think I need some soda water. I cannot find where you kept the baking soda," Boe explains.

Lilly starts to prepare the soda water for Boe. The feeling of urgency finally left. Paul comes into the kitchen. Lilly tells him about Boe's illness. Paul says he will milk the cow and collect the eggs before he leaves. Lilly assures Paul there is nothing wrong. Boe has eaten too fast or too much. Paul makes sure everything is okay before he takes his leave. Lilly cleans the house and prepares for the next day. Boe states that he is better. Boe inquires about Netta. Lilly tells him everything is fine, "Netta had a little girl. Her name is Anna Belle."

Meanwhile on the other side of the county at the lumberyard, Walter receives multiple pats on the back.

"Now you can try for a son," Adley laughs. Walter finds himself liking the attention, along with the offer to have drinks to toast for his first child.

"When is the barbecue?" Adley asks.

"What barbecue?" Walter replies.

"You know, a coming out barbecue!" one of the guys yells.

"Oh, I don't know. I have to see when Lucille feels up to it," Walter says.

"We will chip in on the meat. I will get Martha to make potato salad. Once Martha finds out, she will be over there in a hurry," Adley says. "Lucille is really not up to company yet. Let me get back to you."

Lucille is at home trying to divide her time between the house cleaning, the baby, and Netta. Netta is in pain. The bleeding has increased. Several times during the day, she wishes for Lilly. The baby cries consistently. Lucille is confused as to what to do. Lucille tells Netta she needs to go over to Dean's. Lucille wraps the baby in a blanket, and walks next door. Dean is in the backyard.

"What are you doing, Lucille?" Dean asks in surprise.

"I need help. I don't know what I am doing anymore. The baby is crying, something is wrong," Lucille answers. Dean takes the baby into the house. Dean examines the baby.

"Does Netta feed the baby?" Dean asks.

"No, I squeezed milk from her breasts and mixed it with evaporated milk from the can," Lucille says.

"Help me with the twins. We need to go over to your house," Dean says anxiously.

Lucille and Dean manage to get everyone over to Lucille's house. They can hear Netta calling before they enter. Lucille hurries to Netta's room. Netta tries to get up. There is blood all over the bed. Dean tells Lucille to put water in the bathtub. Dean places the baby on the bed. The twins gather around it; to them, this is a moving doll.

"We have to get Netta in the tub. We need to stop the bleeding," Dean orders.

"What about the stitches?" Lucille questions.

Dean grabs Netta under her arms. "Get her feet," Dean says. They placed Netta in the tub with her nightgown on. Netta screams.

"Get towels and dry clothes. Bring Netta's sheets off the bed." Lucille goes to Netta's room. She snatches the sheets off the bed.

"Let's lift her out. Lay her on the floor. We need pads. Get as many as you have," Dean says. Dean props Netta's feet up in the tub, putting them higher than her body.

"Don't cry, baby. It will be all right," Dean urges. The boys are standing in the bathroom door.

"Lucille, come get the boys!" Dean yells. Lucille's adrenaline is flowing; she is moving at high speed. Everything is turning upside down. Lucille pulls the boys out of the door from behind. She grabs the collars on their little shirts and closes the bathroom door. The baby is crying.

"Go see the baby! Bring her back in here. This is going to take a while," Dean says. The girls are shaking the bed and rocking the baby. Lucille picks up Anna Belle and carries her to the bathroom. Dean changes Netta's clothes. Lucille stands, rocking the baby.

"Lucille, put the baby down and help me," Dean demands. Lucille places Anna Belle on towels on the floor. Dean and Lucille redress Netta.

"Netta, can you walk?" Dean asks.

"I think so, Aunt Dean," Netta replies. Dean helps Netta to her room.

"Sit here on the small bed until we can make your bed." Dean says. The girls, Pauline and Paulette, flank her on each side.

Lucille is in the kitchen with Anna Belle. Anna Belle is still crying.

"Give me the baby," Dean says. Dean undresses Anna Belle to check her umbilical cord. It is okay. Dean redresses Anna Belle.

"Lucille, Netta's bed needs to be changed," Dean says. Lucille leaves the kitchen. Dean walks around the kitchen, holding Anna Belle. Dean tastes the milk Lucille had prepared.

"That's your problem. Your Mama did not dilute the milk," Dean utters. Dean places two pans on the stove with water in them. She adds a can of milk to one pan with half a spoon of honey. In the second pan, she adds mint tea and paregoric. Rocking Anna Belle, Dean says, "Aunt Dean will take care of you." She gently kisses Anna Belle on her head.

With the help of the twins, Lucille places Netta in her bed.

"Mama, I am sorry, don't be mad at me." Netta can feel the stress of her mother.

"I am not upset at you. I just get a lot on me right now. I love you," Lucille replies. Lucille enters the kitchen.

"You did not dilute the milk. Anna Belle's stomach hurts. I will give her some mint tea. It will help her tummy. Give Netta a cup. She needs to rest," Dean advises. Lucille sits down at the table.

"Dean, I am not going to make it. How can I pull this off when I can't even make it through one day?" Lucille feels defeated. Dean places her hand on her sister shoulder.

"Yes, you will make it. You are just tired. Go get some rest. When you wake up, you will think clearer. The twins and I will stay a little while."

Paul comes over to Lucille's house, looking for Dean and the twins.

"Why are you over here?" he asks.

"Lucille was overwhelmed from lack of sleep. Here, hold the baby. I will fix you something to eat here," Dean says. The boys want their father's attention. They try to tell Paul what they had witnessed earlier. Paul just listens. He looks at Anna Belle. He thinks about all that has taken place to get her here.

"Everybody, come eat," Dean calls. Dean takes Anna Belle from Paul.

"I will go lay Anna Belle with Lucille. We can eat and leave," Dean says.

Later Walter comes into the house. He goes to Netta's room. Netta is asleep. He goes to his bedroom. Lucille and Anna Belle are asleep. Walter stares at Lucille and the baby for a minute; he feels a sense of pride. Walter slowly closes the door.

He goes into the kitchen to make a sandwich. He is surprised that there is no bread. He takes the pressed meat, rolls it up, and eats it with a glass of cider. Lucille can hear Walter moving about in the kitchen. She slowly gets out of bed.

"How was your day?" Lucille says to Walter.

"Okay. The fellows want to give us a coming-out barbecue. I told them I have to check with you about when," Walter answers. Lucille gets up from the table. She goes over to the counter. Dean has left a note on how to prepare the milk. "There is four-cup mason jar full of milk for Anna Belle." The note goes on to say, "Do not squeeze Netta's breasts. Do not let her feed the baby. Rub camphor oil and alum water on Netta's breasts. This will help dry up the milk in her breasts." Lucille finishes reading the note.

"We need to get the doctor over here," Lucille says, staring out of the window.

"Are you ready to do that?" Walter responds.

"Yes, I need to get it over with. I will start supper now," Lucille says. They can hear crying coming from the bedroom. Lucille goes to get Anna Belle. She hands her to Walter.

"I need to check on Netta," Lucille says. Netta is still asleep. Lucille returns to the kitchen. She begins to cook. She warms a bottle of milk. She hands it to Walter. Walter is clumsy in handling Anna Belle and the bottle. Lucille helps him adjust.

"Mama," Netta calls. Lucille goes to Netta's room.

"Mama, I need to go," Netta says.

"Here, I will leave this bucket in your room. Try to get out of bed slowly. I will help you, but you need to do it on your own. I will be back to empty it. Are you hungry now?" Lucille asks. Lucille leaves the room.

Netta struggles to use the bucket. A mixture of blood and urine flows from her body. She adjusts a clean pad in her panties. She wants Lucille to spend more time with her. She is sick. Lucille has never left Netta alone before when she is ill.

"I will take the baby to Netta," Walter says.

"No," Lucille answers, "I don't want Netta to have that type of bond with her."

"How are we going to keep the baby away from Netta?" Walter questions. "This doesn't make sense,"

"I know we can't keep the baby away from Netta, but for now, let's just take care of her without Netta's help,"

Walter is puzzled, but he does not question Lucille. Lucille is afraid Netta will feel the bond of a mother. In Lucille's mind, in order for this charade to work, Anna Belle must see only one mother. At this point, Lucille decides to place a block in her mind—she is Anna Belle's mother.

"Give me a minute to take Netta her food then I will come back to get Anna Belle," Lucille says. Netta is sitting up in the bed. "How do you feel?" Lucille asks.

"I hurt down there," Netta replies.

"It will stop soon, we just have to make sure you keep clean to heal," Lucille adds. "Eat. I will empty this for you." Lucille leaves the room. She goes to the bathroom to clean the bucket. She looks into the bucket. All Lucille sees is blood. Lucille is concerned that Netta is still bleeding too much. Lucille returns the bucket to Netta's room.

Lucille enters the kitchen. She takes Anna Belle from Walter. Walter finishes his meal.

"I am going outside to the workshop," he says. Lucille sits, holding Anna Belle. Her thoughts drift over the chaos she went through today. She knows she has to come up with a plan—a plan to deal with the change which has come into her life. Why is this so different from when Netta was a baby? She searches her mind to find an answer as to what went wrong.

Lucille prepares Anna Belle for the night. She takes Anna Belle into Netta's room and places her on the small bed. Netta has finished eating. She is lying on her side.

"Mama, can I see Anna Belle?" Netta asks. Lucille moves the tray; she places it on the floor. Lucille holds Anna Belle just out of reach of Netta.

"You get some rest. I am going to lay her here for now." Lucille places Anna Belle on the small bed. "I don't want her to disturb you. I will take your tray to the kitchen and be right back," Lucille says. Lucille rushes the tray to the table and goes back to get Anna Belle to place her in Lucille's bedroom.

As Lucille returns to Netta's room, she can hear Netta crying from the hall. "Netta, are you okay?" Lucille says with concern.

"Mama, I'm hurt." Netta says. Lucille goes to Netta's side. "I know you are. I can make you some tea to help you sleep," Lucille says. Lucille leaves the room.

Netta buries her face in the pillow to scream and cry. Netta does not know how to tell her mother she is hurting inside. She does not know how to tell Lucille she is still afraid—afraid with a fear sometimes so horrible that she cannot explain it, but it makes her feel sad inside. Netta feels sad inside. She does not need tea. She needs her mother to pay attention to her and love her. All she wants is for Lucille to hold and reassure her.

Chapter 9

The next morning, Lucille seems to have a better grip on her routine. Now she is faced with the doctor's visit. Lucille hopes her monthly period would happen before the doctor comes, but it does not. Today Lucille will have to cut a square from a feed sack. After Lucille completes her nightly routine, she goes into the bathroom, taking with her the feed sack and rock salt. Lucille wets the feed sack and ties up the way Lilly has instructed. She puts one hand on the bathtub. She squatted down, spreading her legs. She reaches under her body and begins to rub as hard as she can. Soon she can feel the stinging and the burning of the feed sack against the most delicate part of her body. Once she starts to bleed, she takes a cold wet rag and applies it to her raw skin. Lucille wears a pad to bed that night.

The next morning, Lucille gets up early. She feeds Anna Belle. Lucille knows she needs to get Netta dressed and sitting up when the doctor comes. Netta is slow to move. Lucille has removed the stitches two days ago. Netta is still bleeding heavily and having pain.

Lucille placed Netta at the kitchen table. Lucille puts on her best nightgown.

Lucille places Anna Belle in the middle of her bed.

Soon there is a knock on the door. "Who is it?" Lucille yells.

"Doctor Hill," he answers.

"Come in." Lucille listens for the door to open and says, "We are back here, doctor."

"Good morning. How are you, Mrs. Jones?"

"We are good," Lucille answers.

"I need to wash my hands," Doctor Hill says.

"You can go into the kitchen, Netta is in there. Netta, show the doctor where he can wash his hands!" Lucille yells. Netta is nervous. Lucille has told her earlier not to move until the doctor leaves.

"Yes, ma'am."

Doctor Hill follows Netta's voice.

"How are you this morning, little lady?" he says to Netta.

"I am fine," Netta says.

Doctor Hill returns to Lucille's side. "Okay, you need to lie down. Open your legs." Doctor Hill notices swelling and abrasion in the vaginal area. This can happen during natural birth. He inserts his finger inside her and presses down on her stomach with the other hand. "You are coming along fine," the doctor says. He washes his hands again.

"Come here, little one." He undresses Anna Belle down to her diaper. He examines the umbilical cord. "Who cut the cord for you?" he inquires.

"My mother acted as midwife," Lucille answers.

"She did a good job. The cord should fall off soon. Just keep it dry. How is her appetite and her bowels?"

"Everything is fine so far," Lucille says. "Doctor, can I have some penicillin pills? I am having night sweats."

"I think I have some with me. Yes, here you go," he says. "You will be just fine. What's the baby's name?"

"Anna Belle," Lucille answers. He gives Lucille the baby document to be filled out and filed at the county seat. Lucille pays the doctor and escorts him to the door.

Lucille goes to the kitchen where Netta is waiting. Netta stands. She leans on the table for support. "Let's get you back to bed. I will bring you some tea and medicine in a few minutes." Lucille goes back to the kitchen. She feels so much relief. She has passed the new mother test. Her stress is less for now.

Lucille takes Netta a penicillin pill and a cup of mint tea.

"Here you go. I will make lunch soon." As soon as Lucille says that, Anna Belle starts to cry. "Mama is coming baby," she says, leaving the room swiftly. Netta has never heard Lucille call herself "Mama" for anyone else. It made her feel strange. Netta is not used to sharing her mother with anyone else.

There is some resentment there.

Lucille changes the diaper and gives Anna Belle her lunch. Netta hears the back door close. She moves her tray away. "Mama," she calls. There is no answer. Netta manages to get out of bed. She walks along the hallway, leaning on the wall for support. She looks in the kitchen, but no one is there. She looks in Lucille's room, but no one is there. Netta goes back to the kitchen just in time to see Lucille carrying Anna Belle to Dean's house. Netta doesn't understand why Lucille just leaves her without saying something.

"Hello," Lucille says, "It's us, me and Anna Belle."

"Where is Netta?" Dean asks.

"She is at home in bed," Lucille replies.

"How is she? Has the bleeding stopped?"

"No, it seems to be slowing some."

"She needs to get more sun," Dean advises. "You have got to get her up, so she will be strong."

"I got medicine from Doctor Hill this morning. He came to examine me and Anna Belle. He says we are just fine," Lucille says with a smile.

"Of course you are. You did not have a baby," Dean says. "What is happening to you? You need to focus on getting Netta well."

"I am thinking about taking her to Mama for a while."

"Why?" Dean asks. "Netta is just twelve years old, Lucille. You need to be careful. She just went through a difficult birth. Her poor mind must be overloaded with questions. Questions about the different emotions she is going through, and now you want to send her away."

"Well, anyway, this weekend we will be having the coming out barbecue," Lucille says, changing the subject.

"I know. Paul told me," Dean says.

"Well, bye, we have get to go."

Lucille and Anna Belle leave the house. Dean watches her sister as she walks away; to her it seems Lucille is acting strangely.

But what would I do, or how would I act if my twelve-year-old daughter gave birth? she thought to herself.

Lucille is surprised to see Netta in the kitchen when she opens the kitchen door.

"Mama, I was calling you," Netta responds.

"What did you want?" Lucille asks. "I am glad to see you out of bed. Did you wipe your breasts like I told you?"

"Yes, ma'am," Netta answers. "Can I hold Anna Belle?"

"No, you need to make sure your breasts are not leaking first. She will smell the milk on you. Go get two pads and put them in your bra to make sure you are not leaking milk. Then you can hold her."

Netta walks slowly down the hall to her room. Lucille knows that Anna Belle is sleepy. She takes Anna Belle to her room and sits in the rocking chair. This way, she will put Anna Belle completely to sleep before Netta finishes dressing.

It is hard for Netta to get dressed. She struggles with the bra. The pads make it hard to put on the bra. Netta finally gets dressed. She goes to the kitchen, yet no one is there. Netta goes to Lucille's bedroom.

"She is asleep now. You can hold her when she wakes up," Lucille says. Netta goes into the kitchen, waiting for Lucille. Netta is excited she is finally getting time alone with her mother.

"Can you cut up some onions for me?" Lucille asks. "Netta, this weekend we are having a barbecue. Remember that Anna Belle is your sister. You cannot tell anyone about the secret."

"Mama, do you still love me?" Netta asks.

"Why would you say something like that?"

"You aren't with me anymore."

"I am busy with Anna Belle right now. It just seems that way. She needs more attention than you," Lucille says. Netta becomes silent. That is not the answer she wants to hear.

Walter is happy to see Netta up. "I have not seen much of you lately. Are you feeling better?" Walter asks.

"Yes, sir," Netta answers. For a few minutes, everything is like the way it used to be with just the three of them.

After supper, Netta becomes tired. "Mama, will you come to my room with me?" Netta asks. Lucille follows Netta to her room. Netta wants her mother with her like old times. Lucille uses this time to check Netta's breasts. Netta wants to cry. She still is not getting the kind of attention she wants. Lucille kisses Netta on her forehead and leaves the room. Lucille and Walter talk about the upcoming barbecue.

The days pass quickly. People come to the house early this Saturday morning. The men want to start cooking the meat in advance. More likely they want to start drinking early.

"Walter, keep them out of the house. It is early. They will wake Anna Belle," Lucille commands. Walter gets dressed and joins the men in the backyard. Lucille watches out of the window. She can see that Walter is acting like a proud daddy.

"Netta, Netta!" Lucille yells. Netta lies quiet and still in bed. She hesitates to answer. "Netta, are you still asleep?" Lucille says, standing in the doorway. Netta slowly turns over to say, "Yes, ma'am."

"You need to get up and get dressed early. People are coming around here today. Netta, don't jump rope today. Stay on the porch or close to the stairs. You cannot run or jump. It's just too soon," Lucille says, leaving the room.

This is the only time Netta wants to stay in her room. She doesn't understand the effect of child's play on her body now. All she understands is that she cannot play.

The crowd grows, so the backyard is full of people. Netta notices how everybody is making a fuss over Anna Belle and Lucille. No one seems to notice she is there. She cannot play with the children. It has been months since she attended school. Most of her friends have new friends, and they do not notice her.

Netta gets up from the stairs. She goes to her room. There she sits on the small bed, playing with her doll. "You are my Anna Belle," she says as she strokes the doll's head. Netta soon falls asleep as she plays.

Outside everybody is commenting on how pretty Anna Belle is. Most of them say she looks a lot like Netta. Walter is tipsy from the cigars and whiskey.

Dean asks Lucille where Netta is. She has not seen her for hours. Dean looks for Netta in the kitchen. Dean goes to Netta's room. There she finds her asleep in her clothes on the small bed. Dean takes off Netta's shoes and places a blanket over her. Dean kisses her on her forehead and closes the door as she leaves the room.

Netta is getting stronger as the days pass. Anna Belle is growing. Lucille teaches Netta how to prepare Anna Belle's bottles and food. Lucille has taken some time off because of childbirth. Netta will have to prepare the bottles and be responsible for Anna Belle while they are at Dean's house during the day.

Tomorrow will be Lucille's first day back at work. That night, Lucille packs Anna Belle's bag. The bag contains a change of clothes, diapers, diaper cream, a wash towel, crackers, milk, and a bottle. Walter is in the kitchen with Lucille, holding Anna Belle. He is amazed at Anna Belle's progress.

Netta sits at the table; she feels so invisible. Netta gets up from the table. She goes to her room to play with her dolls. Lucille and Walter retire to their room. Walter tells Lucille she looks so peaceful rocking Anna Belle to sleep. Lucille goes to sleep that night with anticipation.

Early the next morning, Lucille is up. She moves through the house anxiously. "Netta, come get your sister! Walter has to go," Lucille yells. Walter kisses Anna Belle and hands her to Netta.

"Bye, Netta," Walter says.

"Netta, take Anna Belle in your room with you. You need to finish dressing." Lucille scolds. Netta places Anna Belle on the small bed. She puts on her shoes. "Here, dress your sister," Lucille says, handing Netta a small top and bottom.

Soon it is time to go over to Dean's. Lucille can see Martha from the walkway. "Good morning, stranger. I have not seen you since the barbecue. Let me see the baby?" Martha says.

"Come inside, I don't want her to catch a chill," Lucille says.

"Hi, Netta, are you losing weight?" Martha asks. Netta does not answer. She walks ahead. "Hi, Aunt Dean," Netta says.

"Martha, I thought you had left." Dean says in surprise.

"Lucille told me to come in if I want to see Anna Belle," Martha responds.

"Hi, Netta. I am sorry I did not answer you," Dean says. "Martha, do you want to come for the Fourth of July? Mama and Uncle Boe are coming."

"Yeah, I get to run. Lucille, you want a ride?" Martha asks.

"Sure," Lucille says. She kisses Anna Belle and leaves.

"Netta, did you eat?" Dean asks.

"No, ma'am," she answers.

All day Netta plays and helps Dean around the house. Dean takes care of Anna Belle. Dean knows the importance of letting Netta be a child. Dean knows Netta misses being a little girl. The children play in the warm spring day. Dean sits on the porch with Anna Belle. As evening grows near, Dean calls everyone in to eat. Netta says to Dean, "Aunt Dean, I am glad you still love me."

"I will always love you, Netta," Dean replies.

"Mama and Walter don't," Netta says.

"Why do you say that, Netta?" Dean asks.

"They just don't," Netta says.

"Hello, I am here." It is Lucille. "Where is my baby? Look what I have," Lucille says. Lucille is holding a small teddy bear. Netta waits for Lucille to notice her and give her a kiss, a hug or something.

"Are you ready to go, Netta? Get Anna Belle's things. Let's go," Lucille orders.

"Goodbye, Aunt Dean," Netta says.

"Night, Netta," Dean says. Dean can see the sadness in Netta's eyes. This routine is reenacted for several weeks.

It is the Fourth of July. Netta is very excited. Soon she will see Lilly. Netta is in the yard playing with the twins. Dean, Lucille, Paul, Adley, and Martha sit on the porch.

"Here comes Granny!" Netta yells. Netta runs to meet Lilly. "Hi, Granny," Netta says. Netta hugs Lilly.

"How are you feeling, baby?" Lilly asks. The twins surround Lilly.

"Hi, Mama," Dean says, hugging Lilly. Lucille hugs Lilly, then Martha. Everybody stands in the yard, greeting her.

Beep, beep. It is Walter driving a car. Everybody is surprised. "Hello … Hello, I say!" Walter yells from the road. Everybody is still in shocked surprise. Walter does not let anyone know his intention of buying a car. Lucille walks to the car, holding Anna Belle.

"Where, when, who?" Lucille fumbles through her words. "I have been saving money from the furniture I made. Paul taught me to drive. How do you like it?" Walter says. Netta and the twins want to see. They climb into the car and bounce on the seats.

"Paul, did you know?" Lucille asks.

"Yes," Paul answers.

"Why didn't you tell me?" Dean asks.

"Because, if I tell you, it would be just like telling Lucille. Walter wants this to be a surprise," Paul says. "How about a ride?" Walter and Paul climb into the car and drive away.

Lilly enters the house with all of the children behind her. Lilly has brought all of her grandchildren a gift.

"Netta, I brought you something special," Lilly says.

"What … what is it?" Netta says, bouncing up and down. Lilly hands Netta a dream catcher.

"It's pretty, Granny. What is it?" Netta asks.

"It's a dream catcher," Lilly answers. "You hang it above your bed, and all your good dreams will come true. All the bad dreams will be caught and thrown away forever."

Netta is happy. It has been a long time since she got a gift. This is the best day Netta can remember in a long time. Today should last forever. The music, food, and fun last late into the night.

The next day, Lucille is up extra early. She wants to get the girls up early. Lucille and Walter decided last night that he would drive Lucille to work. Netta will walk Anna Belle next door.

"Netta, take care of Anna Belle. See you later tonight!" Lucille yells, getting into the car. Netta watches as Lucille and Walter drives by. Netta manages to make it to Dean's house.

"Hi, Aunt Dean," Netta says, sitting down with Anna Belle.

"Where is your Mama?" Dean asks.

"Walter drove her to work," Netta answers. It kind of upset Dean that Lucille has not come in before she leaves for work.

"Where is Granny?" Netta asks. "Mama and Uncle Boe had to leave." Dean answers. Netta is disappointed. Netta wants to spend time with Lilly.

Lilly and Boe leaves early. Boe needs to see a doctor. He has trouble sleeping. Lilly worries about his health. Lilly also worries about Netta. She intends to have a talk with Lucille. Netta's spirit is very needy and wanting. *This can lead to Netta misunderstanding what love is,* Lilly thinks to herself.

Chapter 10

Boe comes out of the doctor's room, shaking the doctor's hand. "Well, what did the doctor say?" Lilly asks.

"Oh ... he says I need to get more rest," Boe answers. Paul takes Lilly and Boe home to the farm.

That night, Lilly dreams of Boe in a field of white light. Small white and pink lights dance around him. She is in the dream. She is out in back of the house calling for Boe. He never comes.

The next morning, Lilly gets Boe's best suit to clean it.

"Why are you getting my suit out?" Boe asks her. Lilly does not answer. Lilly starts to hum a church song. She will do this all day long. That night, Lilly reads her Bible. From time to time, she holds the Bible to her chest, rocks, and cries. Boe notices his sister. He knows something is weighing heavy on her mind. This is not the first time Lilly has done this. Boe knows that once the praying is over, Lilly will tell him what is on her mind. Boe decides to go to bed early.

"Good night, I think I will go to bed," Boe says. Lilly does not answer. Lilly does not hear him. Lilly prays late into the night.

The next day, Martha delivers sheets to Dean.

"Ms. Helen is talking about leaving town again," Martha says, drinking coffee.

"Well, you say she talks about this all the time," Dean says.

"I know. She wants me to come."

"You don't have to go if you don't want to."

"I know that. Ms. Helen is the only job I ever had. Mama worked for her before she died. She took care of me. That's the reason I never came out to the farm to live with Aunt Lilly," Martha says. "Ms. Helen gives me money. I have a closet full of clothes. I drive her car. I live in her house. I know her secrets. She trusts me. She protects me. I feel like I owe her."

"Hi, Aunt Dean." It is Netta.

"Good morning, Netta. Bring Anna Belle over here. She truly is growing up fast. Well, I have to go," Martha says, handing Anna Belle to Netta.

"Bye." Netta places Anna Belle in a highchair.

"These sheets always smell sweet," Netta says.

"Yeah, it's the perfume the ladies wear. When someone sweats on a sheet, that sheet will smell of their skin," Dean answers. "You can take Paul his lunch today. How would you like that?"

"I can go by myself?" Netta asks.

"I think it will be okay. It's just at the corner." Dean says. Netta is excited.

She always has Anna Belle with her. This will be a moment alone.

At lunchtime, Dean hands Netta a brown paper bag. Netta skips and kicks rocks on her way to the store.

"Here you go, Uncle Paul," Netta says.

"Thank you," Paul says. Netta walks slowly, picking flowers. In the distance, she can see the white sheets. She stops at the gate and takes a deep breath. At that moment, everything seems right.

That night at home, Netta wants to tell Lucille about the adventure she had today. It is overshadowed by Lucille's driving lessons. Walter teaches Lucille how to drive. Tomorrow the whole family will drive out to Lilly's house for Lucille to practice away from traffic.

Lilly and Boe cook as if it is a holiday. This will be the first time the whole family spends the night. Because Lucille and Walter never had a car before, a trip like this is unheard of.

"We have been waiting for you all to get here," Boe says. "Lilly baked a cake, Netta," Boe teases.

Everyone has a big lunch. Boe and Walter go to the barn. Walter will repair a table Lilly wants to move into the house. Netta helps Lilly complete a quilt. Lucille and Anna Belle are swinging in the swing. Netta loves the attention Lilly gives her. She starts to sing.

In the barn, Boe talks to Walter about having someone sharecropping the farm.

"Have you made up your mind on this?" Walter asks.

"Lilly was always against it before, but now she is bringing it up," Boe says.

"Why don't you just sell the farm?"

"I don't think Lilly will ever sell this farm. There is another house on the other side of the farm. I used to live there with my wife. I came to live here when she died. Lilly was a widow, the girls are gone, and it seemed like the right thing to do. We work and sold the vegetables to get by," Boe says. "They will have to fix up the house, it needs repairs," Boe adds.

"Uncle Boe, will you come and pull on this as hard as you can?" Walter asks.

Boe stands up and falls to the ground. Walter drops his tools.

"Boe, Boe," Walter says, slapping him lightly on the face. Boe opens his eyes.

"What happened?" Boe says.

"You passed out," Walter answers. "Let's go back to the house."

"No, just wait. Don't talk to Lilly about this. She is worried about something right now. I don't want to worry her anymore," Boe begs. "Just let me sit down for a minute. I just stood up too fast. That's all," Boe adds. Walter continues to repair the table. He keeps a watchful eye on Boe.

Later that night, the family sits on the porch. Netta is in the front yard, chasing lighting bugs. Lilly notices how Lucille is so attentive to Anna Belle. "Lucille, Netta is feeling unloved. You need to spend more time with her. She is growing up. Even with what she has been through, she still needs to be guided," Lilly advises.

"Mama, Netta is just fine. She is just lazy. I can never get her out of her room. Every time I look up, she is in her room," Lucille says.

"Lucille, why is she in her room?"

"She plays with her dolls. Mama, please, I know my own child," Lucille becomes upset. "I am going to go to bed. Don't let Netta stay out there all night." Lucille takes Anna Belle and goes to her room.

"Boe says you are thinking of sharecropping," Walter says.

"The time is right. Now I just need the right person," Lilly says.

The next morning Lilly is the kitchen. Netta comes into the kitchen.

"Good morning, Granny," Netta says."

"Morning, baby did you sleep well?" Lilly asks.

"Yes, ma'am," Netta replies.

"Do you want some flap cakes with honey?" Lilly asks.

"Morning, Lilly. Morning, Netta." Walter says. Soon everybody is seated at the table. After breakfast, Lucille and Netta help Lilly with cleaning the house.

"Mama, Walter told me last night that Uncle Boe passed out in the barn yesterday. Uncle Boe asks him not to tell you because you are worried about something, and he did not want to worry you anymore," Lucille says. "Mama, what is it? What are you worried about?"

"I am just worried about Boe. That's all, nothing else," Lilly answers.

"Are you ready?" Walter yells from outside.

"Yeah, here I come," Lucille answers. "Netta, take Anna Belle and swing with her. She will be sleepy soon. Then you can play," Lucille orders.

Lucille leaves the house with excitement. This will be her first driving lesson. Netta follows alone. She goes to the swing as Lucille instructed. Lilly can see the look on Netta's face.

"Give me the baby. You go play," Lilly says. Lilly sits on the porch rocking Anna Belle. She sees Boe making his way to the barn. Lilly knows Boe is sick. She begins to rock and pray for strength when she needs it.

Walter has been teaching Lucille for the majority of the day. "It's time to go back and get the kids. We can get home before dark if we leave now," Walter says. Lucille changes place with Walter so he can drive back to Lilly's house.

"Walter, I think I will let Netta stay with Mama and Uncle Boe for this week. If Uncle Boe is sick, maybe someone needs to stay." Lucille says.

"Did you ask Netta if she wants to stay?" Walter asks.

"No, she won't mind. She likes being out here with Mama," Lucille says. Arriving at the house, they can see Netta is playing catch with the dog. "I will tell Mama that I am leaving Netta." Lilly is in the kitchen.

"I saw you all coming. I was warming up dinner for you. How was your lesson?" Lilly asks.

"Walter says I did well. A few more times and I can drive without him," Lucille explains. "Don't warm the food. We can take it with us. Mama, I want to leave Netta with you for the week. I will have Paul bring her some clothes when he comes on Monday"

"Did you tell Netta this?" Lilly asks in surprise. "Lucille, Netta doesn't need to be out here. She wants to be with you. I am not saying she can't stay. I am saying to ask her if she wants to stay. That's all." Lilly begs.

"All right, I will ask her." Lucille agrees.

Lucille walks to the tree where Netta is drawing in the dirt.

"Netta, Uncle Boe is sick. I am leaving you here with Granny in case she needs help," Lucille tells Netta.

"Mama, I don't want to stay out here. There is no one to play with," Netta begs.

"This is for only one week. I will send your clean clothes back with Paul," Lucille says. "Now stop pouting, and act like a big girl. Don't start crying. You will make Mama think you don't want to be with her. Don't you love your granny?" Lucille walks away.

Netta turns her face away from the porch. She cannot help the tears. Once again, Lucille is leaving her when she doesn't want to stay. Lucille reaches the porch. Lilly stands there with the food wrapped up for travel.

"Told you, Mama, Netta will be just fine." Lilly hands her the food. Lilly helps by carrying Anna Belle to the car.

"You all be careful on your way home," Lilly says. Netta watches as they drive away. As Lilly starts up the steps she turns. "Netta you okay?" Lilly shouts.

"Yes, ma'am," Netta answers. Afraid of hurting her grandmother's feeling, she stays near the tree until her tears dry. Netta feels betrayed and helpless.

Chapter 11

The next morning, Paul is there at his usual time. "Here are the clothes your Mama sent you." Paul says, handing Netta a bundle of clothes. "Your aunt Dean told me to tell you hello, and the twins too. She says she will miss you," Paul adds. Netta leaves the porch to go to her room.

"Walter says you all are thinking about share cropping?" Paul questions.

"Yes, I have made up my mind. The time is right," Lilly answers. "Will you put up a sign at the store for me?" Lilly asks. "They can make a good living. I will rent out the little hut that sits up front near the gate. It sits on the highway. People pass there all the time. We stopped selling food there some time ago. There is a house down the private road. We will rent it out if someone wants to live in it. Boe and his wife lived in it before she died. It will need some repairs."

"Boe is seventy-six now. We grow more than we eat. We give most of the food to the church. Just make the sign as soon as you get back, please. I will be so thankful," Lilly says."

"Yes, ma'am. I will do that as soon as I get back to the store," Paul says. "Is Uncle Boe in the barn?"

"Yes," Lilly answers. Lilly watches Paul as he walks toward the barn. "Netta, are you in there?" Lilly calls.

"Yes, ma'am," Netta answers.

"Come out here with me," Lilly suggests. "You feel all right?" Lilly asks. "What is the matter, Netta?"

"Nothing, I just miss the twins," Netta replies.

"Well, soon you can go back to school," Lilly says.

Going to school is the furthest thing from Netta's thoughts. Netta's thoughts drift to her home where she longs to be. Netta wants to go home with Paul. She knows that without her mother to say "yes," she will have to stay until Lucille comes for her.

"Granny, I don't know what grade I will be in when I go back to school," Netta says.

"You have done all your lessons. Your uncle Paul can vouch for you if there is any doubt." Lilly assures her.

"The children will make fun of me."

"Why do you say that? No one will make fun of you." Lilly says, hugging Netta. Lilly sees that Netta cannot separate the truth from the lies. *All Netta's life, we taught her to tell the truth. Now we have to teach her how to lie,* Lilly thinks to herself.

"I will see you later this week," Paul says as he gets into the truck. Netta screams inside for Paul, *Turn around, come back, and get me.*

"Let's go and start lunch. I have a few pieces of cloth to make a dress. How would you like that?" Lilly says, leading Netta by the hand.

By the time Paul returns to town, it is lunchtime. He goes to his house. In the backyard, he can see Dean and the children.

"How is Mama?" Dean asks. "She and Netta are fine. They send their love," Paul answers.

"How is Netta? Did she seem sad?" Dean asks.

"Come to think of it, she was quiet. How did you know?" Paul asks.

"I just feel it," Dean says. "Maybe I will make a new dress for her. School will be starting soon. She will like that," Dean adds. Dean picks up Anna Belle. Paul gathers the twins. They all go into the house for lunch.

After lunch, Dean rocks Anna Belle to sleep. The twins are reluctant to go to bed. Dean allows them to skip nap time today. She has only a few sheets to wash. This is the lightest load of sheets Martha has ever brought for washing. The smells of the sheets make Dean think about Netta. The sweet smell of perfume hangs on every thread.

Dean and the twins return to the house to start supper. Anna Belle is crying. Dean places her in the highchair while the twins entertain Anna Belle. Dean hums while the twins sing to Anna Belle. Anna Belle laughs and beats on the chair with the spoon as a drum.

Soon Dean completes her cooking. She feeds the children. She fills the bathtub with water for the evening bath. Soon the house is quiet. Dean gathers her sewing gear and the cloth.

"Hello." It is Lucille.

"Hello, how was work?" Dean answers.

"Where is Anna Belle?" Dean leaves the room to retrieve Anna Belle.

"There's Mama's baby," Lucille says as she holds out her hands. Lucille showers Anna Belle with kisses and hugs. "Thank your aunt Dean. We have to go. Your daddy is waiting in the car," Lucille says. "Thank you." Lucille kisses her sister on the head and leaves.

Walter waits in the car. He smiles to see Anna Belle. Dean watches out of the window. To see Lucille, Walter, and Anna Belle without Netta seems strange; in the same eyes, it looks natural. Dean knows she is looking at the divide.

Walter, Lucille, and Anna Belle decide to go to the café near Main Street. Lucille sees some old friends she has not seen in a long time. Lucille and Walter portray the proud parents, enjoying the attention Anna Belle receives. Life is going well. Lucille likes this feeling of being a new mother. Her first husband did not stick around. He left before Netta was born. She has never shared this feeling with a man before. She has never seen Walter happier. Lucille seems to forget about Netta and that October night.

Netta sits by the fire with Lilly. Lilly sits by the fire and pours out her wisdom for Netta to learn. The right rules to live by. Boe tells her of adventures and secrets from his boyhood.

The days repeat themselves over and over. The weekend has finally come. Netta is excited. She knows Lucille will be there on Saturday morning. Lilly watches Netta become increasingly anxious as the day passes. When nightfall comes, Lilly is very concerned. She is hoping everything is all right. Lucille knows better than to stand Netta up like this. Uncle Boe is upset also. He needs Walter to finish the table from his last visit.

The three worry long into the night. Lilly asks everybody to say an extra prayer. That night, Lilly dreams of angels holding a white cross. Behind the cross is Boe on a white horse. He is smiling. He rides out into the light.

Early the next morning Lilly is up first. She waits for Boe to come out of his room. She is relieved when he comes for his cup of coffee. "How are you this morning?" he asks.

"Oh, I did not sleep really well," Lilly answers.

"Getting ready for church?" Boe asks.

"Well, I need to see if Lucille and Walter are coming out here today," Lilly says. "But on the other hand there is nothing we can do if something is wrong."

"There is nothing wrong with them. They just had something to do," Boe says.

"Something more important than Netta?" Lilly asks. "Okay, let's get ready for church. If they are not here by the time we leave, I will leave a note," Lilly says to Boe.

The church services are long. Netta is anxious. She does not want to eat at church today.

"Granny, can we eat at home? I want to see Mama, Walter, and Anna Belle," Netta says. Lilly, Boe, and Netta pack up food and go home.

Lilly is very upset now. She sees Lucille and Walter are not here. Now she has mixed emotions. Should she be mad, or should she be sad?

Beep, beep. It is Lucille, Walter, and Anna Belle. Lilly remains sitting in her chair; she is so angry. She does not stand up to greet them. Netta runs to the car. "Mama, where have you been? Granny was worried something had happened to you," Netta says with excitement.

"Oh, Mama, Walter had to work yesterday. I am sorry. I should have had Paul to bring me or sent a note," Lucille says, kissing Lilly on the head. Walter is carrying Anna Belle. Lilly notices something has changed.

"Are you hungry?" Lilly asks. "Hi, Walter, can I hold Anna Belle?" Netta asks, reaching for Anna Belle.

"Sit down. She has gotten big. I don't want you to drop her," Walter says. Netta goes to the swing. Anna Belle cries; she does not want Walter to let go.

"Okay, give her to me," Lucille says.

"Mama, do you want to see my new dress Granny made for me?" Netta says.

"Sure," Lucille says, swinging Anna Belle. Netta leaves the porch.

"Lucille, what has gotten into you? Netta needs you. She needs some attention," Lilly says.

"Mama, it has only been a week," Lucille replies. "She has stayed longer than this before."

"Just don't make her compete for your affections," Lilly answers.

Lilly goes to the kitchen. She starts to warm food for dinner. She listens to Netta trying so hard to put one week into one sentence. Netta cannot comfort down. She wants to show Lucille the new flowers she has helped plant. Lucille is more concerned with putting Anna Belle down to sleep.

Once Lucille puts Anna Belle to bed for a nap, she joins Netta and Lilly in the kitchen. "Now, honey, why are you so excited?" Lucille says. "You acted as though we had been gone all year long." Lucille jokes. To Netta it seems like a year when she is in some place she doesn't want to be.

Lilly listens to the conversation and looks out of the window. She sees Walter running from the barn. Lilly drops the pot of food in the sink. She can feel the wind blowing through her soul. "What is it Walter?" Lilly shouts.

"It's Uncle Boe. He has passed out, and this time I cannot bring him here." Walter says, catching his breath. Lilly jumps off the porch. She runs to the barn. She sees Boe lying on the ground.

"Boe, Boe, please not today," Lilly is rocking Boe's head back and forth on her chest. She knows she may never his eyes again.

"Mama, move back. Let Walter put him in the car. We need to get him to the doctors right away," Lucille stresses. Boe's breathing is very shallow.

"Netta, you will have to stay here alone. There is not enough room. I will be back to get you as soon as we get Mama and Uncle Boe to the doctors," Lucille says. Lucille grabs Anna Belle. She runs to the car.

Netta watches in terror as they drive away. Netta sits. She cries; she has no idea what to do or how to react. Everything happens so fast. Netta sits on the porch, afraid to move from the swing.

The day turns into night. No one returns to get her. Netta closes all the doors to the house, trying hard to secure herself. Every noise sounds magnified ten times. Netta goes into her room. She places a chair against the door. She watches out of the small window in the room.

Soon she can hear a car coming down the road. She struggles to remove the chair from in front of her door.

"Netta, Netta, where are you?" It is Walter. "Lock up the house and come with me," he orders.

"How is Uncle Boe? Where is Granny?" Netta asks.

"Uncle Boe is in a coma," Walter answers.

"What is a coma?" Netta asks.

"He is in a deep sleep, and no one can wake him," Walter answers.

"Where is Mama and Anna Belle?" Netta asks. Walter does not answer; he is trying hard to concentrate on the road.

Walter and Netta reach town. Walter takes Netta to Dean's house. Only the twins and Paul are at home.

"Where is Aunt Dean?" Netta asks.

"She is with your mother and Lilly at the hospital," Paul answers.

"Netta, I need you to stay here with Paul and the twins until I come back with Lucille," Walter says as he leaves.

When Walter returns to the hospital, everyone is in the small waiting area.

Dean is holding Lilly's hands. Lucille is rocking Anna Belle with tears in her eyes.

"Has the doctor come out to talk with you all?" Walter asks.

"No, did you get Netta?" Lilly answers.

"Yes, I have taken her to Dean's house," Walter says.

It seems like hours. Soon the doctor walks toward them down the hall. Lilly stands up to meet him.

"He has suffered a stroke. He is stable now, but we will need to keep a close watch on him. You need to go home and get some rest. There is nothing more you can do here," the doctor says. Lilly wants to see Boe. "I need to see him," Lilly pleads.

"Mama, we have to leave now. Come with me," Dean says, wrapping her arms around her mother.

On the drive to Dean's house, Lilly stares out of the car. She looks to the heavens, silently praying for her brother's life. Lilly knows all the signs have been revealed to her.

"Just a little longer, Lord. Just a little longer." Lilly repeats this until the car stops in front of Dean's house.

"Tell Netta I will come for her in a minute," Lucille says. Dean and Lilly get out of the car. Walter and Lucille drive down the road to their house.

"Granny are you okay? Is Uncle Boe okay?" Netta asks in a childlike manner.

"Uncle Boe is resting. He is sick. We have to pray for his soul now," Lilly says.

"Mama, lots of people have strokes. Uncle Boe just needs to be more careful. He will recover from this. He may have limitations, but he will be all right," Dean urges. Lilly sits down at the table. She knows that Boe will be walking with the angels just like she dreamed soon—if not tonight.

"Hello, it's me." It is Lucille. "How is Mama?" Lucille asks Dean in a whisper.

"Mama, is there something I can do?" Lucille asks.

"No, it's all up to the Lord now," Lilly answers.

"Netta, come. Let's go home" Lucille says.

"I will see you in the morning," Lucille says, as she and Netta leave the house.

Dean prepares tea and watches her mother as she drinks it. She seems almost childlike in her pain. "Mama, you need to get some rest," Dean says.

Lilly does not answer, she sits in a trance staring at the floor. Her thoughts are with Boe. Lilly goes into the bedroom. She kneels and prays most of the night.

When Lilly finally goes to sleep, she dreams of Boe. He tells her to be strong. He will always be there by her side. He takes her by the hand

and leads her back through time. He tells her she has always been the one who protected the family. Boe and Lilly sit on the bank of a river. She can smell the flowers and feel the rays of sun on her face. He tells her he will leave soon. He tells her she will not be alone. Netta will be with her. He tells her, "Netta is a broken child. She will have her rewards in the future. Guide Netta. Her generation will make the difference."

Boe stands up and tells Lilly he has to go across the river. Lilly cries; she knows that if he crosses the river, she will never see him again. He assures her he will come back to get her in due time, but for now, she must concentrate on the task she has before her.

Lilly asks Boe, "what task?"

Boe says, "You will know when the time comes." He walks out into the water. Two beautiful angels come to meet him. He smiles and appears on the others side of the river. Lilly wakes with tears in her eyes.

It is morning. Lilly comes rushing out of the room. "We have to go, we have to go now!" Lilly says.

Paul can see the look in Lilly's eyes. Dean says, "Take her, Paul. Take her to the hospital now." As soon as Lilly reaches the hospital, she goes to the room where Boe is. Boe is lying in the bed. Lilly goes to the bed and starts to cry.

The nurse comes in behind her. "You will have to leave."

"No," Lilly says.

"The doctor says not to allow visitors," the nurse says. "I am his sister. I am not leaving." Lilly holds tight to Boe's hand.

Soon the nurse returns with a doctor. The doctor asks Lilly to step outside so he can talk to her.

"Your brother needs rest. He is showing great improvement. The nurse tells me last night he was talking in his sleep," the doctor says.

"Did he open his eyes?" Lilly asks.

"No, but that is not uncommon," he replies. Lilly turns she walks to the sitting area. Paul is there.

"Lilly, do you want to go back to the house?" Paul asks. Lilly does not say a word. She walks out of the hospital. Paul pulls the car in front of her. She does not move. Paul gets out of the car and takes Lilly by the arm to assist her into the car.

Lilly asks Paul to take her to the funeral home. Paul asks, "Why?" He heard the doctor say Boe is showing improvement. Lilly knows she must get things in order. It does not matter what anyone says; she knows the spirits have spoken to her. There have been three dreams. It is time for her to face the facts and get her business in order. Boe is the last of her brothers and sisters. No one else is left to take care of this. As hard as it may seem, she must be prepared. Paul obeys. He does not understand the logic behind the detour. Lilly goes in alone. Paul waits patiently. Soon Lilly returns with a handful of papers.

Dean and the twins wait for Lilly and Paul to return.

"How is Uncle Boe?" Dean asks.

"He is the same," Lilly answers.

"The doctor says he is showing good improvement," Paul adds.

"See, Mama, I told you he would be all right," Dean says.

"Hello." It is Lucille and Netta. "Hi, Mama, how did you sleep?" Lucille asks. Netta is holding Anna Belle. She walks over to the table; she places Anna Belle in the highchair.

"Morning, Granny," she says, hugging Lilly around the neck.

"Walter is waiting for me outside. I have to go to work. You come and get me if you need me," Lucille says leaving the room.

"Granny, should we go the hospital to see Uncle Boe?" Netta asks.

"I have been to the hospital," Lilly answers. Lilly gets up from the table. She starts to pour water for tea. Looking out of the window, she sees the early morning sun. A large white feather floats down onto the porch. Lilly walks to the door to make sure she is seeing this large white feather. She slowly bends over to pick the feather up. Upon touching the feather, Lilly starts to shout and cry. Dean and Netta are surprised to hear Lilly cry out. They rush to the door to see what the matter is. There is Lilly, standing, holding this white feather, and crying.

"Mama, what is it? What is the matter?" Dean asks. Lilly turns to Dean. Dean can see in Lilly's face the shadow of death. At that instant a bone-chilling breeze blows through them. Dean hugs her mother. She knows what Lilly is feeling. Dean helps Lilly to sit in a chair on the porch.

"Netta, go to the store and tell Paul to come here," Dean says. Netta runs to the store. The store is closed. A sign reads that Paul is out making deliveries. Netta returns to the house.

"Aunt Dean, Uncle Paul is not there. The store is locked," Netta says. Dean panics.

"Don't fuss now. Boe is with the Lord," Lilly says. "Go feed the children. I will be all right. Just let me sit here for a while," Lilly says.

"Aunt Dean, what is the matter with Granny?" Netta asks. Dean cannot explain. She tries so hard not to cry herself.

Dean asks Netta to prepare food for the twins and Anna Belle. Dean goes to her bedroom. She needs to get dressed and be ready when Paul comes home for lunch. Dean knows Lilly tells the truth. There is no need to wait for anyone to verify the death. Uncle Boe has passed away; she knows because he passed by here.

When lunchtime comes, Paul returns to the house. He sees Lilly sitting on the porch.

"How are you doing, Lilly?" he asks. Dean stands at the door. She beckons him to come in. Once Paul is in the house, Dean leads him to their bedroom.

"Uncle Boe has passed away," Dean says.

"Who came by to tell you all?" Paul asks.

"No one has come by. Mama knows he is gone," Dean answers. Paul finds this hard to understand.

"How can you just say he is dead without being there?" Paul argues.

"We need to go to the hospital. I will get Netta to stay with the children. Go get your lunch. It is ready on the stove. Then we can go to the hospital," Dean says. Paul rushes through eating his lunch. He shakes his head in disbelief. He wonders how the women can be so sure without someone coming by to tell them.

On the way to the hospital, Lilly is quiet. When they arrive, Lilly says, "You need to go tell your sister. I will be all right."

As soon as Lilly enters, the hospital the nurse approaches her. "We tried to find someone who can come for you. I will tell the doctor you are here." When he comes to talk to Lilly, she tells him she knows what he is about to say.

"Can I see him now?" Lilly asks. The doctor walks with her to the room where Boe's body is. "Can I be alone? I will be all right," Lilly asks. The doctor slowly closes the door.

Paul drives to the store. He tells Dean to take the truck. He is so puzzled at the events that have taken place. Dean goes to Lucille's job. Lucille tells her boss about the loss in her family. Her boss gives her the permission to leave.

Lucille and Dean go to the hospital. Lilly is still in the room with Boe. "Mama, you have to leave now," Lucille says. Dean takes care of the paperwork. Lilly hands Dean the papers from her purse. Dean is surprised Lilly has already made arrangements. Dean gives the papers to the nurse. Lucille and Dean are shaken, but Lilly seems calm now.

"Let's go see to the children now," Lilly says.

Netta and the children are in the backyard.

"Granny, Mama!" Netta yells.

"Mama needs to rest. She will see you later," Lucille says. Lilly bends over and kisses Netta on the head. She goes into the house. Lucille takes Anna Belle from Netta. Netta and the twins see Dean approaching. The twins run to meet Dean.

"Where is she?" Dean asks.

"Mama is in the house. I think she wants to be alone," Lucille answers. For a minute, the world stops. Dean and Lucille stand in the backyard, silent and dazed. Neither one of them moves; the children circled them. It seems like a ring of life.

"I am going to take Netta and Anna Belle home," Lucille says. Dean sits on the porch. She wants the twins to wear themselves down. They will be so asleep, and Lilly will not be disturbed.

Lucille and Netta reach the house. Netta knows something has happened. "Mama, is something wrong?" Netta asks.

"Uncle Boe has died," Lucille answers. Netta has never known anyone close to her die. Anna Belle is asleep. Lucille takes Anna Belle to her bedroom. Netta goes out to the back porch. She sits. She tries to remember what Uncle Boe looked like the last time she saw him. What did he say to her?

Chapter 12

As hours pass, Lucille stands at the door.

"Are you hungry?" Lucille asks.

"No ma'am," Netta answers. Netta goes into the house.

"Mama, will Granny come and stay in town now?" Netta asks.

"I don't know. She has a strong will," Lucille answers. Lucille never questions the thought of Lilly's living arrangements. If she comes and stay in town, there will be no problems. She can live between Dean and Lucille. On the other hand, if she will not move, who will move to her? Dean cannot move with Paul and the twins with the store here in town. She thinks about it. Lucille knows she does not want to live outside of town. She dismisses the thought when she hears Anna Belle crying.

"Hi, Netta." It is Walter. He has come out from work.

"Hi, Walter. Uncle Boe is dead," Netta says. Lucille can hear Walter's voice in the kitchen.

"When did it happen?" Walter asks.

"Sometime this morning. Dean says Mama knows when she woke this morning," Lucille explains. "Your dinner is on the stove. I am going over to Dean's house."

"Can I go with you?" Netta asks.

"Sure baby," Lucille answers.

"I will come over later," Walter adds.

Lucille, Netta, and Anna Belle walk next door to Dean's house. From the backyard, Lucille can see Dean and the twins sitting at the table.

"Hi, where is Mama?" Lucille asks. "She made tea some time ago. She is lying in bed. I don't think she is asleep," Dean adds.

"Do you think I should check on her?" Lucille asks. "No, if she wants to come out, she will. She knows we are here," Dean answers.

"Daddy, Daddy," the twins all say. Paul walks into the house.

"Hi, everybody," Paul says, picking up one boy and one girl. "How is Lilly?

Where is Lilly?"

"She is lying down," Dean answers. "Lucille, is Walter home?" Paul asks.

"Yes."

"I think I will go over there."

"Are you hungry?"

"No, not now, I will eat later," He answers. Paul leaves the house. He feels anxious to leave. He thinks many times about what happened this morning. He thinks about Lilly's uncanny ability to know things without doubt. This is the second time she has known the outcome without being there. The first time was in October.

Walter is in the workshop. He can hear Paul calling for him. "I am in here!" Walter yells.

"Hey," Paul says.

"Hey yourself," Walter replies, working on a piece of wood.

"I know they need to sort things out over there at my house. I hope you don't mind the company."

"I am way ahead of you," Walter says, handing Paul a bottle of whiskey with a tiny glass.

"I don't know if I am ready for all the sadness."

"Well, you have a very short time to get ready."

In the kitchen Lucille and Dean are trying to organize everything. Lilly comes to the kitchen.

"Dean, did Paul come home yet?" Lilly asks.

"Yes, ma'am. He is with Walter at Lucille's house," Dean answers.

"I will need him to take me home tomorrow," Lilly says. Dean and Lucille are against the idea of Lilly going home by herself. Lilly will not take "no" for an answer.

"Mama, you cannot go out there by yourself—not now," they argue.

"I have things I need to take care of at home," Lilly says.

"Will you stay out there alone?" Dean asks.

"Yes," Lilly answers.

"Mama, if you must stay out there, I will send Netta with you. I will feel better," Lucille adds. Once again, Netta is forced to leave without having any say in the decision. Netta sits quietly. She knows to say anything will cause problems.

The next morning, Martha brings sheets to Dean's house. She is surprised to see Lilly in the kitchen.

"Nobody told me you are coming into town," Martha says, hugging Lilly.

"I know, Martha. Boe has passed," Lilly says.

"What do you mean, Aunt Lilly? Do you mean Uncle Boe is dead?"

"Yes," Lilly starts to cry. Dean comes into the kitchen. She forgets about Martha coming today. From everybody's reaction, Dean knows Lilly has told Martha. Martha reaches for a chair to sit down. She drops the bundles of sheets to the floor.

"Why didn't somebody tell me?" Martha asks.

"It happened so fast. We just forget," Dean says.

"Good morning, Martha," Paul says. "Lilly, let me know when you are ready to leave."

"Netta is going with her," Dean says. Paul continues out of the house. He can see Netta, Lucille, and Anna Belle coming down the walk.

"Morning, Paul," Lucille says. Netta passes Paul without speaking. She enters the kitchen.

"Good morning," Netta says.

"Good, now we can go," Lilly says.

"Mama, I wish you would come back here today. Paul can always come back for you and Netta in the evening," Dean pleads.

"No, I need to do things before Friday," Lilly says. Lilly and Netta leave the house. Lilly and Lucille hug each other in passing.

"Netta, you mind Mama," Lucille says. Netta does not reply.

When Paul reaches the farm, Lilly just sits in the truck. "Granny, you coming?" Netta asks. Lilly is staring at the barn. This is the last place she saw Boe. She can see him entering the barn in a cloud-like form. "Granny, Granny, you okay?" Netta asks.

"I will be all right," Lilly says as she gets out of the truck. Paul helps Lilly up the stairs. Today she looks so fragile to him.

"I will go and see if everything is okay in the barn," Paul says. Lilly never turns around. Lilly goes to the kitchen to throw out the food that was left on the stove. It has started to smell, sitting out in the heat for two days. Netta moves about the kitchen.

"Granny, what do you want me to do?"

"Nothing, baby. I just need to be busy," Lilly answers. Netta goes to the porch. She can hear Lilly singing *Amazing Grace.*

"Tell Lilly I am leaving," Paul says. He can hear her singing. He has never heard the song sound sadder than the way she sings it. Netta waves bye to Paul.

Netta swings and plays with her doll Anna Belle.

"Let's go to the barn and get out the buggy. We need to go to the church."

It is a warm summer day. Netta has never been to the little white church during the week. It looks so empty.

"Pastor," Lilly calls.

"Yes," a strong voice answers from the back of the church.

"Hello, Sister Hill. What do I owe this blessed occasion to?"

"Pastor, I need a going home service for my brother Boe."

"Oh, Sister, when did this happen? No one told me he was sick."

"He went in a hurry yesterday morning. I did not have a chance to say goodbye," Lilly says with tears in her eyes.

"Sister, come into my office," the pastor says.

"Netta, you can come too."

"No, ma'am. I will go outside if that is okay?" Netta asks. Netta goes outside. She picks four-leaf clovers and ties them together to make a halo to fix on her head. She walks around to the back of the church. A small wading pool is bordered by a cemetery on the right.

I guess this is where Uncle Boe will rest now, she thought to herself.

"Netta." It is Lilly calling for her. Netta runs around to the front of the church.

"Here I am," Netta answers.

"Goodbye, Pastor. Thank you," Lilly says.

On their way home, Lilly makes a detour. She stops at a small farmhouse down the road from the church.

"Hello, Lilly." It is Ms. Hattie, Lilly's long-time friend. They sit together every Sunday at church.

"What are you doing out here today?" Hattie asks.

"I had to see the pastor. Boe has gone home with our Lord," Lilly says.

"Oh my lord, come down from there. Come sit down for a while. Katy, Katy," Hattie calls. She is calling her granddaughter, who lives with her. Katy is fifteen years old.

"Yes, ma'am," Katy answers.

"Get some cold water for Sister Hill and her child," Hattie orders. Katy runs off to the kitchen.

"We cannot stay. There are a lot of things I need to take care of. I just wanted to be the one to tell you. Thank you for the water, but we have to leave," Lilly says. Netta and Lilly ride off down the road.

Soon they are home. Lilly and Netta unhitch the buggy. "Are you hungry?" Lilly asks.

"Just a little," Netta answers. For the rest of the day, Lilly cleans. Lilly tells Netta she can play outside. Lilly works her grief out. She cleans and mops most of the afternoon.

Soon Netta can see a car coming up the road. It is Hattie and Katy with two other ladies.

"Where is your granny?" Hattie asks. Netta points to the house.

"Katy, stay out here with Netta," Hattie says.

"Yes, ma'am," Katy answers. "I see you sometimes at church," Katy says.

"Yeah, when I am out here with Granny, I go with her," Netta replies.

"I don't like it here. Everything is so boring," Katy says. Katy moved in with her grandmother when her mother and father were killed in a fire two months ago. Katy is from the west. She talks about beaches and white sand, a place where the warm season lasts all year long.

She paints a picture for Netta of a world where every day is a new adventure. Katy is mentally mature for her age. Katy wears painted fingernails, and she talks like an adult. She dresses differently. Netta is fascinated by this creature—half woman, half girl. Netta notices that when Katy is in the present of her grandmother, she acts like a little girl. When she is alone with Netta she acts entirely differently.

Soon the ladies are ready to go. Katy tells Netta she will see her again tomorrow. Katy explains that every time someone dies, the good sisters come by every day until after the funeral.

"You will have so much food, it will be running out of your ears," Katy says.

"Bye, see you tomorrow," Netta says. Lilly sits in the chair by the fireplace.

Lilly is quiet. She reads her Bible most of the night.

"I am going to bed, Granny," Netta says. Netta kisses Lilly on the head.

The next morning, Paul is early. Lucille and Anna Belle are with him.

"Good morning," Paul says to Lilly.

"Where is Netta, Mama?" Lucille asks.

"She will be out. I heard her stirring in her room."

"Mama," Netta says in surprise.

"Hi, Uncle Paul," Netta adds. "Anna Belle come to me," Netta begs. Anna Belle is reluctant to leave Lucille. "Okay, stay there," Netta says as she leaves the room.

"Paul, would you please take Boe's suit to the funeral home? Here is a note to give to Mr. Brown. These are instructions for Friday," Lilly says. "All the arrangement has been made. Everybody can stay here on Thursday night. The funeral will be at one o'clock, Friday afternoon."

"I will go to the funeral home as soon as I get back to town," Paul replies.

"Paul, Brother Tom will come and pick the vegetables this morning. We will have to pay him something. I told him he can have all you don't take," Lilly says.

"Yes, ma'am. I will talk with him about his terms," Paul replies. "I am going to the barn to get eggs," Paul says. Netta follows along behind him.

"Mama, what are you going to do about the farm?" Lucille asks.

"What do you mean?" Lilly replies.

"You cannot stay out here alone. Dean and I think you should move into town with us."

"I have no intention of moving yet. Maybe later, but not now."

"We will worry if you are here alone."

"Paul will come out every other day as he does now," Lilly says, trying to reassure Lucille.

"That is not good enough." Lucille gets frustrated.

"I am leaving now!" Paul yells.

Netta is under the tree, swinging. She sees a car coming up the road. *Here come the good sisters*, she thought to herself. Netta is excited because she can see Katy again. She likes to hear Katy talk about the different things she has seen.

"Hi, Netta," Katy says. "Who are the lady and the baby?" Katy asks. "That is my mama. She came here with my uncle Paul," Netta answers. "You want to go to the barn?"

"Sure," Katy answers.

"Netta, come get your sister!" Lucille yells.

"Ah, I have to go and get Anna Belle. We will have to stay under the tree. Mama doesn't want her in the barn," Netta explains.

"She looks like you." Katy observes.

"That is what everybody says. I am going to sit in the rocking chair on the porch. She will fall asleep if I can rock her," Netta says, upset. Katy stayed under tree, swinging. Netta sits on the porch with Anna Belle. Netta rocks and holds Anna Belle tightly to gain control. Soon Anna Belle is asleep. Netta slowly takes her to the bedroom.

All day the good sisters cook, clean, and sing. Netta and Katy walk around the farm. Netta is learning so many things from Katy; she forgets why she is stuck on the farm. Soon Hattie calls for Katy to go home.

"Bye, Katy, see you tomorrow," Netta says, waving her hand. Netta takes a seat on the step.

"Mama, can I get my ears pierced?" Netta asks Lucille.

"No, you are too young, Netta," Lucille says.

"Katy has pierced ears," Netta complains.

"You can wait until you are sixteen." Lucille reinforces. Netta doesn't understand the logic. A few months ago she gave birth, but now she has to wait to get her ears pierced.

Netta sees a car coming down the road. It is Walter.

"Hey, Netta," Walter says. "We miss you at home." This makes Netta feel good. She has been feeling like an outcast lately.

"Netta, you need to get ready for bed. You will stay here again with Mama," Lucille says. Netta is upset. She wants to go home. Lucille says it would be just one night.

"I will bring you clothes to wear to the funeral tomorrow," Lucille says. Netta goes into the house without saying anything. Netta looks into the mirror, wondering what has happened. This time last year, life was so different.

Chapter 13

Early on Thursday morning, the house is busy. The good sisters prepare the house for Boe's wake. People are bringing foods and drinks. A relative Netta has never met is coming from a nearby town. Netta and Katy entertain themselves playing in the barn. Katy shows Netta a small pouch. The pouch contains rolling paper and tobacco. Katy takes the tobacco and rolls it up in the paper. Netta sits patiently; she watches Katy as she lights the cigarette and takes a draw.

"Here, go ahead and smoke it," Katy urges.

At first, Netta is afraid.

"It will not hurt you, watch." Katy takes another puff.

Netta decides to try. Netta takes the homemade cigarette; she holds it all wrong.

"No, hold it like this between your fingers," Katy instructs. Netta takes a pull of the cigarette. She breaks out into a whopping cough.

"Now try it and hold the smoke in," Katy says.

Netta follows her instruction. Netta feels her head starts to spin. Her eyes start to lose focus. Netta lies back in the hay, looking upward. She feels funny, kind of strange, in a happy way.

"Netta, you cannot tell your granny or Mama about this. We will be in trouble if they find out," Katy says.

There are those words again: "you cannot tell." It changes Netta's mood about what she is doing. Netta gets up and walks to the barn door. In her altered state of mind, she can hear Lucille telling her the same words about Anna Belle.

"What are looking at?" Katy calls to Netta.

"Nothing," Netta replies.

"Do you want to smoke again?" Katy asks.

"No. I don't like the way it makes me feel. I am going to swing." Netta says, leaving the barn.

Soon Walter, Lucille, Dean, and the twins are driving up to the house. "Netta, Netta," the twins all call. Katy is surprised to see so many little people that all look alike.

"Are they twins?" Katy asks.

"Yes, they are my cousins," Netta answers. "Hi, Aunt Dean, Pauline, Paulette, Paul, and Dean. I miss you," Netta says greeting them. Netta takes the twins to the tree. They play under the tree until the evening comes.

"Come in and get dressed!" Dean yells to Netta and the twins. Katy and the good sisters leave. It is time for the wake service. Netta helps the girls get dressed. The family follows one another to the small white church. The music is playing; the little church looks bigger at night with the lights on. Lilly stands in the doorway, looking straight ahead. Dean and Lucille flank her arm in arm. They walk toward the front of the church. There is a white casket draped in blue. The casket is open, and one can see Boe's face. It looks so stiff and pale. Lilly sits down in the first pew. Her face is blank, showing no emotion. People are moving up and down the narrow aisle between the pews. Occasionally, someone will come up to Lilly, hug her or hold her hand, and give words of peace. Walter and Paul go outside and stand with the other men.

Netta sees Katy. She would like to go outside with her, but she is babysitting. The twins are so busy; they have no idea what is happening. Anna Belle is being handed from person to person who has never seen her before.

Soon the pastor asks for everyone to be seated. He gives the final prayer and informs everyone about the time for the funeral tomorrow.

Once the family reaches the farm, Dean tells Lilly she wants her to come and stay at her house after the funeral. Lilly never says a word. She takes her Bible and goes into her room.

Walter and Paul are on the porch, drinking cider and whiskey. The twins and Anna Belle are asleep. Dean, Lucille, and Netta are in the kitchen. They are putting covers on all the food that people have brought to the house. Netta listens as Lucille asks Dean if Lilly has said anything about where she will live after the funeral. Dean tells Lucille she doesn't know. From Lilly's room, they can hear her crying and praying. It brings a strange quietness to the house.

The next morning Paul goes to the barn. To his surprise, Lilly is there. "Lilly, are you okay?" Paul asks.

"I am just fine. I needed time for myself. I need to think," Lilly answers. Lilly kisses Paul on the head and leaves the barn. Dean can see Lilly coming up to the house.

"Why is Mama out in the barn so early?" Dean says. Lucille joins her, looking out of the window.

"She looks so sad," Lucille says.

"Okay, when she comes in, let's try and cheer her up," Dean says. Lilly never comes into the house. She stops on the porch and sits in her rocking chair.

Walter has joined Paul in the barn.

"This is the table I was working on when Boe collapsed," Walter says. "We need to move it under the tree. There will be a lot of people here today. This will help when the eating starts." They each grab the ends of the table and move it out to the tree.

The hours move fast. Soon the time has come for everybody to get ready. A big black car drives up to the steps. Lilly tells everybody to get into the car. Paul and Walter will take Walter's car and follow behind.

Once they reach the church, Dean and Lucille take Lilly's arms as they did the night before. Netta and the twins walk hand in hand, followed by Paul, Walter, and Anna Belle. Martha and other family members follow. The church is full of church members who have come to pay their respects. The funeral is long and sad. The pastor talks about Boe and his many good deeds.

Soon the adult Deacons line up to carry the casket to the small cemetery behind the church. The casket is placed under a large tree close to the wading pond. Several chairs are lined up next to a deep hole in the ground. Lilly sits, rocking and staring into the dark hole. The good sisters are singing low in the background.

"Dust to dust. Ashes to ashes," the pastor says. Each family member must throw dirt on top of the casket as it is placed in the ground. Finally, everyone gets back in the car.

When the family returns home, there are women preparing the table Paul and Walter placed under the tree. There is so much food. The yard is filled with people. Lilly is escorted to the porch. She sits on her rocking chair.

People come and go late into the night. Once everybody leaves, the subject on where Lilly will stay comes up again.

"Mama, on Sunday, we must go back home. Are you coming with us?" Dean and Lucille question. "No," Lilly says.

"You cannot stay here alone," they insist.

"Why?" Lilly asks.

"Because we will worry about you out here alone," they argue.

"Don't worry. I will be all right," Lilly replies. Without thinking, Lucille says the words Netta never wants to hear again.

"Mama, if you are really set on staying, I will leave Netta here with you until school starts. This will give you time to decide," Lucille says. Netta overhears the conversation from where she is sitting on the steps. She never turns around. She knows the decision has been made, and no protest will change it.

Chapter 14

The next day, Paul and Walter return to town. Netta and the twins occupy their time playing around the tree. Dean, Lucille, and Lilly are sitting on the porch. Netta can see a car come down the road. It is Martha. She has come to spend the day.

"Hello, everybody," Martha says as she kisses Lilly on the head.

"How are you doing Martha?" Lilly asks.

"Okay, I guess."

"You sound like something is wrong," Lucille says.

"Well, Ms. Helen is planning on leaving town. She is leaving on Monday to go out west to buy a house. I guess I will be leaving soon," Martha says.

"You don't have to leave," Dean says. "What about Adley?" Lucille asks.

"We have talked about it, but he is not making any promises about marriage. Too bad, I really like him," Martha adds.

"We'll pray about it for the right decision," Lilly says.

"You know, I can see how a new town might be good. I have never gone twenty miles from where I was born. This will be a new adventure and a new life," Martha says.

"Do you know where she is going out west?" Dean asks.

"She told me the name of the city, but I don't recall it now," Martha answers.

"Martha, you are young. You should have adventures in your life. Never live in regret. You are my sister's child. You will always have a home here with me," Lilly says.

"Thank you, Aunt Lilly. You are so wonderful," Martha says with a smile.

"Lucille, Ms. Helen will sell the house to you and Walter. She will need the money to relocate," Martha explains.

"Do you know how much she will sell it?" Lucille asks.

"Not yet, but she told me to let you know so you could be prepared," Martha says. The women chat and visit all afternoon. Soon Martha is ready to leave.

"I guess I need to head back to town before dark," Martha says. "You have a safe trip back," Lilly replies.

Dean walks over to the tree where the children are playing. Lucille and Anna Belle walk Martha to her car.

"Time to eat and get dressed for bed." Dean says. Lucille and Anna Belle join Lilly on the porch. They can hear Dean and the children in the house.

"I hope we have enough money to buy the house," Lucille says. "Everything will be all right," Lilly says.

On Sunday morning, Lilly is in the kitchen, preparing breakfast for the family.

"Are you going to church this morning, Mama?" Dean asks with the boys by her side.

"Yes," Lilly answers.

"I will see if Lucille will stay here with the children, and I will go with you," Dean says. Lucille and Netta come into the kitchen.

"Lucille, will you watch the children while Mama and I go to church?" Dean asks.

"I want to go," Netta says. Lucille agrees to stay at the house. Netta, Lilly, and Dean will go to church.

At church, many of the church members are concerned about Lilly's recovery from her grief. Netta and Katy sit together in the back of the church. Netta tells Katy that she will stay with Lilly until school starts. Katy wants Netta to come over to her house after church. Netta tells her she will need to get permission from Lilly. After church, everyone is gathered in the churchyard. Netta asks Lilly if she can go home with Ms. Hattie and Katy.

Lilly tells her, "Not today. Maybe tomorrow I will take you over to Hattie. Lucille and Dean have to leave today. You need to be there when your mother leaves."

Netta and Katy are disappointed. Netta does not care to see Lucille leave her again.

On the ride home, Lilly asks Dean.

"Do you think Lucille is neglecting Netta?"

"You know, Mama, I was not going to say anything, but I have noticed how Lucille has pushed Netta to the side since Anna Belle was born," Dean answers. Netta is listening to the conversation, she is glad someone else has noticed the way her mother has been treating her.

"She has forgotten what the truth is and what is not. I know she must act like Anna Belle is her child in front of other people, but she forgets Netta is just a child too," Dean adds. Lilly looks in the back seat. She sees Netta is listening to the conversation.

"We'll discuss this later with Lucille," Lilly says.

When the threesome reaches the farm, they can see Walter and Paul have arrived. "Mama, Mama," the twins call.

"How was church this morning?" Lucille asks.

"It was just fine," Lilly says, walking up the stairs.

"Lunch is ready." Lucille says.

After lunch, everyone is preparing to leave. Dean, and Lucille are busy packing to return home.

"Walter, did Lucille tell you about Ms. Helen and the house?" Lilly asks. "Yes, ma'am," he answers.

"Let me know if you need help," Lilly says.

"Thank you, but I hope we can handle it. I have saved money from the furniture I have sold," Walter replies. Soon everyone is ready to go. Netta is upset. She goes to the barn before Lucille comes back to the porch.

"Mama, where is Netta? I want to tell her goodbye," Lucille says.

"Netta, Netta," Lucille calls. Netta does not answer. She can hear her mother clearly, but she chooses not to answer.

"Mama, tell Netta we have to leave," Lucille tells Lilly. Lilly remembers she wants to talk with Lucille about Netta, but Lucille rushes off to the car. Just like that, she is gone.

Netta waits almost an hour before walking to the house. She sits on the swing on the porch. Lilly comes out and sees her.

"Where did you go? Your mother wants to say goodbye to you," Lilly tells her. Netta does not respond.

"I need to clean out Boe's closet. I am going to give his clothes to the church. Maybe someone will be able to use them," Lilly says. Lilly turns and goes into Boe's room. Netta follows behind her. Lilly and Netta take Boe's clothes out of the closet.

"Be sure to check all the pockets before putting the clothes in the boxes," Lilly instructs Netta. Lilly starts to sing as she works.

"Look, Granny!" Netta holds out her hand. In it is a large roll of money.

Lilly takes the money from Netta.

"Boe was always hiding his money," Lilly says. Lilly counts the money; it is two thousand dollars in five, ten, and twenty-dollar bills.

"Thank you, Lord. Thank you, Boe," she says. Lilly places the money on the top of a dresser. They continue with the packing. Before they finish, they find a total of five thousand two hundred dollars. Lilly and Netta take the boxes to the barn.

That night Lilly thanks the Lord for letting her find the money. She intend to have Dean and Lucille clean out the closet, but they left before she can ask. Lilly and Netta soon retire for the night. Lilly dreams of Boe's smiling face. She knows he is at peace and has placed the money there for her to find.

The next day, Hattie and Katy come over. Lilly asks Hattie to help take the boxes to the church. Once at the church, the pastor is there to greet them.

"This is a good thing you are doing, Sister Hill. So many people are in need. The Lord will truly bless you," the pastor says. While the adults are inside the church, Netta and Katy are outside. Katy is upset because she has received a letter from her cousin. This made Katy homesick. She wants to go back to live with her cousin. Hattie says she will get over being homesick, but Katy says she never will.

Netta can relate to what Katy is feeling as she is here against her will too.

Katy says, "School here will be boring for me." Hattie wants to make her clothes for school. Katy is used to go shopping for school clothes. Her whole world is spinning out of control.

She tells Netta, "One day I will run away from here." Netta does not understand how someone can run away from where they are staying. Soon they are on their way to Lilly's house.

Lilly offers to pay Hattie for her help.

"You can give me some lunch. That will be good enough," Hattie says. Lilly and Hattie go into the house. Netta and Katy go into the barn. Katy rolls a cigarette. Netta refuses to smoke. She does not like the way she feels when she smokes. Netta listens to Katy as she vents her emotions.

"Katy, Katy." They can hear Hattie calling from outside.

"I guess we are leaving," Katy says. Netta and Katy walk toward the house. "Say goodbye, Katy. We have to go," Hattie says. Lilly and Netta wave goodbye.

"Granny, Katy doesn't like it here. She says she is going to run away," Netta says.

"She is just going through a lot now. Katy just lost her Mama and daddy. She had to move to a strange place. This is a lot for someone so young. She will adjust," Lilly says. "Time will heal everything."

The days pass. Netta is getting excited. Next week, school will start, and she can go back home.

On Saturday morning, Lilly can see Netta's excitement. "Granny, are you coming back to my house?" Netta asks.

"No, baby. I will stay here. I will be all right," Lilly answers. "You need to go to school. I will miss your company," Lilly says, helping Netta pack.

"Hello." It is Lucille. Lilly and Netta move to the front of the house.

"Hi, Mama, Anna Belle," Netta says happily. Netta takes Anna Belle from Lucille. Netta walks to the porch. On the porch, there are two bags. Netta sits in the swing. She recognizes the bags from the closet at home. Lucille and Lilly are in the house, talking. Netta can hear Lilly protesting about something. She hears her name. Lucille is upset when she walks through the door.

"Netta, I have to tell you something," Lucille says as she takes Anna Belle out of Netta's arms.

"Come to the car with me," Lucille says. "You will go to school out here until Christmas. I have been to the school to enroll you. You will like it. The teacher is really nice."

"Why, Mama? Why?" Netta begs.

"I have taken a second job to help buy the house. Mama does not need to be out here alone. It will only be for a little while." Lucille says.

Lucille and Anna Belle drive away. Netta watches with tears in her eyes. Lilly walks to meet her; she knows Netta is not prepared for this. All morning, Netta has been excited about going home. Lilly cannot find the words to tell Netta how sorry she is. Netta spends most of her day under the tree, drawing in the dirt. *How can Lucille keep her away? Why is Lucille keeping her away?*

Chapter 15

The first day of school is hard. Netta is the new girl in the class. All the other girls are looking at her and talking about her. At lunchtime, she sees Katy. Katy is surprised to see Netta.

"What are you doing here?" Katy asks.

"My Mama made me stay. I don't like it here. The girls all talk about me," Netta says.

"Don't pay them any mind," Katy says. "Wait for me out front after school." After school, Katy and Hattie take Netta home. Lilly is surprised to see Hattie drive up.

"Hi, Granny," Netta says, getting out of the car.

"We brought your baby home. I am glad she is going to school with Katy. Maybe she will adjust faster now that she has someone at school she knows," Hattie says. Lilly invites Hattie to sit and visit a while.

For the next few weeks, Netta and Lilly barely see Lucille, Walter, and Anna Belle only two visits before Thanksgiving. After Thanksgiving, they did not come at all. Paul would come for his weekly trips to get supplies for the store. Paul will often take a note or bring one.

Lucille likes the routine she has established with Walter and Anna Belle. Lucille does not want to change the way things are going now. Dean takes good care of Anna Belle. Netta is with Lilly. Lucille and Walter have plenty of time to themselves. Anna Belle is walking and trying to talk now. Walter is very attentive to Lucille and Anna Belle. Things are changing, Lucille is buying new items for the house. She and Walter entertain more. Their first anniversary is near.

On Christmas Eve, Paul brings Netta and Lilly into town. Netta is very withdrawn. It will be a surprise if she can stay at home. She is hoping, but she knows deep in her heart that Lucille has not said anything about her coming home.

On Christmas Eve, everyone is gathered at Dean and Paul's house. Everybody greets and hugs one another. The twins pull Netta to the Christmas tree. Anna Belle slowly stumbles behind them. Dean, Lilly, and Lucille go to the kitchen to finish cooking the Christmas feast.

"The twins and Anna Belle are growing," Lilly says.

"Mama, how have you been?" Dean asks.

"Just fine. Netta and I are good company for each other," Lilly says.

"That's good. I have decided to let her stay out there to finish this year of school," Lucille says. Lilly did not say anything. She and Netta has already come to that conclusion.

"Merry Christmas." It is Martha.

"Hey there, Merry Christmas yourself," Dean says. Martha hugs Lilly and Lucille.

"Can I lick the bowl?" Martha says. "Aunt Lilly, I have told Dean and Lucille I will be leaving the day after Christmas. I will be taking a train out west to live. Ms. Helen has bought a large house there. She left last week with four of her girls. I had to stay behind to make sure everything is packed and on the train. I will miss everybody. I will write and send pictures as often as I can."

"I will say a prayer for you to have a safe trip and a good life," Lilly says.

"What did Adley say?" Lucille asks.

"He says he will come out there soon. Men always promise you the world and deliver nothing," Martha says.

It is getting late. The women talk and cook late into the night.

"I am going home now," Walter says.

"Take Anna Belle with you and put her to bed." Lucille responds.

"What about Netta?" Lilly asks.

"I will take care of her," Lucille says. There is that difference again. Lilly just observes; she does not say a word.

On Christmas morning, Netta is up early. Netta goes to the Christmas tree; she sees only three gifts with her name on them. There are so many gifts, but only three are for her. She moves the other gifts around; they are for Anna Belle. *Anna Belle, how can she have so many, she can hardly walk?* Netta thinks to herself. Netta knows she has to act happy, or Lucille will think she is ungrateful.

"Mama, can I go next door to see what the twins have gotten for Christmas?" Netta asks.

"Yes, get dressed. Tell them your Mama and your aunt Dean will be over soon," Lucille says.

Netta can hear the twins before she goes into the house.

"Look, look, Netta." All of them are trying to show Netta their Christmas toys.

"Here, Netta. This is for you." Dean says, handing her a box wrapped in green and red paper.

"And I have this for you," Lilly says. "Go ahead and open it." It is a beautiful gold necklace.

"Oh, thank you, Granny. It is so pretty. I love it," Netta says. "Help me put it on." Netta runs to the mirror to see how the necklace looks on her neck. This is the first grown-up gift she has ever owned. Netta feels things are changing inside her. She looks in the mirror; the reflection of a little girl is fading.

She moves her head from side to side with her hair held up in her hand. She can see how slender her neck has become. She strokes her neck and chest with the other hand. Her hand follows the outline of the necklace between her breasts. She tilts her head upward. The light reflecting off the necklace lights up her face. She sees a stranger in her own eyes.

Christmas is soon over. Netta and Lucille return to the farm. This time, Netta is happy to go. She gets all the attention she needs from Lilly. Over the next few weeks, Lilly notices the change in Netta. Lilly decides the time is right to teach Netta the wisdom of women as she knows it.

The days pass quickly. Soon it is Netta's birthday. Everyone comes out to celebrate. Hattie and Katy are invited. Lucille notices the change in Netta— the way she talks and the way she has started to reason things out. Lucille finds herself alone in the kitchen with Lilly.

"Mama, I don't like the influence this little girl has on Netta," Lucille says. "Listen, Katy is the only friend Netta has. You cannot interfere with that."

Lilly says. "She is not from around here. That's all I mean," Lucille replies. "Lucille, this time last year, Netta was standing right where you are standing. Her belly was full with Anna Belle. Her life was changed forever. Through all that she never stopped loving you. She never stopped believing in what you thought was best for her."

"I have waited a long time to tell you this. Don't get mad because she is happy. She is not the reason for the shame. She is the one person who suffered. So whatever brings a smile to her face, don't try to take it away from her." Lilly puts down the dish cloth and leaves the room.

For the next two years Lilly and Netta lived together, learning from each other.

Lilly has sharecropped the farm off to a family. They are new to the area. She found them through Brother Tom at the church.

The family is a good God-fearing family. They have joined the church. Their son goes to school with Netta. The wife and Lilly are good friends. Netta rides to school with Johnny. He is sweet on Katy. Every day after school Johnny teaches Katy and Netta to drive.

Netta will soon be fifteen. Katy and Johnny want to take Netta into the next county. "Granny, can I take a ride with Johnny and Katy into the next county on my birthday?" Netta asks.

"You know your mother is coming out to see you with your sister." Lilly answers.

"I will go into town with Johnny and tell her not to come." Netta says. Lilly is surprised. The next day after school Johnny, Katy, and Netta drive into town. Netta knows Lucille will not be home. Netta instructs Johnny to take her to Dean's house.

"Hey, Netta," little Paul is the first to see her.

"Hi, Netta, what are you doing here?" Dean asks. "Does Mama know where you are?"

"Yes, ma'am," Netta says. "Here is a note for Mama. I will be gone on my birthday, so there is no need for her to come out to the house," Netta says. Dean looks in at her surprise. She takes a look at Netta. Dean can see she is maturing. Netta has never ventured out with anyone other than the family.

"Okay, I will tell her," Dean says.

"Netta, Netta," it is Anna Belle. She is almost three years old.

"Netta, she looks just like you," Johnny says.

"We need to go." Netta says. Today Netta is happy. She does not need to be reminded of Anna Belle.

The next day, Netta is excited. She puts on her prettiest dress. *Beep, beep.* Netta sees Johnny coming.

"Granny, I am leaving now," Netta says, running out of the house. "Ready to go?" Katy says.

Forty-five minutes later, they arrive in the city. This is the first time Netta has ever been out of town. A whole new world has opened up. The people look different. Johnny drives up to a corner café. Netta has never seen the inside of a café. This is the best birthday Netta has ever had. Netta has never seen a menu. She does not know how to order. Johnny orders a hamburger and french fries.

"I will have the same," Netta says. Netta is tapping her feet underneath the table; she is so excited. The whole day is filled with excitement. The threesome walks up and the down the sidewalk, looking into shop windows, daydreaming, and wishing.

On the ride home, everyone talks about how they want to go back to the café. Soon they reach Lilly's house. Lilly is sitting on the porch. Johnny and Katy wave and yell, "Hi, Ms. Hill!" Netta races up the steps. She starts talking about her adventure of the day. Lilly has never seen Netta this happy. That night in her room, Netta pretends she is sitting in the café, ordering every dish she can remember.

The next few days, Katy, Johnny and Netta go into town after school. Lilly is concerned; Netta is getting home later each day. Lilly makes Netta come home right away after school. Now she is worried about the effect of Netta's birthday trip.

"Netta, Katy and Johnny are older than you are. Their parents do not mind them staying out after dark. You cannot do that. I will not allow it," Lilly says. This is the first time Netta does not agree with what Lilly says. Netta goes to her room.

Later that night, Netta apologizes for leaving without asking permission.

Lilly is proud. She knows Netta understand.

"Do you want to read the letter I got from Martha? She sent a picture postcard of the ocean," Lilly says. Netta takes the card in her hands. She is mesmerized, looking at this picture. Katy has told her over and over again about the ocean and how it looks. Now Netta can see it; she thinks this is heaven on earth. The people look so different. Netta starts to read the letter. She hangs on every word. She can imagine this large house Martha writes about.

"Granny, can I write back to Martha?" Netta asks.

"Yes, please do. She will like that," Lilly answers. Netta spends the remainder of the night writing to Martha.

On Sunday, Lilly and Netta are getting ready for church. There is a knock on the door. It is Sarah and John. John and Sarah are Johnny's parents.

"Hi, Sarah, John. You ready for church already?" Lilly asks.

"No!" Sarah answers.

"We want to talk with Netta," John adds. Lilly can see they are upset.

"What is the problem?" Lilly asks.

"Johnny did not come home last night," Sarah says. "We need to ask Netta if he said anything to her and Katy about what he was going to do last night," John says.

"Netta," Lilly called. Netta has heard the whole conversation from the other room.

"Yes, ma'am," Netta answers.

"Netta, Sarah and John need to talk with you about Johnny," Lilly says.

"Did you talk to Johnny yesterday? Did he say where he was going? Was there someone in the car with him?" They grilled her.

"I saw him yesterday evening. He was going over to Katy's. That is the only time I saw him." Netta answers. Lilly asks if Sarah wants to sit down. She is visibly shaken. Johnny is her only child. Sarah and John are getting on in years. Johnny is their miracle child. Sarah was in menopause when he was born.

"Netta, go get a glass of cold water," Lilly orders.

"We can stop on our way to church and talk with Hattie and Katy," Lilly says.

The trip takes only a matter of minutes.

"They maybe at church already," Lilly says as the car stops in front of Hattie's house. "Netta, go knock on the door." Netta goes to the door and knocks.

To her surprise, when Hattie opens the door, she says, "Netta, good. I was getting ready to come over to your house. Have you seen Katy?" Hattie does not wait for her to answer; she can see John and Sarah in the car. She runs to the car.

"Your boy came here last night and got Katy. Now she has not been home all night!" Hattie shouts.

"We are looking for Johnny too." Sarah responds.

Netta is standing on the porch. Her thoughts are running wild.

"Netta get over here," Lilly calls.

"Did they say anything to you?" Hattie asks.

"No, ma'am," Netta answers.

"Are you sure?" John asks.

"Granny, I am just as surprised," Netta says.

"I am not going to church. The sheriff is on his way out here." Hattie says.

Everyone decides to stay at Hattie house.

Netta is hurting inside. She cannot understand why Katy did not let her know what was going on. *Did she run away? Is she okay? What happened?*

Netta sits on the porch while the adults are inside, blaming one another. She sees the sheriff coming up the road.

"Does someone here need the sheriff?" he says. Hattie rushes out of the door.

"Sheriff, my daughter has not come home all night. She is only seventeen years old," Hattie blurts out.

"My son has not come home all night. He is eighteen years old," Sarah says. "Okay, wait a minute, let's get this straight. Did they leave together?" the sheriff asks.

"Yes," Hattie says.

"Do you know any of their friends?" the sheriff asks. "Johnny only had Katy and Netta as his friends," John and Sarah say.

"Who is Netta?" the sheriff asks. "Netta is standing right there." Hattie points.

The sheriff grills and questions Netta for almost an hour. Netta feels like she is on trial. Everybody expects her to know. The only thing Netta is feeling is hurt and desertion.

After the sheriff leaves, Lilly, Netta, Sarah, and John leave Hattie's house. The sheriff asks them to contact him if they come home. That afternoon, Lilly and Netta sit on the porch. Netta gets up to go to the barn.

"Where are you going?" Lilly asks.

"Just to the barn," Netta answers.

"Do not leave this yard today."

"I am not going anywhere, Granny."

Netta walks to the barn. She sits on a bench outside the door. She kicks her feet in the dirt. She searches her mind for answers. She raises her face to the sun.

"How could they leave me here? If they have run away, why didn't they take me with them? Everybody thinks I know. The one thing I know is I am out here alone again." Netta's concentration is broken when she notices a car drive up to the house.

It is Lucille, Walter, and Anna Belle.

"This is all I need," Netta says to herself. Netta stays seated. She watches as Lucille takes a seat on the swing. Netta watches as Walter takes Anna Belle to the tree and places her in the tree swing. Netta knows Lilly will tell Lucille about Katy and Johnny. Netta sits; she watches Lucille's body movements. She can tell what is being said by the many times that Lucille turns to look her way.

"Netta, come up here!" Lucille yells. Netta stands up and dusts off her backside. She walks slowly toward the house. Netta knows Lucille will have something to say. It is nobody's business if they ran off. The only regret Netta has is that they did not take her with them. Netta can see Lucille is mad before she climbs the stairs.

"Netta, what is this Mama is telling me about that girl and boy you hang around with?" Lucille asks.

"Nothing. All I know is that they did not come home last night," Netta answers.

"Don't you lie to me! I told Mama I did not like that Katy," Lucille argues. "Now you tell Mama what you know about this."

"Mama, I told Granny all I know," Netta pleads. Lucille shouts and calls Netta a liar.

"Lucille, stop talking to her like that!" Lilly says, raising her voice. "Netta is not lying. I know she is telling the truth. I was here with her last night, and I saw her face this morning. She found out about them the same time I did." Lilly defends her. "Why are you angry at Netta about this anyway? She is still here with me." Lilly scolds.

Lucille knows Lilly is right. She cannot stop being angry. There is tension and misplaced anger throughout the visit.

On the way home, Lucille tells Walter.

"Maybe I will bring Netta home. She is getting out of control. She knows what happened. She can fool Mama, but she cannot fool me." Lucille says.

Months past but still no words about Johnny and Katy. Hattie is sick with worry. John and Sarah are in a state of depression. Sarah has taken to her bed. John is inattentive to his crops. Lilly brings food to them. Netta feels she is under suspicion. Some days Sarah will ask her, "Where are they?"

Lilly tells Netta to stay home. She cannot go with Lilly to visit John and Sarah. Netta's presence is upsetting Sarah, who is going mad in her despair.

One day while Netta is waiting for Lilly to return from Sarah and John's house, Netta goes to the mailbox. She sees three letters from Martha. One letter looks different from the other two. She opens it first.

Netta, we ran away.

Tell my grandma I am okay. Sorry I did not tell you about it. Johnny and I are married. I am going to have a baby. I

*know they will never let us stay together. I am going home. I
will stay with my cousin when I get there. I miss you. If it is
a girl, I will name her Netta.*

The letter is not signed. There is no return address. Netta's heart fills
with joy. Katy and Johnny are okay, and they live together. She sits on the
swing under the tree. Netta starts to laugh until the tears come to her eyes.
Netta is laughing so hard, she fails to see Lilly approaching.

"What are you laughing about?" Lilly asks. Netta has to adjust herself
in a hurry. She does not want to tell Lilly about the letter just yet. "I am
reading a letter from Martha. She sends her love." Netta is lying. She really
doesn't know why. She feels she needs to protect the truth about Johnny
and Katy for now.

John and Sarah are talking about leaving. John says he will take Sarah
to her sister in the next county. He found her standing in her nightgown
in the middle of the yard late at night. She was waiting for Johnny. Netta
and Lilly walk to the porch. Lilly rocks in her chair. Netta can see the
tiredness in Lilly's eyes. Netta picks up her letters. She begins to read the
letters from Martha.

Chapter 16

By the Fourth of July, John and Sarah have moved. Lilly and Netta are alone in the farm. Paul only comes out once a week now. He only comes for eggs. Paul and Walter grow enough vegetables in the field behind Lucille's house.

Today Lucille will come to take them into the city. Netta and Lilly will stay in town for the next two days.

The twins are talking and playing school. The boys are teaching the girls their ABCs. Dean says, "They get it from their daddy." Netta has isolated herself. She feels she has outgrown the games the twins play. She walks to the corner to get away from her family. Netta sees the changes, which has taken place in the neighborhood in the last three years. She looks at the corner store. Walter and Paul have made changes to enlarge it. Everything has changed. Netta knows she has changed. _I feel I don't belong here anymore_, she thought. She knows she does not belong on the farm either.

"Netta, Netta," she hears someone calling for her. She feels as though she is doing time, caught up between here, there, and nowhere. It is Lilly calling for her. Every day since Johnny and Katy ran away, Lilly has become overprotective. "Netta, I was looking for you. You tell me when you are going for a walk," Lilly begs.

"I was just bored," Netta answers.

"Netta, you want to help me make ice cream?" Dean asks. Dean can see something is bothering Netta.

"Granny is afraid I am going to run away," Netta says.

"Yeah, Lucille told me about your friends. Have you heard from them yet?" Dean asks.

Netta knows she has to make a decision before she answers. For a minute, she hesitates. "Yes, ma'am," Netta answers reluctantly.

"Did you tell Mama yet?" Dean asks.

"No, she has been so busy helping everybody. I think they will blame me. Everybody thinks I have something to do with Johnny and Katy running away," Netta says. "Katy sent me a letter about two weeks ago. The letter says Katy and Johnny are married. She is going to have a baby."

The ice cream is ready. The twins have more on their faces than in their cups.

The fireworks light up the night sky. Lilly and Dean are in the kitchen. Lilly wants to make tea. Lilly watches out of the door. She smiles at the expression of Anna Belle and the twins as they watch the fireworks.

"Mama, I want to tell you something," Dean says, putting water in a kettle.

"It's about Johnny and Katy."

Lilly moves toward the table. She takes a seat.

"Go ahead," Lilly responds.

"Mama, you cannot tell Netta I told you," Dean adds. "Katy wrote Netta. Johnny and Katy are married and are having a baby. Netta did not tell you because in her mind, everyone blames her for them running away."

"Don't say anything to her about this. I want to keep Netta's trust. You can decide what you want to tell Ms. Hattie. This is hard for Netta. She feels she has to hide the truth because everyone thinks she is bad. I don't want Netta to punish herself about this," Dean says, moving the whistling kettle off the fire. Lilly drinks the hot tea and meditates on what Dean has told her. Lilly doesn't want Netta to be a victim again. She makes up her mind never to ask Netta about Johnny and Katy again. Katy is the only friend Netta really has. Sometimes, things should be left alone.

The days pass fast; soon Netta will return to school. She dreads the idea. School will not be the same without Katy. Netta and Lilly talk about her first day of school. Netta hates everything about school. Lilly has never seen this side of Netta.

"Netta, what is wrong?" Lilly asks.

"I just don't fit in at school. I never have," Netta says in a fading voice. Netta notices a letter from Martha on the table. She picks up the letter and starts to read it. Netta takes the letter into her room. She imagines herself living with Martha, going to dances, and dressing up in silk dresses. Lilly can see the hurt in Netta. Lilly wishes she could stop her pain.

Later that night Netta is asleep. Lilly is sitting, reading her Bible. The wind is blowing. Even though it is Indian summer, a chill flows through her body. Feeling she is tired, Lilly says her prayer and goes to bed.

Lilly dreams she is walking in a beautiful green pasture. Netta is there, she is swinging in a tree swing that is just like the one in her front yard. Sandwiches, lemonade, and fruits are on a blanket surrounded by Dean, Lucille, the twins, and Anna Belle. She stands beside a fence; in the blink of an eye, she is standing on the other side of the fence. She can see everybody enjoying the perfect picnic. Lilly hears the wind whisper her name. She turns her face to see who is calling to her. When she looks back to the picnic, the distance has grown. She hears someone call her again. Each time she looks back, her children are farther away. Soon she is standing in the middle of a road.

"Lilly," it is Boe.

"Boe," Lilly is happy to see her brother. Lilly moves to touch Boe. She instantly wakes up. The old rooster is crowing to greet the day. Lilly goes to the kitchen. She starts her coffee. Lilly sees a flash of light and drops to the floor. Lilly lies there not moving, unconscious, and unable to move or to speak.

Netta is in her bed, asleep. She dreams of fireworks like the ones she remembers from the Fourth of July. In her dream, she can hear someone calling, "Come to me, come to me." Netta can hear her, but she cannot see her.

Netta wakes when the rooster crows a second time. Netta can feel a strange quietness in the house. She gets dressed.

When Netta goes into the kitchen, she sees Lilly lying on the floor. Netta hears Paul's truck coming down the road.

"Granny, Granny," Netta says, shaking Lilly. Netta rests Lilly's head on the floor softly. She runs to open the door. She yells to Paul, "Come quick! Something is wrong with Granny." Paul runs up the steps. He goes into the kitchen. He sees Lilly on the floor. He lifts Lilly from the floor and takes her to her bed. He checks her pulse.

"Get me a mirror," Paul orders. He places the mirror under Lilly's nose. He holds it there, but the mirror does not fog. He knows Lilly is gone.

"We have to take her to the hospital now." Paul carries Lilly to the truck. Netta follows. Paul speeds to the hospital. He runs inside. He tells the first nurse he sees.

Once Lilly and Netta are at the hospital. Paul goes to get Dean. He knows Lilly is dead, but he cannot say it.

Paul runs into the house suddenly. Dean and the children are surprised.

"Netta, need you at the hospital. Lilly is sick. You need to get Lucille from work," Paul says anxiously.

Dean changes her clothes in record time. She goes to Lucille's job and tells her of the emergency. Lucille and Dean arrive at the hospital. Outside the hospital door are Netta and a nurse. Netta is bending over in a sick desperate manner. They can hear her crying.

"No, no," Netta is in a hysterical state. Dean has a sick feeling in her stomach.

"Netta, stop it. What has happened to Mama?" Lucille asks, placing her hands on Netta shoulders. "Mama, they say Granny is dead," Netta cries.

Without a word, Lucille and Dean push through the doors of the hospital with a nurse in pursuit.

"Ladies, please wait," the nurse calls.

"Where is she? What room? Show me, show me now!" Lucille and Dean scream.

"Tell me the truth. She is not dead. Just tell me the truth," Dean says, dropping to her knees. Another nurse comes to the aid of the first nurse to help restrain the two.

"Please, listen to me. You have get to calm down," the nurse says.

"Okay, okay. Just take me to my mother," Dean says with anger.

Slowly they walk to a room. There they can see a body covered from head to toe.

"Oh, Lord, don't let this be. Mama, Mama … please, God. Please." The sight of the body brings them to reality.

Dean moves to Lilly's side. She leans over and kisses her. Her lips feel the touch of a cold body. Dean takes Lilly's hand and strokes it. She holds Lilly's hands to her lips. She kisses Lilly's hand.

Lucille looks in disbelief, clutching her hands to her chest. She moves closer to Dean. Lucille touches Lilly's arm. Time stands still. It all seems surreal.

"Ladies, please. We need to step outside," the nurse says. Netta runs to hug Dean and Lucille when she sees them coming out of the room.

At this point, Dean knows someone needs to take control, no matter how bad the pain is.

"Lucille, take Netta over there and sit down," Dean says.

"Come with me," the nurse says to Dean. Trying hard to hold on to her composure, Dean signs the necessary papers.

"Let's go. We have business to take care of," Dean says.

Dean, Lucille, and Netta drive to the funeral home. Netta refuses to go in. Dean and Lucille go inside. They are greeted by Mr. Brown, who remembers them from Boe's funeral.

"We need to make arrangements for our mother, Mrs. Lillian Hill."

"Yes, I remember your mother. She was a very nice lady. I am sorry for your loss. Mrs. Hill has made arrangements for this day. She made the arrangements the same time she made her brother's. Just tell us where to go to pick up her remains. Bring her dress and get some rest. She has taken care of everything," Mr. Brown says.

Dean and Lucille are in absolute shock. They thank Mr. Brown and walk out of the door. Netta can see the look on Dean and Lucille's faces.

"Are you through all ready?" Netta asks. No one answers. They walk to the truck like zombies.

The drive home is strangely silent. Paul can hear the truck stop outside. He goes to the porch and watches the women. Paul knows what has happened. He sends the children to their room. Lucille and Netta go home. Dean walks with her eyes straight ahead; she never looks at Paul on the porch.

Dean takes a seat on the steps. She touches her lips with her fingertips. Dean is recalling her kiss to Lilly's face. She starts to shake. She opens her mouth to scream. She screams so long. She becomes light-headed form the strain. Paul holds her around her shoulders from behind. He can only hold her until she stops.

Netta walks over to Dean's house at the request of Lucille. She sends Netta to bring Anna Belle home. Netta stops and sits with Dean and Paul. Netta becomes confused with the hurt. She sits, staring out into the garden Paul and Walter are growing. The twins and Anna Belle are at the door looking out.

"Netta," Pauline calls.

"Bring me Anna Belle. Please, Pauline," Netta requests.

Netta takes Anna Belle home. Lucille is sitting on the porch, watching Netta and Anna Belle make their way home.

"Mama, Mama," Anna Belle calls.

"Is Dean all right?" Lucille asks Netta, looking across the yard.

"No, Mama. She ain't all right." Netta sits Anna Belle down and runs to her room crying. This has to be the saddest thing Netta can imagine. No one will love her now. She is crying for her broken heart. The tears come like an ocean of water. Netta cries herself to sleep.

When Netta awakes, it is dark. She can hear Walter's voice. Now she hears Lucille crying loudly. Walter is standing at the door. Lucille is crying, sitting at the kitchen table.

"What is wrong, Netta?" Walter says. "Lucille starts crying. All I said was how was her day," Walter says in confusion.

"Granny is gone," Netta answers with tears in her eyes. Walter's face turns pale. He goes over to Lucille.

"Baby, I am so sorry. Where is Anna Belle?" he asks. Lucille points in the direction of her bedroom.

"Come over here, Netta." Walter motions. He hugs her and comforts Lucille at the same time. The night is very restless.

Chapter 17

The next morning, Lucille, Netta, and Anna Belle go to Dean's house. Anna Belle will stay with Dean and the twins; Lucille and Netta will go to the farm. Dean instructs Paul to send a wire message to Martha.

Arriving at the farm, Netta slowly enters the house. Lucille follows closely. "Did Mama ever say anything about what clothes she wants to be buried in?" Lucille asks. Netta has never anticipated she would ever hear these words. She cannot answer. Netta walks to Lilly's room. She is being led by an unseen force.

As Netta opens Lilly's closet, a white feather floats down from an overhead shelf. Netta picks up the feather. It smells like her Granny. On the shelf is a white box with pink ribbon tied around it. Netta reaches to get the box down. Netta feels tearful as she brings the box to Lilly's bed. Lucille watches Netta as she unties the ribbon. Inside the box is a beautiful soft pink lace dress. Under the dress is a small box and pink ballerina slippers. In the small box are earrings and a matching necklace. Lucille knows Lilly had placed the box there for them to find.

Netta leaves Lilly's room. She goes into the kitchen. She gazes at the floor where she found Lilly that fateful morning.

"Get some clothes to carry home, Netta. We need to go. We will come back later," Lucille says, holding the box in her hand. "We need to go to the church and talk to the pastor."

"And Ms. Hattie," Netta says. Netta knows Lilly would want Hattie to be the first to know. Lucille drives to the church. The pastor is outside, sweeping off the front steps of the church. He looks up as Lucille and Netta get out of the car.

"Hello, Pastor," Lucille says.

"Hello, ladies. How are you on this blessed day?" the pastor asks.

"Where is Sister Hill?" he asks. Netta hangs her head.

"We need to make arrangements for Mama's going home services," Lucille says. The pastor is visibly shaken.

"Sister Hill will be missed. She did so much good for others. Please come in and sit down." The pastor ushers them in. Netta remains outside. She sits on the bench under the tree in the churchyard, gazing at the glistening water.

She can think only of Lilly. Lilly had been everything to Netta. The thought of living with Lucille is frightening to her. Netta feels the only person in this world that cared about her is gone. This time, she does not want to go home with Lucille.

On the way home, Netta sits, looking at the road that lies ahead. Her mind drifts. She remembers Katy and herself sitting in the barn smoking a homemade cigarette. Just like a puff of smoke, her life has changed. How can she live with Lucille? There is no buffer between them now. Netta knows Lucille is her mother, but she is not her friend.

Life as she knows it has changed and nothing can change it back. Lilly is dead, and a piece of herself has died along with her. She is crying inside with every waking moment.

Netta is now lost. She has never had to walk through life alone. In her trancelike state, she can hear Lilly say, "Prayer can conquer all. Just pray. I will be with you." For the rest of the ride, Netta closes her eyes and prays.

When they reach Lucille's house, Netta goes to the back steps and sits there until dark comes. Netta cannot explain why she is feeling so much anger. She has no idea why she is so mad or who she is mad at. She searches the boundaries of her world. Netta can see no way out. Her grief is full of resentment at what she cannot explain. *No one to talk with, no one to love me*, she thinks.

"Netta, come into the house. I am going over to Dean's," Lucille says. Netta goes into her room and cries herself to sleep.

The next day, the good sisters from the church start coming to the houses. Netta tries hard to stay invisible. This reminds her of the first time she met Katy. Now it serves as the reason to say goodbye to Lilly.

"How are you doing, Netta?" It is Hattie. "Lilly is singing with the angels now. I will miss my friend," Hattie says.

When Netta hears the word "friend," she decides to tell Hattie about Katy's letter.

"Ms. Hattie, you don't have to worry about Katy. She is with Johnny. They ran away to get married. She sent me a letter. I am sorry I did not tell you, but everybody was blaming me. You can find her with her cousin," Netta says.

"I wrote to her cousin. She never answered. Thank you," Hattie says, hugging Netta. Netta begins to cry into Hattie's chest, burying her face.

"Go ahead, baby. Let it all out," Hattie says. It is so ironic—two different people missing the same two other people at the same time for the same reasons.

"You just sit here. I will bring you something to drink," Hattie says.

"No, please don't. I will just stay here for a little while," Netta says. Hattie leaves Netta alone.

Netta can see the twins playing in their yard. There are people over there as well. The twins wave and call to Netta, but she keeps her head down. She really wants to be alone. Netta walks to the garden. She is concealed by the large tree in the yard. How small this garden seems, compared to the one on the farm. Netta sits by the tree; she closes her eyes. She tries hard to remember Lilly's smile. Netta starts to cry. *How can I get over this? Why is it so hard? Why does it hurt so much?* she thinks. Netta hides there until late into the evening.

"Where have you been? I have been looking for you." Lucille says in haste.

"What do you want?" Netta shouts.

"What do you mean 'what do I want'?" Lucille answers in anger. "Who do you think you are talking to? You must have forgotten I am your mother," Lucille says. Netta does not answer.

"Did you hear me?" Lucille says.

"Yes, I heard you," Netta replies.

"You wait until everyone leaves." Lucille threatens. Netta looks Lucille in the eyes and runs off to her room. Netta reaches the house; she passes through the crowd of people in the kitchen. Netta closes her bedroom door and places a chair against it.

Soon everyone has gone home. Lucille goes to Netta's room. The door doses not open. Lucille pushes.

"Netta, open this door. Open it now!" Lucille shouts, waking Anna Belle who is in her arms. Netta gets up from the bed and opens the door.

"What has gotten into you?" Lucille asks, placing Anna Belle in her bed. "You better behave or I will—"

"Or you will send me off to Granny!" Netta says before Lucille can finish.

"Don't you talk to me like that. You are still in my house and you are not grown yet!" Lucille shouts.

"I am only here because Granny is dead!" Netta shouts back. Lucille walks to Netta and grabs her by the arms. Lucille shakes Netta.

"Don't talk to me like that as long as you live in my house!" Lucille screams. Netta pulls backs and sits on the side of the bed, looking at the floor. Lucille leaves the room.

"What is going on in there?" Walter asks.

"I don't know what has gotten into Netta. She must have forgotten who is the mother. I will not be talked back to in this house," Lucille says.

"Everybody is upset right now. Maybe she is just grieving for Lilly," Walter adds.

"Grieving or not, she will not raise her voice to me in my house," Lucille declares.

Netta wakes the next morning to Anna Belle tugging at her hair. Netta rolls over, sees Anna Belle, and covers her head.

"Go away," Netta says. "Go get Mama." Anna Belle leaves the room. She goes down the hallway to Lucille's room. Anna Belle tugs at Walter and Lucille.

"Tell Netta to feed you," Lucille says. Anna Belle returns to her room. Netta has heard what Lucille says. She is holding the covers tightly over her head.

"Netta, Netta, Mama said to feed me," Anna Belle says. "Feed me, feed me ..." Anna Belle cries and screams these words until Walter gets up out of bed just to stop her from crying. Lucille is angry.

"Netta, Netta, get in here!" Lucille demands, calling from the kitchen.

"Did you hear Anna Belle? Why didn't you get up and just give her some milk?" Lucille inquires. Netta has no answer.

"What is wrong with you Netta? Answer me!" Lucille demands.

"Nothing is wrong with me," Netta answers.

"Why are you going against me?" Lucille asks. Netta cannot answer simply because she has no answer. Netta walks to the kitchen to give Anna Belle her milk. Walter is looking at both of them. He sees Netta is angry.

"Morning, Netta." Walter says.

"Good morning," Netta replies. Netta hands a small cup of milk to Anna Belle. Netta goes to the bathroom. She begins to cry. She misses Lilly so much. Her life is changing, and she has no control over it.

Netta goes to her room. She makes her bed and gets dressed. Netta goes to the back porch. Without saying anything, she walks over to Dean's house. Netta can see Dean in the window. Dean waves to her from inside the house.

"Hi, Aunt Dean." Netta says. Dean can tell Netta has been crying.

"Good morning, Netta. You want some breakfast?" Dean asks. "No, ma'am," Netta answers.

"Martha will be here tonight on the train," Dean says. This news makes Netta feel happy. She can talk to Martha about all the things they have written about over the last three years.

"Martha will stay with us for the funeral." A hush falls over the room. Dean has finally says the word everybody is trying to avoid.

"Netta, hi, Netta." It is Pauline and Paulette, standing at the door.

"Come in here and eat. Where are your brothers?" Dean asks. Pauline leaves the room. Paulette goes to Netta's side. The sound of laughter and running can be heard coming down the hallway. The boys are teasing Pauline.

"Dean." It is Lucille calling. "Have you seen—oh, there you are. I was looking for Netta," Lucille says. "Why didn't you tell me you are coming over here? I want you to watch Anna Belle. I need to go to the store for some things."

"Anna Belle can stay here with the twins," Dean interjects. Lucille leaves the house after thanking Dean. Dean can sense the tension between Lucille and Netta.

"Netta, did you tell Lucille you are coming over here?" Dean asks.

"No, ma'am," Netta replies. This explains Lucille's reaction to Dean.

"Do you have a dress to wear to the funeral?" Dean asks.

"I am going to wear the dress Granny made for me," Netta says.

"Help me get the twins dressed. The women from the church will be here again today," Dean says. Netta and Dean dress the twins. Soon the good sister from the church arrives with food. Netta sits on the porch swing, trying to be invisible. Seeing all of Lilly's friends without Lilly seems strange.

Why Granny and not one of them? Netta thinks. Netta knows to think this is wrong, but anything would be better than what she has to face.

All day there is activity and people going and coming. Soon a taxi pulls up in front of Dean's house. It is Martha. Netta runs to meet her. They embrace.

"Martha, you look so pretty. Aunt Dean will be glad you are here," Netta says.

"You have grown up to be a young lady. Who are all these people here?" Martha asks.

"Let me help you," Netta offers. "Aunt Dean, look who is here." Dean runs to hug Martha. They embrace each other until they cry.

"Oh, look at the babies. They have grown so much in three years," Martha notices.

"Come hug your cousin," Martha says, holding out her hands. The boys run to Martha. The girls and Anna Belle cannot remember who Martha is.

The women are standing on the back porch looking on. Netta bypasses them with Martha's bags. Tucked in the side of Martha's canvas bag is a magazine. Netta places Martha's bags in the bedroom. She quickly grabs the magazine. The pictures and the clothes are fascinating to her.

Netta never hears Dean and Martha comes into the room.

"Netta, what are doing reading Martha's book?" Dean scolds her.

"That's okay, Netta. You can have it if you like," Martha says.

"Thank you," Netta says. She kisses Martha on the cheek and leaves the room.

Netta goes to sit on the swing again. This time, she can occupy her thoughts with the many articles in the magazine. The pictures of the new line of swimsuits with the ladies lying on beach towels catches her eye. The whole picture comes to life. The two ladies become Katy and herself. Netta's fantasy is short-lived. She can see Lucille approaching the gate.

"Did Martha come yet?" Lucille asks.

"Yes, ma'am," Netta replies.

"Go home and try on the dress I bought for you to wear to the funeral," Lucille orders. Netta is surprised. She has made up her mind to wear the dress Lilly made for her. Netta knows to say anything will only lead to a fight. Netta just obeys.

The next day everyone travels to the farm. The family will stay there until after the funeral. Netta unlocks the door. The twins rush in past her as though they are running to greet Lilly. Netta turns to look at the adults who are unpacking the cars. As she stands in the door, a sweet breeze strokes her face.

Netta goes to Lilly's room for the sole purpose of getting Lilly's Bible. She quickly moves it to her room.

"Netta, come help." It is Lucille. Netta goes to the front of the house. Lucille is standing there with bags in her hands.

"Put these in the kitchen for me, please." Lucille says. Netta goes into the kitchen, placing the bags on the table.

She gazes out of the window at Adley, who is trying so hard to impress Martha, who has outgrown his country ways. Martha has a new sophistication about her. She has been exposed to a different world, and it shows.

Netta looks on as the good sister drives up to the house with food. She watches as the men help unload for them. The sound of the twins and of Anna Belle coming into the kitchen changes her thought pattern.

"Go outside and play under the tree," Netta tells them.

"We want water," Little Paul says. Netta reaches to get glasses for the children.

The day passes quickly. Soon it is time to get dressed to go to church for Lilly's wake. The twins are reluctant to change their clothes. Dean asks Netta to dress the girls while she and Paul take care of the boys. Soon everyone is ready for the ride to the church.

The church looks like a beacon in the night. There are so many people that the crowds overflows out into the churchyard. Netta feels hurt and embarrassed by the looks the family receives from the crowd. She does not want to get out of the car. The car door slowly opens. A large hand reaches out to offer assistance. It is one of the male church members. Netta can see his hand and the shape of his body, but his face is invisible with the light at his back. He is to her a faceless man in a black suit. Netta reaches for his hand.

"Thank you," she mumbles. After one leg then the other, now she is standing. Fear starts to well up in her mind. The church is only four steps away, but to Netta, this short distance seems like a mile to the door.

"Netta, move." It is Anna Belle as she pushes her way out of the car.

Move, all I have to do is move one foot in front of the other, Netta thinks. Netta can feel her breathing changing; her hands are trembling. Her body is cold in the middle of the hot summer night.

The family lines up—Lucille and Dean are with Walter, and Anna Belle and Paul are close behind them. Next come Netta, the twins, Martha, and other family members. Netta can feel the eyes of the people on her. The feeling of sorrow and sadness drapes the room like black curtains. Walking toward the altar of the church, Lucille becomes weak. Walter holds her waist from behind.

"Mama, Mama," she sobs.

There it is. The lights and candles create a smoke-haze halo around Lilly, whose peaceful look makes you wonder why she will not open her eyes. *Doesn't she know everyone is here to see her?* Netta feels.

Dean gets up from her seat; she goes to Lilly. She is touching and kissing her mother's face. She is crying. She whispers, "I hope I was a good daughter to you. It would mean the world to me if you could answer." Dean is praying and crying. She realizes this is the last time she will ever touch or kiss Lilly's face again.

Netta finds herself standing. She notices a large white feather in the flower arrangement.

"Where are you going Netta?" Paulette asks. Netta does not hear her. She shuffles her way to the end of the pew. Netta walks to the casket. She takes the feather; it smells like Lilly. She looks into the casket. There is no sound in her ears. She can only hear loud screaming and crying. Netta feels Dean's hand on her chest. She is supporting Netta from behind. Netta realizes the screaming is coming from her.

Dean leads Netta to the front pew. The ushers descend upon her with great urgency. Netta pushes the usher away. She runs out of the church. She reaches the tree and throws up.

Martha comes out after Netta.

"I am not going back in there," Netta says, gasping for breath.

"You don't have to." Martha assures her.

It is still early when the wake ends. The house is crowded with people. Netta slips away to go to the barn, only to find it occupied by Walter, Paul, Adley, and the other men.

"Do they need us?" Paul asks.

"No, I am just walking around," Netta says. She backs out of the door. She goes around to the side of the barn and sits on a wooden crate. Netta leans backward, looking upward at the stars. As she gazes, she sees a shooting star. *Granny, is that you?* she questions in her thoughts. Netta returns to the house once most of the cars are gone from the yard.

Martha and Adley are in the porch swing. They are talking about the past and the present. He tells her how he is in love with Martha, and his new love is just a substitute while he is away from her. Netta does not care if they want to be alone. She sits on the stairs.

"Netta, you okay?" Martha asks.

"Yes, I am okay," Netta responds.

"You don't want to go in?" Adley adds.

"No!" Netta answers sharply. Adley wants to persuade Martha to make out with him.

Netta could care less; she is only thinking about how tomorrow will be the saddest day of her young life. Sleep is not an option for her. Netta goes to her room. She prays for tomorrow to come and go quickly.

Chapter 18

Morning arrives. Soon the house is busy. Netta has to help the girls with their hair and dressing.

"Now go sit down and stay clean," Netta orders. Everyone is apprehensive after last night at the wake.

The big black car pulls up in front of the house. The family arrives at the church. The good sisters form two rows on each side of the church stairs. They are all in white dresses with white scarves circling their heads. Netta is reminded of the white sheets dancing as the wind blows between them. It makes her feel a sense of calm. The music is peaceful. In the church there is standing room only.

The family is seated. The funeral service begins. The pastor is speaking and weeping as he talks about Lilly.

"Sister Hill loved this song and, choir, I want you to sing it loud and with feeling so Sister Hill can hear you in heaven." The music plays, the choir starts to sing *Amazing Grace*.

The crying and the fainting are too much for the ushers. The ushers are forced to recruit people from the pews to help. Dean and Lucille are crying hysterically. The twins and Anna Belle are crying because Lucille and Dean are crying. Paul and Walter are trying to console everyone.

Netta gets up from her seat, walks to Lilly, and gives her a kiss. Netta turns and walks slowly out of the church. She walks to Lilly's gravesite. She sits in one of the chairs there. Humming and rocking, she just gazes. The wind is blowing through the trees. The sound is soft, like Lilly calling her name.

The pallbearers are walking with Lilly's casket high upon their shoulders. They place her above the open hole. Dean, Lucille, and the family are seated. The final words cannot be heard from the crying, drowning out every word the pastor says. "Dust to dust, ashes to ashes." Now it is says.

Dean is so overwhelmed that Paul has to carry her to the car. The twins are screaming for her, running behind.

"Let's go, Netta." It is Martha placing her arm around Netta's shoulders. Netta looks at Martha. She slowly stands. She takes one last look into the ground. She smiles. Resting on the top of the pink and white flowers, she sees a white feather.

When they arrive at the farm, the crowd is huge. Netta rushes to her room.

She closes the door. Minutes pass.

"Netta, you in there?" It is Martha. "Can I come in?" she asks. Netta gets up from the bed. She unlocks and opens the door.

"You can come in," Netta says, opening the door. Netta holds onto the doorknob. She closes and locks the door behind Martha. Martha sits on the bed. Netta sits on the vanity chair in front of the dresser mirror.

"You don't want to eat?" Martha asks. "They are worried about you and I am worried about you too. I know it is hard. I was your age when Mama died. I was not a woman and not a little girl anymore. Fifteen can be an awkward age. You can make bad decisions if you don't think clearly. I have seen a lot of girls become women before their time."

"Netta, are you all right? I don't mean the funeral, I mean everything. How are you and your Mama getting along? I can tell from your letters that you are upset with her for leaving you out here on the farm with Aunt Lilly. I know you and Aunt Lilly are close. She loved you so much. She was so proud of you."

"Lucille can only handle one child at a time. She never wants another baby after you. We used to joke about what would happen if she gets pregnant again. She swore she would never have another child. You are all she needed. So don't be upset with her, she can only do one child at a time."

"You are fast becoming a young lady. All the boys will like you. Maybe some time, you can come and visit me when you are older," Martha says. Netta becomes excited at the idea of seeing all the things she and Martha write about.

There is a knock on the door. It is Adley looking for Martha.

"I have a new love. I just don't want to hurt Adley or make him sad, but he is becoming a pest. I will see you outside, okay?" Martha says, unlocking the door. Netta watches Martha leave the room. She turns and looks into the mirror. Around her neck is the necklace Lilly gave her at Christmas. She holds it tight and smiles. Netta walks slowly out of the room.

So many people, she thinks.

"Netta, are you hungry?" It is Hattie. "Yes, ma'am," she answers.

"Come to the kitchen with me," Hattie offers. "I gave your Mama and aunt Dean tea with paregoric," Hattie adds.

Netta looks out of the window. She sees Adley and Martha by the fence. Even from this distance, she can tell that Martha is only tolerating Adley. Netta takes her food back to her room for privacy.

Soon the crowd thins. The twins and Anna Belle are asleep. Everyone is on the front porch, overflowing into the yard. Netta is sitting in the tree swing. She hears the conversations that are drifting in the wind. She hears Adley trying so hard to convince Martha to stay. He tells her how she is not like the other women he dates. Netta laughs to herself. She knows Martha can stop Adley's pleading at any time, but she chooses not to.

He should be telling Martha something she does not already know, Netta thinks.

Two hours later, Netta walks back to the house.

"Netta, you will stay here with Dean tomorrow. The house must be prepared to be boarded up until we decide what to do with the farm," Lucille says. Netta is in shock.

How can this keep happening? Every chance Lucille gets, she leaves me behind, Netta thinks. She doesn't respond; she goes to her room and closes the door. Netta leans on the door, staring at the floor.

The next day, the farm is busy. People are coming by to help or take things away. The remaining livestock are sold to the surrounding farms. The twins and Anna Belle are playing and running around the big tree in the yard.

"Netta, can you come help?" Dean calls as she climbs onto a chair to clean off the shelf in Lilly's closet. There are boxes of papers and pictures.

"This is a picture of Mama and Daddy when they are young," Dean says. Netta takes the picture in her hands. She looks and comments, "How pretty Granny was."

Packing and cleaning consume most of the day. Paul returns in the evening with Lucille. Lucille's focus is only on Anna Belle, as usual. Netta is extremely nervous. The house is not finished, and Dean is preparing to put the twins to bed for the night. Paul will be leaving soon to go back to town. Netta knows she will wake up here in the morning. Her question to herself is, *How long will I have to stay at the farm again?*

It takes Dean and Netta several days to complete the packing. This Saturday, Walter, Adley, and the men from the lumber mill work all day to secure the farm.

The adjustment overwhelms Netta most of the time—not only moving back home, but changing schools and trying hard to fix in. Netta's body is very shapely for an adolescent. The young girls are envious of her body. On the other hand, the boys are very vocal. Netta has an adult body with an innocent, protected mind. No one has ever told her about the different games boys play or the boyish things they will do. Games like the one Jimmy Ray plays with her.

One day at school, Jimmy Ray sees Netta walking alone from one side of the school to the other. He has a serious lust for Netta, but she always rejects him. Netta is walking slowly, reading; she is deep in thought. Jimmy Ray approaches her from the rear. He puts his hand over her mouth; he grabs her around her waist. He pulls her to the side of the building. He pushes her against the wall.

"Do not scream. All I want is a little kiss from you. Have you ever kissed a boy before?" he says. This is déjà vu for Netta. Out of fear, Netta reaches for a pencil from her sweater pocket. Netta thrusts the pencil into Jimmy Ray's arm and breaks it off.

She grabs her things and runs off. Netta does not stop running until she reaches home. She sits on the back steps. She is panicking, trying hard to contemplate her actions. She tries to recall, but her fear blocks her thoughts. Netta's thoughts shift to Lucille. How can she explain being home early? Maybe Lucille will not know if Dean doesn't see her on the back steps. Netta moves quickly into the house. She starts her daily chores inside the house. Netta knows she needs to go over to Dean's house. She needs to see if Dean has notice her coming home an hour early.

It is overcast this October day. The children have been inside all day; the door is closed. Netta waits until it is the usual time for her to go to Dean's house.

"Hi, Aunt Dean," Netta says, entering the house.

"Hi, Netta," everyone says. The twins and Anna Belle are busy playing. Dean is cooking.

"Netta, how was school today?" Dean asks. "Your Mama tells me you don't like it there."

"It's okay," Netta answers. She feels relieved she feels Dean is unaware of her coming home early. Netta opens up her writing tablet and begins to write a letter to Martha.

"Netta, Netta." It is Lucille in a panic.

"What's wrong?" Dean asks in surprise.

"There is some woman over at my house talking crazy. She says Netta has stabbed her son in the arm with a pencil. They had to take him to the hospital to have the pencil removed from his arm," Lucille explains.

"Is this true, Netta?" Dean asks.

"Mama, I can explain!" Netta says with fear. "It was all his fault. He tried to make me kiss him behind the building. I stabbed him with the pencil so I can get away," Netta explains.

"That's not what he is saying," Lucille responds.

"Leave Anna Belle here. Go ahead and take care of things," Dean suggests. Lucille is angrier than concerned with Netta. She is pulling Netta along by the hand, saying, "It is always something with you."

Netta feels defeated. She feels no one will believe her. She is always being blamed for something she did not do. Netta can see the silhouette of three people on the front porch. As she gets closer, she can see Walter inside the front door. He is talking to the male figure, but she cannot make out what is being said.

Jimmy Ray has his head down, hiding behind his Mama like a little girl.

Netta and Lucille walk past the three and stand next to Walter.

"Tell them what you told me, Netta," Lucille orders. Netta looks at Jimmy Ray as though he is the only person there. Her fist are clenched. She starts to speak slowly.

"I was walking and reading my book. Jimmy Ray grabbed me and tried to kiss me," Netta says.

"I did not try to kiss you. You stabbed me for nothing. Nobody likes you," Jimmy Ray argues. "You are lying. Why did you run off the school grounds? The teachers were looking for you."

"Is that true, Netta? Did you leave school today?" Lucille inquires.

"I was afraid. I just picked up my books and ran," Netta explains.

"Why did you not tell someone what had happened?" Lucille asks.

"I don't know," Netta replies.

"She could not tell because she knows no one would believe her," Jimmy Ray says.

"Well, what are you going to do?" Jimmy Ray's mother asks.

"Netta says she was attacked," Lucille replies.

"She is lying. The school went looking for her. She had run off, just like Jimmy says," Mrs. Ray replies. "The doctor said the bill is high. We need to know when will you give us money."

The women argue back and forth. Walter can see the smirk on Jimmy Ray's face. Walter suggests everyone stop the arguing for now. He, Lucille, and Netta will talk and get back to them after Lucille visits the school tomorrow.

As soon as the Ray family is gone, Lucille starts in on Netta in a non-supportive way. Netta argues for justice until she can hardly talk.

"You just go to bed, and everything better be the way you say, or I will punish you," Lucille declares.

Netta is afraid. The whole day happened so fast. Netta never wants to hurt anyone. She tries every day to be nonexistent. She just goes to school and comes home as her daily routine. Netta sits on the side of her bed. She goes to her closet. She looks through the closet to prepare her wardrobe for the next day. She notices a box on the shelf. In the box are pictures of Lilly, and underneath the pictures is Lilly's Bible. Netta has never opened the Bible, but tonight it is just what she needs. Netta opens the Bible to the Twenty-Third Psalms.

When Netta opens the Bible, there is money in it used as a bookmark. Netta looks through the Bible; there is a total of fifteen hundred dollars in various bills. She knows this will make Lucille happy. She decides to hide it until the storm blows over. Netta says her prayers and readies herself for tomorrow.

The next morning, tension is high. Lucille is upset. She must take time away from work to go to the school with Netta. On the ride to school, Lucille reminds Netta her story must be true. Netta tries to reassure Lucille of her innocence.

Walking down the hallway of the school, Netta can feel all the whispering eyes. The heads turning and frowning.

"Good morning, we are here to see the principal," Lucille says to the office clerk. The office clerk asks Netta her name.

"Oh yes, we are looking for you yesterday afternoon," the clerk says. "Just have a seat. Mr. Robers will be with you soon."

Netta is wringing her hands. Her thoughts are racing. She is trying hard to recall everything that happened yesterday. The door to the principal's office opens. Netta sees Mr. Robers walk to the counter. He is talking with the school clerk. He motions toward Netta and Lucille.

"Hello, I am Mr. Robers, the school principal," he says. Lucille introduces herself. Netta, Lucille, and Mr. Robers go into his office.

"Mrs. Jones, we have a very serious problem here. Jimmy Ray's arm requires five stitches. He will be permanently scarred. The family is very upset. In saying that, we have no other choice but to suspend Netta," Mr. Robers says.

"This is all wrong. Netta is the person who was attacked," Lucille argues. "We searched for Netta once Jimmy Ray came into the office bleeding. He and his friend told a different story," he says.

"Netta, tell me you side of the story?" Mr. Robers asks. Netta tells in detail how Jimmy Ray assaulted her. Mr. Robers questions why she did not report the incident to the office. Netta cannot think of a reason other than fear. By the end of the hour, it is clear that no one believes Netta's story is true.

"Mrs. Jones, I feel I need to research this more. Until that time, Netta must remain at home," Mr. Robers says as he stands to indicate the meeting is over.

Lucille drives Netta home. "Netta, what has gotten into you? I will talk with you to night. I am going to work. I don't know what to believe," Lucille says.

"Please believe me," Netta begs. Lucille drives off.

Chapter 19

Netta stands at the gate. She has tears in her eyes. All her life, she feels she is always being blamed for something she did not do. Now this. Netta is so afraid of what Lucille will do. Netta goes to her room. She is crying. She kneels to pray.

"Why, what can I do?" She cries. Netta sits on her bed. She sees the letter from Martha. Without thinking, Netta takes a canvas bag from her closet. She packs some clothes. Netta takes the money from the Bible. She counts out one hundred dollars. She takes the rest of the money and places it in a sock. She pins the sock to her bra. Netta leaves by the front door. She looks to see if Dean's door is closed. She walks slowly past Dean's house.

Netta arrives at the train station. She inquires about the next train going west. The ticket agent informs her the next train leaves in an hour. Netta shows Martha's address to the ticket agent. She asks how much it will cost to get there. The cost is forty-five dollars. Netta pays for the ticket.

Netta sees an elderly lady waiting for the train. She sits beside her. Soon the lady is talking with Netta. They are going to the same town.

"Good, I hate to travel alone. My daughter is having a baby, and I am going to help," The old lady explains.

Netta tries hard not to show how she is feeling, or that anything is wrong. She tells the elderly lady that her sister is getting married and she will be in the wedding.

"My name is Clara Walker." Netta tells only her first name. Netta tells Ms. Walker this is her first trip on a train. They form a bond for traveling. Ms. Walker assures Netta everything will be all right; she will guide her.

Soon the whistle blows.

"All aboard!" the conductor shouts. Netta knows once she steps onto this train there is no turning back. Her heart is pounding. She thinks it can be heard over the noise of the train.

"Are you okay? You don't get travel sick, do you?" Ms. Walker asks.

"No, ma'am," Netta answers. "You go first. I will hold your bag," Netta says. Ms. Walker climbs up onto the train; she turns to Netta to take her bag. "Climb on up, child. Let's find a good seat. The train is not crowded. That is good." Ms. Walker observes. Netta slowly steps up onto the train. She follows closely behind Ms. Walker.

The ladies place their bags overhead. Ms. Walker has a picnic basket with food. Netta looks out of the window across the tracks. She sees another passenger train. She marvels at the massive cars made of steel.

How can it move? Should I go? Maybe I should tell someone? To whom can I tell? Mama will be mad. She is already mad. With that thought, the train makes a forward jerk. The whistle blows, and it is too late to turn back now. Netta closes her eyes and prays. She feels fear and excitement at the same time. Netta watches as the landscape speeds up before her eyes.

"Is this your first train ride?" Ms. Walker asks.

"Yes, ma'am," Netta answers. Ms. Walker smiles. She opens a canvas bag. She pulls knitting needles and yarn from the bag. Netta's eyes are fixed on the view out of the window. She sees one world passing and the beginning of an uncertain world she knows nothing about. Netta tries to think at what point in this day she has decided to run away.

Can I go back? I cannot stop this train. It is moving so fast. If it did stop, could I find my way home? Netta thinks. Netta sits back. Soon she falls asleep from the consistent rhythm of the train on the tracks.

For two and one half days, Netta marvels at the many towns and railway stops. This is an adventure she will never forget.

Meanwhile, Lucille's anger has turned to worry. It has been two days, and no one can find Netta in the small town. Lucille has looked high and low. She and Walter have looked for her, even going to the farm. They go to Hattie and Netta's old schoolmates. No one knows where she is. The sheriff takes a report. Hattie tells Lucille to just pray. The truth will come out.

"We need to get ready. We will be getting off in an hour," Ms. Walker tells Netta. Reality sets in for Netta. She knows when the train stops this time, her trip will be over. The destination she wants will be staring her in the face.

"Will your sister be waiting when the train stops?" Ms. Walker asks.

"No, ma'am. I will get a taxi," Netta answers.

Netta watches as the city comes into focus. She has no idea that a city this big and this modern exists. The light, the people, the cars—Netta suddenly feels fear. How can she find her way around this town?

The train slowly pulls into the station.

"There is my baby," Ms. Walker says with excitement. Netta reaches for the bags. Stepping slowly down to the ground, she looks around in amazement. The train station is huge. Ms. Walker introduces Netta to her daughter and son-in-law. The couple asks what side of town she will be staying on. Netta takes out the letter from Martha and shows them the address. Ms. Walker's son-in-law comments that this is a very private and affluent part of town. Ms. Walker makes the suggestion to take Netta to her sister's home. She will feel better knowing that Netta made it to her destination safely. Her son-in-law agrees.

Once Netta walks out of the train station, the weather seems moist to her skin. She is overwhelmed by the sophistication of the city. It is late into the night, but the city is so alive. As they walk to the car, Netta's excitement can be seen in her reactions.

As they drive closer to Martha's address, Tom, Ms. Walker's son-in-law, asks, "What type of work does your sister do to live in this neighborhood?"

"I don't know," Netta answers. Netta sits back in her seat. She is captivated by the large houses. The houses are as big as the city hall building in the small town she comes from.

On the top of the hill over the city stands a large double gate. Over the crest it reads "Mason Estate."

"May I see your sister's address again?" Tom asks. "This is the right place." Tom drives through the gate. At the end of a tree-lined road stands a huge mansion with a large gas lantern that lights up the night.

"We will wait to make sure your sister is home," Ms. Walker says. Netta steps out of the car. Never once did she think, *what will happen if Martha is not at home?*

Netta walks to the door. There is a large lion's head door-knocker in the center of the door. A thick, twisted red rope is at the right of the door. Netta knocks on the door. No one answers.

"Pull the rope," a voice calls from the car. Netta pulls the red rope. She can hear bells from inside the house. Netta sees a light turn on; she hears footsteps. The doorknob turns and so does Netta's stomach. Everything slows down to a crawl. A large, well-dressed man opens the door.

"May I help you?" he asks. Netta clears her throat. "Does a Martha Hill live here?" Netta says.

"Who may I say is calling?" he asks.

"Netta, her cousin," she says.

"Wait here." He closes the door behind him. Ms. Walker and her family are looking on with curiosity. Minutes pass. Suddenly the door swings open. It is Martha.

"What, how did you get here? Is that Lucille and Walter in the car?" Martha asks.

"No," Netta answers.

"Who are these people?" Martha asks as she walks down the steps to the car. "Hello, my name is Clara Walker. I traveled here with your sister on the train.

"We offered to bring her here to your house. This is my daughter and her husband. Now that Netta is safe, we can leave," Ms. Walker says.

Martha is confused, but he will not let the strangers know it. Martha looks at Netta's face. She sees something is wrong. Martha thanks Ms. Walker. She steps back from the car and says goodbye. Netta waves goodbye.

As soon as the car is in motion, Martha says, "Okay, Netta, what is going on? Where is your Mama? Why did they send you here? What has happened at home?" Netta drops her head.

"I just leave. They don't know I am here," Netta says.

Martha is speechless. "You mean you ran away?" Martha asks.

"Yes, ma'am," Netta answers.

"Why, Netta? What happened?" Martha asks.

Netta explains to Martha about the attack at school. She tells Martha how she fears Lucille. Martha stands in shock with the cool October wind blowing on her face.

"Let's go inside. If anyone asks you a question, don't say anything. I will do all the talking. It is a good thing Ms. Helen is out tonight," Martha says, leading Netta through the large double doors.

Chapter 20

Once inside the door, Netta is in awe. The beauty of the house is more than she can ever imagine. Just inside the door is a grand foyer with a large glass table with fresh cut flowers. Her head tilts back as she looks upward to the ceiling. She slowly brings her eyes down, looking at the twin staircases with red carpet on them. Martha notices how amazed Netta is, looking at the majesty and elegance of the house.

Martha leads Netta through the house. Off to the leaves, they walk past a formal room where a fireplace is burning. Down the hallway, they pass a large room with a piano and a card game table with chairs. The room is so big that there is room for dancing and for lounging. They pass into another room with a formal dining table and pantry through a swinging door that leads to the largest kitchen Netta has ever seen. In the front of the window is a small dining table. Three beautiful women, all dressed in very lacy robes, are sitting drinking, laughing, and talking.

"Martha, who is this?" one of the ladies asks.

"I will tell you later," Martha answers. Through the kitchen, out of the back door, a well-lighted pathway leads to two small houses at the end. The path splits into a V-shape with one house on the right and one house on the left.

Martha leads Netta to the small house on the right. Netta hears unfamiliar sounds. She has never heard the ocean crashing against the rocks. The wind sings high in the palm trees. Netta turns to look backward up the path. She realizes they have just walked through a huge garden with cement benches and large statues.

Martha knows the urgency of the situation. She is trying hard to stay calm. Thoughts are racing through her head. *Lucille must be out of her mind with worry. What happened to make Netta run away like this? There must be more to the story,* she thinks.

Martha opens the door to her house. She holds the door open as Netta walks in.

"You live here alone?" Netta asks.

"Yes," Martha answers.

"It is nice," Netta remarks.

"We have to contact your mother to let her know you are okay," Martha informs Netta. Netta does not respond.

Martha knows there is no telephone in Lucille's house.

"We will send her a wire the first thing in the morning," Martha says. "Now tell me again why you did this."

Netta retells Martha how Jimmy Ray tried to hurt her. She explains how she defended herself by stabbing him in the arm. Netta tells Martha how Lucille did not believe her.

"She says she would punish me when she came home. I was afraid. I did not know what Mama would do to me. She hates me," Netta explains.

"Lucille doesn't hate you. I know things have been distant between you two since Anna Belle was born. And now, Aunt Lilly is gone. You feel you lack support. Grieving and change can do a lot of things to a young girl. I know, I was young when my mother died." Martha seems to relate to Netta for a minute. "Nevertheless, you need to get washed and change your clothes. You can sleep in this bedroom."

While Netta is taking a bath, Martha is trying to decide how to explain this lifestyle to Netta. "How can I explain Netta to Ms. Helen? Children have no place here, especially one so innocent." Martha pours herself a drink and turns on music to help her relax. Maybe she can come up with a plan until she can get Netta back on the train to go home.

"I am finished," Netta says in a childlike voice.

"Okay, Netta we need to talk. Sit down. Tomorrow we will send a wire to Lucille. I will give her a telephone number so she can call here. When you meet Ms. Helen tomorrow, you will say you are eighteen years old if she asks. Let me do all the talking about why you are here. She may remember you from home. In any regard, she has her rules. You will spend most of your time here in the house until I can get things sorted out. Do you understand?" Martha questions.

"Yes, ma'am," Netta says.

"Are you hungry?" Martha asks.

"No, ma'am," Netta answers. Netta retreats to her room. Netta kneels down to pray. Maybe her coming here was not the best idea or thing to do after all.

Martha's telephone rings, it is David. David is Martha's lover. She has completely forgotten about her date. Martha explains to David that something has come up. She must cancel her date with him. As she hangs up the phone, she pours herself a drink. She sees things will change for her if Netta stays here.

The next morning, Martha can see Ms. Helen sitting at a small table on the patio. She is drinking coffee and going over her book of receipts. Netta is asleep. Martha puts on her robe and walks down the short path to where Ms. Helen is sitting.

"Good morning," Martha says.

"Collin tells me you have a guest," Ms. Helen responds.

"That is why I came over here—to tell you my young cousin from home arrived last night."

"You never mention to me anything about her coming here."

"I did not know myself. She will not stay long. It seems she did not tell anyone. Netta ran away from home. As soon as I contact her mother, we will make plans to get her back home," Martha explains.

"Good, we don't need any trouble with a runaway. How old is she?" Ms. Helen inquires. Martha knows she must lie. If Ms. Helen knows Netta is only fifteen, she will be angry.

"Eighteen," Martha lies.

"How long will it take, and what can she do while she is here?"

"Netta has washed sheets for you before. You say they are the whitest you have ever seen,"

"Oh yes, I do remember. Okay, good, she can help with the laundry but only for now," Ms. Helen orders. "Bring her to meet me after lunch. In the meantime, you need to prepare a special treat for Captain May. His son is coming home from West Point. It is his birthday and the captain wants to give him a private party. Tell Antoinette to prepare herself. We can finish the details later. This will be on Friday night. We have four days to prepare. Use the parlor upstairs. In the meanwhile, go to the bakery and order a cake. I will see you this afternoon."

Netta is looking out of the window. She sees Martha talking with Ms. Helen. To Netta, Ms. Helen looks like the ladies you see in the magazines, even in her robe. Netta watches Martha walk the short path back to her house.

"Good, you are up. We need to get dressed to go into town. I have things to do. Most of all, we need to send the message to your mother to let her know you are safe," Martha says.

As Martha and Netta walk to the garage to get a car, Netta can see the majesty of this large estate. It is so overwhelming that she feels intimidated by its grandeur. As they drive toward the huge gate, Netta sees the driveway is surrounded by beautiful grounds that were hidden by the darkness last night. The huge gate seems to open into a road that slopes like a curving snake. Along the curving road to one side is another large gate with a driveway. On the other side of the curving road is the ocean. The beautiful blue water seems to extend forever. Netta sees the water crashing against the rocks. For the first time, she can understand the noise she heard last night. It is all like a dream; her heart is racing with excitement. At the end of the road, a town starts to take form. The town is hilly. The rising and falling of the drive send surges of butterflies through her stomach.

Netta sees people of different cultures that she has never encountered before. Her head is spinning from all the newness. There are so many buildings and a railway down the middle of the street. Martha smiles as she watches Netta turn her head from side to side, trying to absorb everything she sees.

"Do you like what you see?" Martha asks.

"Yes, ma'am," Netta answers with excitement. By this time they arrive at the telegraph office.

"Sit here. I will be right back," Martha says as she exits the car. Netta looks on as the people pass her sitting still. The people, the sounds, the city, all the new smells—Netta is mesmerized. She does not hear or see Martha getting back into the car.

After all the errands and a small tour of the city, Martha and Netta are taking the long ride up the coast to the hillside estate.

The main conversation is about how Netta should address Ms. Helen.

"Netta, how do you like the big city?" Martha asks.

"It makes home seems so small. It is a big place," Netta responds.

"Now that we are going back home, you will meet Ms. Helen. Remember what I told you last night. Listen and be polite. You are eighteen years old. We have sent a wire to your mother. You are going home as soon as Lucille gets the train ticket for you to return. Do you understand?" Martha asks.

Arriving at the estate, Martha parks the car in front of the house. Martha pulls the red rope. The tall man who opens the door last night answers. "Hello, Ms. Martha," he says.

"Hello, Collin. This is Netta. You met her last night. She will be staying here for a little while," Martha explains.

"I know, Ms. Helen informed me. Ms. Helen is waiting for you in the study," Collin says.

"Thank you, Collin. Please take this to the kitchen," Martha says, handing Collin a package. Netta watches as Martha inspects herself in the large mirror. Then Martha turns and adjusts Netta's clothing and hair.

"Okay, let's go meet Ms. Helen," Martha says, exhaling.

The house is even more beautiful with sunlight shining in through the large windows. The colors of the crystal chandelier look like hanging rainbows. The room seems alive. Martha leads Netta to a room located in the south wing of the house. Martha knocks on the door. Slowly Martha opens the door.

"Come on in," a voice says.

There she is, the infamous Ms. Helen. Netta has heard the women of the family talk about her for years. Sometimes in a good way but always with respect. Ms. Helen is an extraordinary woman—very shapely, with elegance and glamour. Sitting in a chair next to the fireplace, Ms. Helen sits like a beautiful royal queen.

"So this is your young guest?" Ms. Helen asks.

"Yes, ma'am," Martha answers. Netta can see that Martha's body language has changed. Netta has never seen Martha so humble. She always appears to be strong and independent, but not now as she stands before Ms. Helen.

"Come closer, so I can get a good look at you." Ms. Helen motions to Netta with her hand. "Tell me, what made you come here?" Ms. Helen asks.

"She had a problem and ran away. We have just sent a wire to her mother, who will send for her soon," Martha answers, protecting Netta.

"I ask the young lady, not you," Ms. Helen says firmly. "What is your name? How old are you?" Netta turns her eyes toward Martha. She remembers the conversation they had the night before and earlier in the day.

"My name is Netta. I am eighteen years old," Netta answers.

"Good. Martha told me of your dilemma. Has Martha told you what we do here?" There is a pause in the room. Netta shakes her head to say no.

Ms. Helen continues. "We give complete pleasures. Everything you see here, stays here, do you understand? You do not discuss or tell anyone what goes on in this house or on this estate, do you understand?" Ms. Helen stands to get a cigarette holder from a nearby table. "Here is what I am going to do for you. While you are here, you will help with the laundry, washing sheets and my personal things. I will pay you the same as I paid you before. This will help you earn your ticket home. You must obey my rules."

"Now Martha will introduce you to Sissy. She will show you everything you need to know about the linen—where it is washed and stored."

"Netta, you are a very fine young lady, do you know that? Everybody here pulls their weight and contributes to the house. I am the house." In saying that, Ms. Helen excuses them with a wave of her hand.

Leaving the room, Martha is concerned with Ms. Helen's comment to Netta about her looks, but she knows better than to show it. It is more important than ever to get Netta back home where she should be.

As they enter the kitchen, Netta can see three people sitting at the table, two women and Collin.

"Carmen, Sissy, this is my young cousin, Netta. She will stay with us for a little while. Sissy, Netta will help with the linen and Ms. Helen's personal things and nothing else," Martha explains.

"Okay, Ms. Martha," they answer. Martha and Netta sit down for lunch.

Carmen prepares a plate of food for them.

Carmen is Ms. Helen's cook. Sissy is the young maid. Collin is married to Carmen. The three staff lives on the third level of the house. They are available to Ms. Helen twenty-four hours a day, seven days a week.

Sissy leads Netta down the stairs to the basement. The basement fills the foundation of the house. There are several storage areas and two storm door entrances with windows at ceiling level. Netta has never seen such a fully equipped laundry. Sissy shows Netta around the laundry. Sissy educates Netta as to how Ms. Helen likes things done. After the instruction, Sissy and Netta return to the kitchen.

"Netta, Ms. Martha says for you to come to her cottage," Carmen says. "Thank you," Netta says, opening the door. She stands on the step, looking out into the large garden. *How pretty,* she thinks.

"Netta, I have to go out for a while. Please stay in the house. Everything you need is here. I have magazines, music, and food. Leave a lamp on when you go to sleep." Martha kisses Netta on the head and leaves the house. Netta watches Martha walk up the path to the large house. She sits back in the chair, looking around; she picks up a magazine and goes to her room. Netta soon falls asleep on the small bed.

Chapter 21

It has been a few days now since Netta ran away. Lucille is completely out of her mind with worry. She has alienated herself from everyone. She has not gone to work from the time Netta leaves. Everyone is upset and displaced.

Walter worries while he works. Dean and Paul ask the people around town who come into their small corner store if anyone has seen Netta. The twins and Anna Belle sense something is wrong with Netta's absence this time.

Paul is placing a hay bale at the door of his small store. A Western Union courier stops outside his store.

"I have a wire-gram for Lucille Jones," the driver says.

"I will take it," Paul responds. He gives the courier two bits and goes into the store. He closes the door and locks it. Paul goes home.

"A Western Union man just delivered this to the store," he says, handing the message to Dean. "Take this to Lucille," Paul says. Dean looks into Paul's eyes. Without a word, she leaves the house. She runs next door. Dean enters Lucille's house through the kitchen.

"Lucille, Cille. It is me, Dean!" she yells. There is no answer. Dean travels down the hallway to Lucille's bedroom. The room is dark. Lucille is lying on the bed, looking at the window shade.

"Lucille, are you awake?" Dean asks as she moves closer to the bed. Dean opens the window shade to get light in the room.

"Oh, Lucille, you have to get out of this bed," Dean pleads. Dean hates to see her sister in this state of mind. Dean goes to the bathroom and wets a small towel to wash Lucille's face.

"You have to snap out of this. Netta will come home and everything will be all right." Dean reaches into her pocket, she gives the wire message to Lucille. "Read this," Dean says. Lucille sits up in her bed. She adjusts her eyesight. Slowly she opens the seal. Lucille's hands are shaking, wiping the sleep and the tears from her eyes. She moves closer to the window.

Dean is sitting on the bed; this is the first time she sees Lucille without hope. Lucille holds the gold paper and begins to read the message.

Wednesday, October 16, 1929 To: Lucille Jones

From: Martha Hill Netta is safe…Stop.

She is with me…Stop.
Have Central operator to dial SFC O – 0489#2…Stop.
Call after five o'clock p.m….. Stop.

Lucille drops to her knees. She is gasping for breath. Dean rushes to Lucille. Lucille's facial expression strikes fear in Dean's heart. From the pit of Lucille's heart, she screams as if she has been stabbed in the heart. Dean reads the message, she screams with joy. Dean and Lucille embrace each other. They read the message over and over like a chant that bursts out into a scream of joy.

"Thank you, God! Thank you, Jesus!" They shout. Regaining their senses, they move from the bedroom floor to the kitchen table.

"What time is it?" Lucille asks. She has been in the dark and has lost track of time since Netta ran away.

"It is eleven o' clock in the morning," Dean answers. "You have plenty of time to get ready. You need to eat."

"How did Netta get to Martha? Where did she get the money? Do you think Martha sent for her? Did Martha pay for her train ticket?" Lucille questions.

"Martha would never take Netta without getting permission from you.

"No! No! There is some other explanation," Dean says in disbelief.

"Then explain to me how this happened," Lucille says with conviction.

"I don't know how it happened. Don't blame Martha before you know the whole story. You need to eat and take a bath. Anna Belle misses you. She wants to be with you here at home," Dean says, breaking eggs into an iron skillet. Lucille does not respond. She sits gazing at the floor. She is trying to rationalize the past few days.

Once Lucille is taking a bath, Dean leaves to go home. Paul is sitting at the time with little Paul.

"Netta is with Martha," Dean says, coming into her kitchen.

"With Martha? How did that happen?" Paul responds in surprise.

"I don't have a clue. I really don't know," Dean answers. "But we will find out today after five o' clock this evening. Lucille will go down to the Western Union office to make a call to the central operator. Martha sent a number to reach her."

"You know that will cost money," Paul tells her. "Well, I am glad she is safe.

I am going to go back to the store. Maybe I can sell something. I will be back in time for you to go with your sister," Paul says.

"Thank you for being so understanding," Dean says as she kisses her husband on the lips.

Lucille is soaking in her bath and crying. She does not understand why or how Netta would run away to Martha. Lucille believes Netta has never been the same since she moved back home after Lilly died. Lucille imagines in her mind how Netta made the train trip to Martha.

"Why, why would she do that!" she cries.

Lucille makes her way to her room. Standing in the doorway, she sees how she has neglected her surroundings. The day is moving closer to five in the afternoon. By four in the afternoon, Walter arrives. He is surprised and happy to see Lucille dressed and in the kitchen.

"Hi, baby! You are feeling better?" he asks.

"Walter, Netta is with Martha. Read this wire message I get today," Lucille says, handing Walter the gold paper. The room is silent. Walter hugs Lucille. She buries her face deep into his chest.

"We need to go to the Western Union office now. Please stop over and pick up Dean," Lucille tells Walter as she closes the car door.

Anna Belle sees Lucille for the first time in three days. She runs to her with excitement. The twins join in jumping and singing. Lucille holds on to Anna Belle.

"Lucille, we need to go," Dean reminds her. Anna Belle starts to cry after Lucille.

"She will be back soon," Paul says, holding Anna Belle. Paul and the children watch as Lucille and Dean walk away.

The ride to the Western Union office is full of anxiety. Lucille can hardly wait for Walter to stop the car. Once inside, Lucille shows the clerk the telephone number to call. The Western Union clerk explains to Lucille how making a long distance call works. He explains how he must first relay the call down the line to another operator and that operator will relay to yet another operator. Once contact is made, they will ring back to him.

Once the phone rings, he will transfer the call to a telephone booth located on the far wall. He looks up how many relay points and charges her five cents for each relay station.

"That will be seventy-five cents. Please have a seat, it will take about a half- hour. Please have a seat over there," the clerk says.

Walter hands the clerk the money. Dean escorts Lucille to a bench built into the wall. Lucille is very anxious; she can hardly sit still. Dean places her arm around Lucille to comfort her.

"It will be okay. Soon you can talk with Netta," Dean reassures Lucille. Walter goes outside. He is unsettled; he needs to pace back and forth, passing the window glancing in at Lucille and Dean huddled together on the small bench. It seems like hours. Lucille is watching the clock on the wall.

"That clock must be slow. We have been here longer than thirty minutes," Lucille says.

Ring, ring. Lucille rushes to the counter. She stands in silence.

"Okay, miss, go over to the telephone booth and wait until I ring the telephone before you pick up," the clerk instructs her.

Lucille runs to the telephone booth. She has trouble opening the door.

"Are you ready?" the clerk yells from behind the counter.

"Yes," Lucille responds.

Ring, ring. Lucille's hands are shaking and sweaty.

"Hello, hello," she says.

"Lucille, this is Martha," the voice on the other end of the phone says.

"Where is Netta?"

"She is standing here next to me. But she wants me to talk to you first."

"Why?" Lucille questions.

"Lucille, Netta is afraid you will be mad at her. She thinks you hate her," Martha says.

"I don't hate her. Why would she say something like that? All I ever want for Netta is the best. She has become rebellious. Now she has run away. Let me talk to her now!" Lucille says. Dean motions for Lucille to calm down.

Martha turns to Netta with sadness in her eyes.

"Talk to your mother," Martha says. Netta is shaking her head no. Martha takes Netta's hands and presses the phone into them. Slowly Netta places the phone to her ear.

"Yes, ma'am," she says.

"Netta, oh Netta, why did you run away? You have worried everyone out of their minds. Did Martha send for you? How did you get there?

You need to come home as soon as possible. Do you hear me? Answer me, Netta, answer me!" Lucille says in desperation.

Netta starts to cry. All her fear surfaces again. She has no idea what will happen to her when she goes back. She stands looking at Martha in a daze.

"Say something, Netta," Martha says. Netta drops the phone and runs to her room. Martha picks up the phone. In Netta's defense, she questions Lucille about what she says to her.

"Lucille, what did you say to her? Netta has gone to her room," Martha explains.

"Her room. Martha you are the one behind all of this. Did you send for Netta to come there? You need to send her home now! She does not need to be there in that house with you and Ms. Helen. I know what goes on there, and I will not have Netta there." Lucille says in anger.

"Lucille, Netta showed up here on her own. I never sent for her. It was as much of a surprise to me as it is to you. If I had want her here, I would have asked your permission. Netta has a problem with you. You need to trust her and believe her when she tells you the truth. What is wrong with you? You have changed, Lucille."

"As far as her being here, I will never let anything happen to her. I will do everything I can to get Netta back to you, but if she is not happy there, she will leave again. Next time, it may not be to come to me," Martha responds. Lucille is speechless. She stands there holding the phone. Dean slowly pulls the phone from her hand.

"Martha, this is Dean. What is going on? How did Netta get there?" Dean asks.

"Dean, good, talk some sense into Lucille. Netta came here because she was afraid of what punishment Lucille would give her. She was defending herself that day at school. She feels that Lucille does not love her since Anna Belle was born. I don't know how she get the money to come here. A lady helped her find me once she got here from the train. Netta is not dumb. She has a good head on her shoulders. Lucille is wrong. I love her like a sister, but she is all wrong," Martha says.

The clerk yells from behind the counter, "The connections will close soon! A relay station down the road will be closing. If you want to continue the call you will have to reroute, so you will have to hang up and make the call again. We can start the call up again after we reroute, but it will be at additional cost."

While Dean is explaining to Martha, like what the clerk had said, the connection is lost. Lucille is crying. Walter helps her to the car. "No, I want to call her back now," Lucille insists.

"No, Lucille. You need to wait a few days until you can calm down. Maybe send a wire. You have got to get your head straight about this. Netta is going through a tough time, and you are too," Dean says.

In the meantime, Martha is trying to console Netta. "Let's give her a few days, okay? We can try again when you are ready," Martha says, holding Netta. The moment is broken by a knock on the cottage door. It is Sissy. She comes to remind Martha about the card game Ms. Helen is having tonight. Martha has to see to all the preparations and collect receipts from the gentlemen. She has to make sure four of the eight young women at the house are ready to entertain the men.

"Netta, stay here. I have work to do. I will be in the main house. If you need me, have Sissy find me. Don't come looking for me, okay? Just go to the kitchen, and Sissy will find me. Do you understand?" Martha says, leaving the room.

Dean, Lucille, and Walter return home. Lucille cried all the way home. Dean goes to Lucille's house. She can see Lucille may drift back into depression. Walter helps the ladies into the house. Once Lucille is in the house, Walter goes over to Dean's house to see Paul.

"How did it go?" Paul asks, handing Anna Belle to Walter.

"It is all messed up." Walter replays. "Lucille did not really get a chance to talk to Netta. She became angry and upset. She blames Martha for Netta running away."

"What did Martha tell her?"

"According to Dean that Martha told her, Netta just showed up at her house on Sunday night with an old lady who helped her on the train. Martha has no idea where Netta got the money to get the train ticket," Walter explains.

Dean tells Lucille to rest. "Now that you know where Netta is and that she is safe, you can rest better. Next thing to do is to get her home as soon as possible."

"Lucille, you know Martha has nothing to do with Netta running away. The good thing is that she did run to Martha. If she had run away to someone we don't know, we might never have found her. You need to pull yourself together so we can get her back home. Enough with this self-pity. Netta is a good girl surviving in a bad life."

"Stop and think of all the things that have happened to her in her short fifteen years. Her whole childhood has been shattered. She has been breaking down for a long time. We just did not know. She stayed on the farm with Mama for a long time. I will get you some tea so you can rest," Dean says with sadness. Dean will stay with her sister until she is calm. She wishes Lilly was alive to help with this.

It is hard being the strong one, she thinks.

Netta sits. wondering how everything could go so wrong. She cannot think of going home now, but that is the one place she wants to be. The confusion is overwhelming for her. She sees no compromise in what has taken place, and nobody is explaining it to her.

Netta walks to her room. She starts to pray for guidance. "I don't know what to do. Oh, Granny, I wish you are here. Everything would be all right," Netta says with tears in her eyes.

Although Martha has told her to remain inside the small house, she has decided to go outside. She goes to the side of the cottage out of sight of the large mansion. Netta listens as the water crashes against the rocks. It brings her a tranquil, peaceful feeling. For that minute, that second, everything seems okay—a short-lived moment that she wishes can last forever.

Netta knows she has to make her mind up about talking with Lucille sooner or later. Everything keeps rushing back to her mind's eye. The bad dreams, the bad emotions, the secret, and the truth. Soon the crisp October night and the sound of the ocean calms Netta enough for her to rest.

Chapter 22

The next few days are a turning point in everyone's lives.

Dean is gazing out of Lucille's kitchen window. The kids are bobbing for apples, it is Halloween. Looking into the darkness, she duels with herself.

This is my family, but not my problem. My children are here at home with me. I need to let Lucille handle this on her own. This is a mess, and I cannot fix it. Lucille always manages to escape one way or another. Now she is hiding inside herself. It doesn't matter. Lucille and Netta are my blood, so that makes them my problem, she thinks.

Dean walks over to Lucille, who is standing with Walter.

"Have you written Netta?" Dean asks.

"Yes, but I have not mailed it yet," Lucille responds.

Dean can see Lucille is becoming comfortable with Netta being away again. Paul has advised her to hold her tongue about the situation. In her mind, she knows he is right, but in her heart, she knows Netta is in danger of losing a lot more control of her life if she does not leave Ms. Helen's house.

Netta's depression is topped with confusion. She stands watching Collin. She has asked Collin to construct a makeshift clothesline behind Martha's cottage out of view of the main house.

"Good, make the wire good and tight. That's good. White sheets need the light of the sun for them to gleam and glow for the shine to show through," Netta says to Collin as he drives the last nail into the tall palm.

"Thank you," Collin responds.

Netta pulls the first white sheet from the basket. "You can never shine hanging in that dark gloomy basement. You need sunlight," Netta says, talking to the sheets. As Netta hangs the last sheet, her ears hear the familiar sound of sheets dancing in the wind. She walks backward to get a better view of the choreography of nature. Netta gazes at the white sheets, remembering the day she stood at her aunt Dean's gate looking at some of the same white sheets dancing in the wind. The daydream changes as the white sheets form into the dresses of the good church sisters standing at the doorway of Lilly's small church. The daydream is broken by the sight of Sissy moving carefully through the rows of the white sheets.

"Collin told me about the clothesline. Does Ms. Helen know?" Sissy asks.

"Why should she care?" Netta responds.

"Ms. Helen has her rules," Sissy quietly says.

"No one can see them behind this house. Sheets need sunlight to shine. You will see," Netta says, picking up the laundry basket.

On their walk back to the main house, Netta and Sissy see Martha walking with an elderly man. Martha is pointing to the center of the garden. Netta and Sissy continue on to the basement.

"Netta, you want to help me change beds upstairs?" Sissy asks.

"Martha says I should not go upstairs unless she takes me up there," Netta answers. Sissy takes a few steps. She turns and looks toward Netta with resentment. She does not understand the moral protection that Ms. Helen and Ms. Martha are giving Netta. Sissy walks away, mumbling, "Everyone knows what goes on up there."

Netta loads her basket with more wet clothes. She knows that the white sheets will be dry because the wind is high flowing off the hill. On her way down the walk, Netta meets Martha and the elderly man coming up the walk.

"Hi, Netta, still washing?" Martha asks.

"Almost finished after this load dries," Netta responds.

"This is Mr. Washington. He and his son will build a gazebo in the middle of the garden for Ms. Helen," Martha explains.

"How do you do, young lady?" Mr. Washington asks.

"Fine, thank you," Netta responds. "I guess I will finish now," Netta says, slowly walking away.

She walks around to the back of the cottage. She presses her face into the white sheets, feeling the softness and smelling the freshness that has been placed there by the sweet, salt air. Netta removes them from the clothesline one by one, folding each one in such a manner that they seem freshly pressed. She stacks the sheets neatly on a towel while she hangs the remaining wash.

Netta sits on the grass, leaning up against a large palm tree. Although this is November the sun is still warm in this part of the world. Netta sits and thinks of home. She knows everyone back home will soon be preparing for Thanksgiving. Her heart is saddened to think no one has tried to contact her since she and Martha made contact. She thinks how big the twins and Anna Belle must be by now.

She can see Walter and Paul sitting in the backyard, drinking and talking of plans for the future. Netta smiles to think how Aunt Dean and Lucille must be getting ready for Thanksgiving eve baking. The simple thought of Lucille brings tears to her eyes. *Why does Mama hate me? I love her more than anything,* Netta thinks.

Netta gathers the clean, folded laundry and goes back to the house. Netta goes up the stairs to the kitchen.

"Netta, would you like to go to church with us tonight?" Carmen asks.

"Yes, but I must ask Martha if it is okay," Netta answers.

When Netta leaves the room, Sissy makes a comment. "They treat her as if she is a child. Why does she need to get permission to go anywhere?" Sissy remarks.

"You stop that, Sissy. Netta is Ms. Martha's cousin, and she is only here for a little while. Don't go starting trouble where there is none!" Carmen tells her.

"Sounds like you are jealous," Collin says with a laugh.

Netta soon returns to the kitchen in excitement. "Cousin Martha says it will be okay," Netta says.

"Good, we can leave after I prepare dinner," Carmen says.

Netta goes to the small cottage. Netta will wear a dress Martha has given to her. *It is so fine. It feels like silk,* Netta thinks as she spins around in front of the mirror with the dress pressed against her body. After Netta takes her bath and is combing her hair, Martha comes into the house. Martha buttons the back of Netta's dress.

"This dress looks better on you than it ever looked on me," Martha comments. Martha turns Netta around with both hands on her shoulders. She looks Netta in the eyes to say, "Netta, at no time do you talk about family business or anything you have heard me say about Ms. Helen. Remember the talk Ms. Helen had with you—what goes on here in this house stays here on these grounds. If anyone asks you, you are visiting and nothing else. You are eighteen years old, your mother and father allowed you to visit. Do you understand?"

"Yes, ma'am," Netta says. Now she feels insecure about going to church tonight.

"Okay, good. Behave, listen to Carmen and Collin. Please say a prayer for me." Martha says with a smile, not realizing she has put a sense of fear into Netta about talking with new people.

Martha and Netta meet Carmen and Collin at the steps outside the kitchen door.

"Where is Sissy?" Martha asks.

"She changed her mind just now when she saw you coming up the path," Carmen answers. Carmen, Netta, and Collin walk toward the garage.

Martha walks up the stairs to the kitchen. Sissy hurries to enter the basement door. Martha never notices the intent to avoid her. Sissy is still upset from earlier today, and once she sees Netta in Martha's discarded dress, she becomes angry for fear Martha will not hand down her old clothes to her now that Netta is here. This is one of the reasons Sissy decides not to go to church with Carmen, Netta, and Collin.

On the drive into town, Carmen inquires how Netta is enjoying her stay.

"Netta, how do you like the big city? Does make home seem small?" Carmen says.

"You lived back home with Ms. Helen?" Netta asks in surprise.

"Yes, I lived with Ms. Helen before her husband and son died," Carmen replies.

"Ms. Helen had a son?" Netta questions.

"Yes, but, baby, don't talk about that. Never say anything about that, please!" Carmen says with stress in her voice.

"Everybody just sit back and enjoy the ride," Collin interjects.

The ride into town becomes a silent tour into a new side of town for Netta. The houses reminded her of home. Soon Netta can see a small white church with a tall white cross on top of it. The church sits inside a white picket fence, surrounded by a cemetery. Before Collin can stop the car, the sounds of the Holy Ghost spirituals are traveling through the air. Netta can feel excitement well up inside her. It has been a long time since she has heard songs like this.

Once inside the church Carmen leads Netta to her favorite pew. With a silent nod, Carmen greets the woman in the pew across her. Next to the woman is Mr. Washington, the same man Netta had met earlier in the garden with Martha at Ms. Helen's house.

After church, everyone gathers in the church kitchen to eat and for fellowship. Everyone is curious about Netta. Little did Netta know that Carmen and Collin know Mr. Washington; the woman is his wife along with his daughter, Betsy and their son, BoHeim. Carmen and Mrs. Washington hugged and greeted each other. Everyone introduced themselves one by one.

The young people separate themselves from the adults.

"Betsy, BoHeim, take Netta over to eat with you on the young folk's side of the room," Mrs. Washington suggests. The trio finds a place at the end of a table.

"How old are you, Netta?" Betsy asks. Netta stutters over fifteen to say eighteen.

"You don't look eighteen. You look my age. I am sixteen years old." Betsy observes.

"She does look eighteen," BoHeim declares. It is very obvious that BoHeim is very attracted to Netta. For some strange reason, Netta likes the feeling she gets when she looks at BoHeim.

"Don't mind him, Netta. He has been looking at you since you came into the church," Betsy says, sticking her tongue out at her brother.

"Be quiet, Betsy. They always say you talk too much," BoHeim says shyly.

By this time, Netta has gotten the attention of every young male from the ages of twelve to twenty five. Netta looks like a young lady in the silk dress Martha has given to her. BoHeim is aware of the competition he may have to win Netta's affections. He is glad his mother and Carmen are good friends. Now he will not mind helping his father build the gazebo for Ms. Helen.

Netta finds it hard to eat with all of the winks and smiles sent her way. "Netta, you live in Ms. Helen's house? Tell me about what goes on out there.

People are always talking about that house," Betsy blurts out.

"Betsy, mind your own business, or I will tell Mama on you," BoHeim stresses. "Please don't pay Betsy any mind. She is always nosey. You don't have to tell her anything," BoHeim says to Netta.

Soon the time has come for Netta to leave.

"Netta, we need to leave now." It is Carmen, putting her coat on.

"Nice to have met you all, good night," Netta says as she pushes her chair back to stand up.

Once Netta reaches the car, Netta turns to see BoHeim standing in the churchyard. He is looking at Netta getting into the car. Netta takes her seat then she decides to wave bye to him. One can see BoHeim's eyes light up. Netta smiles as they drive away.

On the drive home Carmen asks, "Netta, did you enjoy the church services?

Would you like to come again?"

"Yes, ma'am, I would love to come back," Netta says with excitement.

Carmen began to sing church hymns. Netta joins in. The ride home seems shorter this time.

Once Netta, Carmen, and Collin reach home, they enter the house through the kitchen. In the kitchen Martha, Antoinette, Loretta, and Sissy are sitting at the table having coffee.

"Back already?" Martha notices. Netta is all smiles to see Martha. She can hardly restrain herself.

"Martha, the church people act just like the people back home. I met new friends. The girl's name is Betsy and her brother's BoHeim." Netta never notices Sissy reaction. Sissy's secret is that she has all but offered her body to BoHeim. Sissy says, "BoHeim is a young man, not a boy."

"Netta doesn't look like a little girl in that dress either," Loretta says, laughing with Antoinette. Sissy leaves the table upset.

Netta never stops talking. "And guess what, Martha? Mr. Washington is his father," Netta continues.

Martha looks toward Carmen. Carmen answers her stare.

"Yes, they are good children. Robert and Mary Washington have done well in raising them. Betsy is sixteen, and BoHeim is nineteen or twenty. I am not sure about his age," Carmen tells Martha.

"Netta, it is time for bed," Martha says. Martha and Netta walk to the small cottage. "Netta, your mother sent me a letter today. You can read it if you want to. Lucille says she needs time to get the money for your train ticket home," Martha says with the letter in her hand.

"Is that all she says?" Netta asks.

"Pretty much," Martha answers.

Netta leaves the letter on the small table and goes into her room. Martha follows closely behind her. Martha begins to unbutton Netta's dress. Martha can see the distress on Netta's face.

"You do look all grown up in this dress," Martha says, trying to cheer Netta up. "Get some rest now. Tomorrow you can write to Lucille and tell her how you feel. You will be home soon, we will get the money together somehow," Martha says as she walks out of the room.

Netta undresses. She looks under the bed for the canvas bag with Lilly's Bible, it is still there. *Should I tell Martha about the money and go home? Does Mama, really want me home?* Netta thinks.

Netta slowly pushes the bag under the bed. While kneeling she says her prayers, thanking God for her newfound friends and praying for her family back home.

Chapter 23

The next morning, Netta goes to the main house to have breakfast and start her day. "Good morning," Netta says.

"Netta, I talked with Mary and Betsy this morning. Betsy wants to know if you would like to come and visit her at her home. Mary will not allow Betsy to visit you here. Would you like that?" Carmen asks.

"Yes, ma'am, but I will have to ask Martha if it is okay," Netta answers.

"Good, you need to have young girls more your own age around you. Now eat up," Carmen said, handing a plate filled with grits, eggs, toast, and bacon. Netta finishes eating breakfast and starts down the steps to the basement.

Netta meets Sissy partway up the stairs.

"Guess what, if it is okay with Martha, I am going to Betsy's house," Netta says, with a childlike excitement. Sissy does not comment. She pushes past Netta with a noticeable anger.

Bursting through the kitchen door, Sissy storms over to the stove where Carmen is standing.

"What is this Netta is talking about, going over to BoHeim Washington's house to visit?"

"Wait a minute, why are you so upset about that?" Carmen asks. "Netta is going over to be with Betsy, they are only two years apart. A girl like Netta needs to stay away from here as much as she can. She has a humble soul, and it is none of your business."

Sissy walks out of the kitchen. Collin is approaching, he has just turned the corner of the house.

"You know, sometimes your wife just needs to keep her nose out of other people's business," Sissy says as she passes Collin.

Collin is surprised. He just stands there, watching her walk away. Collin gathers himself and goes into the kitchen.

"What the hell has gotten into Sissy? She just passed me like a whirlwind, talking about how you need to mind your own business. What happened?

"Oh, she is all upset because Mary Washington and Betsy have invited Netta to spend some time with them at their home. Everybody has always known Sissy always wants BoHeim. Now she thinks Netta does. The Washington's never invited her because they don't want BoHeim with a woman like Sissy. They know why she came here. She just wasn't good enough for Ms. Helen upstairs. Ms. Helen likes her girls pure and fresh. Sissy is not pure or fresh," Carmen says, sitting at the table with fresh green beans in a pan. Collin just raises his eyebrows and gets a cup of coffee.

Netta starts to heat the water for the wash. She is happy with the thought of having a friend. She can only remember having one other true friend, Katy— Katy who taught her things about what men and women do in life. She recalls the first time she met Katy. How they smoked a homemade cigarette in Lilly's barn. Katy was the first person to describe the ocean to her. Now she knows Katy was placed in her life to teach her about things to come in her own life. *That is what real friends do*. With that thought, Netta finishes her first load of wash.

Netta takes her first load of wash to Martha's cottage. She places the clean wash outside the door.

"Martha, Martha," she calls. Martha answers.

"Carmen says Mrs. Washington and Betsy want me to come visit them at home. Can I go?" Netta begs.

"Let me talk with Carmen first then we can decide. I am going out for a little while, but I will stop at the main house and talk with Carmen. You will have an answer today, okay?" Martha kisses Netta on the head and walks out of the house, Netta following closely behind her.

Just outside the door all the white sheets are on the ground.

"Netta, did you drop the wash?" Martha asks.

"No, I don't know how this happened. Now I will have to wash them all again," Netta says with disappointment. Martha helps Netta put the sheets back in the laundry basket.

As they finish picking up the sheets, they see Ms. Helen and Sissy standing in the center of the garden. Martha and Netta walk halfway up the path. Ms. Helen calls to Netta to come over to her. Martha walks alongside Netta.

"What do you have there, Netta?" Ms. Helen asks.

"The sheets fell out of the basket," Martha answers quickly.

"You know, that is the second time I heard that," Ms. Helen says. Netta and Martha are puzzled.

"Go ahead, Sissy, tell them how the sheets get on the ground. Tell them!" Ms. Helen says, raising her voice.

"I turned the basket over," Sissy replies with guilt and shame because she was caught.

"Tell Netta you are sorry," Ms. Helen adds. "Now you take that load of wash and clean it the way she does. If I ever see you do anything like this again, you will not like what I will do," Ms. Helen says with authority.

Martha takes the basket from Netta. Martha takes two steps, pushing the basket into Sissy's hands and gives a cold stare into Sissy's eyes.

"Netta, go to the kitchen and tell Carmen I want the chicken tonight. You help her today. Let Sissy do all the washing today. You run on now. I need to talk with Martha and Sissy now," Ms. Helen says.

Netta can feel a strange tension, but she obeys. Netta walks off with confusion in her mind. *Why would Sissy do that?* As she reaches the step, she turns just in time to see Martha slap Sissy across the face. Ms. Helen does nothing. Sissy grabs the basket from the ground and runs off toward the outside entrance of the basement.

Carmen is watching out of the kitchen window.

"What is going on out there?" Carmen asks Netta.

"Sissy threw the white sheets on the ground. Ms. Helen saw her do it," Netta answers.

"Now, why would Sissy do a fool thing like that?" Carmen comments.

"I don't know. Ms. Helen told her to rewash them. Ms. Helen says she wants the chicken tonight and I can help you all day," Netta answers.

"Good, what do you know about cooking?" Carmen asks with a smile.

"My granny taught me how to cook," Netta replies.

"Oh, well then, I know you can cook. Lilly was a good cook. I was sorry to hear she had passed," Carmen says.

"You knew my granny?" Netta springs up in surprise.

At that moment, Martha entered the kitchen.

"Carmen, I need to speak with you outside for a minute," Martha says, standing in the doorway. Carmen wipes her hands on the apron hanging around her neck. "I will be right back, baby," Carmen says to Netta, leaving the room.

Looking through the window in the door, Netta can see the facial expressions and the body movement of the two women as they talk. Netta is unsure about what has taken place with Sissy, Ms. Helen, and Martha in the garden. In any event, she can make out Sissy's name several times in the conversation. Carmen and Martha embrace. Carmen opens the door into the kitchen to walk in. Martha follows closely behind her.

"Good news. Martha says you can come to Mary and Betsy's when I go tomorrow," Carmen says to Netta. Netta is beaming with joy. "Netta, please write to your mother today. Help Carmen and be good. When you finish helping Carmen, please go back to my house, okay? I will be back before dark," Martha says, padding Netta on the shoulder. "See you all later," Martha adds, walking out of the door.

Collin is entering as Martha is leaving. They speak in passing. Collin closes the kitchen door. He is surprised to see Netta in the kitchen at this time of day.

"Hello, Netta, what are you doing in here? I just passed by Sissy going to the basement with dirty wash," he says. He is interrupted by Carmen clearing her throat and turning her eyes.

"Netta, do you know how to clean and cut greens?" Carmen asks.

"Yes, ma'am. Carmen, tell me how you know my granny, Lilly." Netta says, standing at the sink.

"Boe and Lilly came around all the time to deliver vegetables and fresh eggs. Lilly came with Boe to see Annie. You are too young to remember your aunt Annie," Collin explains.

"You knows my granny too, Collin?" Netta asks, lifting a pan full of collard greens from the sink to a nearby table.

"Yes, yes, we always had the best-tasting vegetables and double-yolked eggs for baking," Carmen says, smiling and looking toward the ceiling.

All at once, the whole conversation changes from happy to serious. Carmen sits down at the table directly across Netta.

"Listen to me, Netta. Do not talk about your aunt Annie or about Lilly around Ms. Helen. Something happened many years ago, and Ms. Helen made us swear never to talk about it or speak their names. Your granny and aunt were good people. I often visited Lilly and Boe on the farm. Lilly would read for me. She had a great gift. Something happened long ago, and we cannot bring it forward—not here, not now, not ever," Carmen says stressfully.

"What happened? I promise I will never tell," Netta begs.

"No! We have said too much. Just know that Ms. Helen has accepted you here. She just chooses to pretend that some things never happened. Ms. Helen is good to us and Martha ... well, she loves your cousin Martha, and that's all that matters. If she says don't speak of the past then we don't talk about it. Besides, it is not our place to tell you anyway. Now let's talk about something else," Collin demands.

Standing in the shadows of the basement door stands Sissy. "You are always running your mouth, old lady. One of these days, you are going to get into trouble," Sissy says in anger.

"You need to watch your mouth yourself. That is my wife you are talking to," Collin threatens. Carmen never says a word in her own defense. Carmen simply turns to Netta and says, "Netta, tomorrow Mary, Betsy, Robert, BoHeim, and we are all going to the harvest carnival. Won't that be nice?" Carmen says, looking at Sissy.

"I have never been to a carnival!" Netta says with a childlike excitement. Sissy looks at everyone and leaves the room in a hurry. Carmen and Collin look at each other and laugh. Carmen makes a comment to Collin. "That girl is on thin ice around here. I will tell you later."

Netta is so excited; she hums while she cuts the greens. Netta finishes the greens.

"Carmen, I am going to Martha's house, I have to write a letter," Netta says, placing the pan of cut greens near the stove.

"Okay, baby, you do that," Carmen responds.

"Bye now," Netta says, running out of the door and down the stairs.

Netta tries over and over again to start the letter to Lucille, but she is unable to write anything. Instead, Netta starts a letter to her aunt Dean. The words flow. She writes everything about the reason she ran away. As she reveals her reason, it is as if a big rock is lifted off her. She writes of her new friends. Netta tells Dean she is washing for Ms. Helen. She lets Dean know Ms. Helen and Martha are treating her very well. She writes about Carmen and Collin. She is very careful not to tell too much about the parties and the people who come to Ms. Helen's house.

In closing, Netta places a ten-dollar bill from the canvas bag under her bed in the letter. She ends the letter by writing

> *Take five dollars and give Mama five dollars. Tell her what I wrote. I love her and Anna Belle and Walter. I miss them very much. I want to come home. I love you. Say hello to Uncle Paul and the twins.*
>
> *Love you,*

Netta seals the letter and puts it by her bed so she will not forget it.

Netta prepares her wardrobe for her trip into town tomorrow. Martha has given her a pair of trousers. She has never had a pair of trousers before, only the old overalls she wore on the farm. Netta places a sweater and the trousers on the chair.

Netta can see Sissy hanging sheets out of her bedroom window. She wonders why Sissy is so mad at her. She has tried hard to be her friend. For the first time in Netta's life, she makes up her mind not to care if Sissy likes her or not. All through school, she wondered why the other students did not like her. This time, it doesn't matter if Sissy likes her or dislikes her. Everybody else does. Netta let's Sissy sees her in the window and then she closes the blinds.

Netta washes up for the evening. She turns on music and reads a magazine.

Chapter 24

Time passes. Martha returns with bags from shopping. Netta is lying on the bed, reading with her door open. Netta gets up to greet Martha.

"Look what I have for you," Martha says.

"Oh, thank you so much! These are the nicest shoes I have ever had." Netta says, hugging Martha.

"Try them on. Let's see if they fit," Martha says. "Lace them all the way," she adds.

"Now when you go out tomorrow, you will look like the other city girls. They dress a little differently here. That's a good fit," Martha says, feeling proud like a parent.

"Can I go and show Carmen?" Netta asks.

"In a little while, you need to help me change. I have to host a party tonight. You can eat and show Carmen your shoes, but you must come back here. You will stay inside even if people are out in the garden. Do you understand? Now run me a hot tub of water for a bath. By the way, did you write to your mother?" Martha says, unpacking the shopping bags.

"Yes, ma'am," Netta replies.

While Martha is bathing, Netta goes to the main house to get dinner and show off her new shoes. Carmen is now dressed in a black dress with a white apron. So is Sissy. Collin has on a black suit vest and a white shirt.

"Look at my new shoes Martha bought me," Netta says.

"They are really fine, Netta. I have prepared your plate. We are really busy. Ms. Helen has special guest tonight we have to serve." Carmen says, handing Netta a plate of food.

"I know. Martha told me I have to eat and go back to the cottage right away," Netta answers.

Everyone is in a rush. Loretta comes into the kitchen to get Sissy to help her.

She is dressed in a sheer sky blue dress.

"Sissy, I need you for a minute," Loretta says. They both leave the kitchen. As Netta is eating, she can hear music start to play. She wants so badly to go into the outer room just to see what all the fuss is about.

"Netta, eat up," Carmen demands. Netta finishes her dinner and leaves out of the kitchen door. She meets Martha halfway down the path. Martha is so pretty. She has on a black lace top with a sheer black skirt. Her face is painted with makeup; she looks like she has stepped out of a magazine. She smells like summer flowers.

"Go to the house and stay there. Good night," Martha says in passing.

Netta returns to her room. She is so excited about tomorrow. Hours later Netta can hear voices from the garden. Her curiosity gets the best of her. She goes to the window in the front of the house.

From the window, she can make out only the silhouettes of a man and a woman. They are seated on a bench in the garden. Netta sees the man kissing and caressing the woman. He opens her top to kiss her breasts.

Netta has never seen passion before. She looks on. The act of making love is something she had never imagined, but it leaves her with a hundred questions. Netta watches as the woman leans over the cement bench. She places the palms of her hands flat on the bench. The man stands behind her, lifts up her dress, and kisses her buttocks. He undoes his trousers. The steam of their bodies can be seen rising with the in-and-out movements they make. The noise they make is a cross between pain and laughter. She watches the couple until they both fall weak. Netta knows she cannot ask Martha about what she has seen. If she does, Martha will know she has disobeyed, so she will have to figure this out for herself.

The next morning, Netta is up early. She gets dressed. She notices that Martha is not up. She knocks on the door.

"Martha, it is me, Netta," she calls through the door. A faint voice says, "Don't come in, I am still in bed."

Netta replies, "I am going to the main house to go with Carmen." From Martha's room, she can hear Martha say, "Okay, be safe."

Netta runs up to the kitchen. Carmen is preparing a basket of food. Collin is having coffee. Sissy is nowhere in sight.

"Morning, Netta, I thought I was going to have to get Collin to wake you," Carmen says.

"No, I have been up for a long time," Netta says, eating toast.

Soon Carmen, Netta, and Collin are packing the car for their day of fun. The ride this morning is longer than usual. There is a heavy fog in from the bay. Netta remarks, "It looks like we are driving in the clouds."

Collin has other thoughts about the drive. The fog only makes driving the steep hill much more dangerous. As they drive farther down the hill, the fog dissipates, and the city starts to come into view. Each time Netta comes down the hill, she sees something new. This time, Collin has to drive past the harbor. Netta has never seen a ship. The boats are as big as buildings to her.

"This is where Robert and BoHeim work sometimes, unloading ships from the many ports around the world," Carmen says. Netta is looking at all the people—some in uniform, and some in strange clothes she has never seen before. A mile or two down the docks past the boats are diners and fish shops on the waterfront preparing for the day.

Soon they are driving across a bridge. Netta moves from side to side to see the height of the bridge. She giggles at the butterflies she feels in her stomach. "Look at all the water down there," Netta remarks.

The scenery changes from water to land, buildings, and shops. Soon they come upon a neighborhood. A street vendor is calling his wears, "I get apples, corn, fresh greens, okra, and onions. I get pots, I get pans …" His voice fades farther down the street they drive. After few more turns, Collin stops in front of a quaint little house surrounded by a picket fence. The house has a porch with screens and a screen door. The smell of fried bacon fills the air.

Carmen leaves the car; Netta exits close behind her. They go up the stairs through the screen door to another wooden door. Carmen knocks on the door and calls "Mary Washington" at the same time.

Betsy opens the door. From the background, an unseen Mary yells, "Come on in!" Betsy grabs Netta by the hand and greets Carmen at the same time.

"Come to my room, Netta." Betsy leads Netta down a long hallway to a room that catches the sunlight early this morning. Netta stops at the door. Betsy's room is so light and colorful. The soft white and pink blends into a bay window filled with dolls. Next to the bay window stands a dollhouse. The window is surrounded with white ruffles with pink ties. Her bed has four posts almost touching the ceiling, a white bedspread with a pink ruffle sham, and pillows. A sewing machine sits on the opposite side of the room in front of another window, flanked by a small chair and dresser.

"Come on in, Netta," Betsy says, holding on to a post on her bed.

"Your room is so pretty, Betsy," Netta expresses.

"I like what you have on, Netta. You look nice," Betsy says. This makes Netta feel really good. She feels as though she can really fit in.

"Thank you," Netta says with pride.

"I sew. Do you want to see something I made?" Betsy says, walking toward her closet. Betsy brings out a skirt and a matching blouse. Then she goes over to the dresser drawer and pulls out a matching doll's dress. "I will make you something if you want," Betsy adds.

Mary comes into the room.

"You girls need to come to the kitchen and help."

"Yes, ma'am," they both answer. Betsy places the clothes back in the closet.

She guides Netta back down the hallway to the kitchen.

"Go to your daddy's workshop and get a box, Betsy," Mary says.

"Come with me, Netta." Betsy invites her. Out of the back door and down the stairs is a small garden with a garage type building at the end. Opening the door, they can smell the freshly cut wood. It is a woodworking shop. Before she realizes Netta says, "Walter would love this."

"Who is Walter?" Betsy asks.

"Walter is my father back home," Netta answers.

"Oh, I thought it was your boyfriend or something like that. Because, you know, my brother thinks you are pretty." Betsy reaches under the worktable for the box. Netta stands there, frozen in time. Her whole being blushes to think that someone would call her pretty.

"Okay, let's go. We are going to have a good time at the beach today," Betsy says, closing the workshop door.

"We are going to the beach?" Netta says, smiling.

"Yeah, the city has this big festival there every year. The church people pick a spot on the beach to bring food and fellowship. The children go over and ride on the Ferris wheel and play games at the carnival. A lot of people will be there from everywhere," Betsy says. "Here, Mama, is this big enough?" Betsy asks, handing her mother the box.

"It will do just fine," Mary answers. "Netta, you look nice today. How is your cousin?" Mary asks.

"Thank you, she is doing fine," Netta responds.

"We had better get going. Sister Combs and the others have been out there since sunrise to get a good area to set up in," Mary directs.

"Where is Robert and BoHeim?" Collin asks.

"They left before morning to unload a ship at the harbor. They will join us later," Mary answers.

The car is loaded to the point where it is uncomfortable.

"It is a good thing we do not have far to go," Collin says, closing the trunk of the car. In less than a mile, the white sands start to show. Netta can see what Katy had told her about many times before. In the distance is a large round thing turning around. "I can see the Ferris wheel!" Betsy shouts.

"Turn here, there is the flag Sister Combs put up to find the church group," Mary says. Netta can hear music in the wind. She smells the ocean. So many people are walking, playing, and running—all are happy.

The car stops. "Everybody, out. Everybody, grab something," Carmen says, opening the door. On a large sand dune are several tables with food and pitchers of drinks, under a large canopy. People are waving to them. Some of them walk out to help carry items. Netta stops and stands, looking out over the beach. The white of the sand that covers the ground like a white sheet covers a bed.

"Netta, did you hear me?" Betsy calls.

"No, I am sorry. What did you say?" Netta says.

"Do you want to walk to the Ferris wheel or eat first?" Betsy asks.

"We can go by ourselves?" Netta asks.

"Sure, we can find our way back. It is just over there," Betsy says. Netta feels a sense of freedom and self-responsibility.

"Let's go to the Ferris wheel," Netta says, jumping up and down.

"Mama, we are going to the carnival!" Betsy yells.

"Be back soon and be careful," Mary answers.

The girls run and skip into the noisy crowd. The calls of the sideshows pull in the suckers who would come and play their games.

"Do you have any money?" Betsy asks Netta. Netta pulls three dollars from her pocket. "Let's play a game," Betsy says.

"Okay, over there," Netta directs. *Five rings for a quarter,* the sign says.

Netta hands the man a dollar, "five for me and five for her," Netta adds.

Netta rings the first stick. She and Betsy jump up and down in surprise and delight.

"Pick out a bear," the man says. Netta, jumping and clapping her hands, says, "Oh, the pretty blue over there, yes, that one."

The girls walk on in wonder.

"Look, Netta, cotton candy. Let's get one!" Betsy says.

"It melts on my tongue," Netta says.

"Come on, let's get our ticket to ride," Betsy says, getting in line at the ticket booth.

Standing in line, Netta looks around at all the people. She tries to act as though she has lived there all her life.

Soon it is their turn to ride the Ferris wheel. The happy, unsettled feeling in her stomach starts, as she steps up to the platform to take her seat on the Ferris wheel. Netta clutches the small teddy bear tightly.

"You don't have to be afraid Netta. It is going to be fun, you will see," Betsy says laughingly. Netta holds Betsy's hand and closes her eyes. Her body moves with the jerking motions of the swing. Netta can feel the movement.

"Open your eyes, Netta. Look, look," Betsy says. Slowly Netta opens her eyes. She is so overwhelmed by the view. Everybody looks so small. The wind is blowing across her face. All her fears turned into amazement. The ocean is so big. It looks like everybody in the world is at their feet. They can see the church group. The smoke is rising from the campfire; small children are playing around. Going down, the crowd of people reshapes itself both in colors and in form. Three times in a row they ride, each time seeing something different.

They are standing in the crowd after the Ferris wheel rides, trying to decide what to do next when a hand from the crowd comes from behind and blindfolds Betsy. She turns to see. "Boy, you better not do that again!" Betsy shouts. It is BoHeim and his friend Elmo.

"Mama, says you need to come back now to eat," BoHeim says to Betsy. "Hi, Netta," BoHeim says with a huge smile on his face.

"Hello," she responds.

"This my friend, Elmo," BoHeim adds.

"Hello, Netta. BoHeim was right," Elmo says to Netta.

"Right about what?" Netta asks.

"BoHeim says you are good-looking," Elmo says. Netta grins and looks away to smile.

"What have you all been doing all this time? Who gave you the teddy bear?" BoHeim asks.

"Netta won the bear all by herself. We had cotton candy, and we have been riding the Ferris wheel. Now!" Betsy says with sarcasm.

"Come, Netta, let's ride one more time before we go." Betsy says to show off to her brother and Elmo.

"Okay," Netta replies.

"We are going to ride too," BoHeim says, touching Elmo on his elbow.

"Come on, Betsy, ride with me," Elmo says, pulling her by the hand. Betsy protests. Elmo leans over and whispers something in her ear, and Betsy gives up the fight. Betsy says, "Okay, give me the quarter." Netta silently laughs to herself.

Standing in line this time is a different type of nervousness. This time, Netta acts like a veteran at riding the Ferris wheel. The compartment of the Ferris wheel is much smaller this time. BoHeim is forced to put his arm around Netta.

"You scared?" BoHeim asks.

"No," Netta responds shyly.

The ride starts. Netta squeezes the blue bear.

"How do you like it here?" he asks.

"It's real pretty here." Netta answers.

"How long are you going to stay?"

"Until my mother sends my ticket to come back home."

"I hope it takes a long time for her to send it," BoHeim says. "I guess we will see a lot of each other. Next week, my daddy and I will start digging the spot for Ms. Helen's gazebo," BoHeim says. The ride is over faster this time.

"Come on, Netta, let's go!" Betsy says, waiting on the ground for Netta. The girls wave goodbye and walk toward the entrance of the carnival.

"My brother and Elmo think they are so smart," Betsy says.

Returning to the campsite seems so boring compared to the fun and adventures that they have just had.

"Betsy, Netta, get yourself some real food. You have been gone for hours," Carmen says.

"Carmen, look at the bear I won." Netta says, pushing the bear forward.

Mary and Carmen start to clean up their area as Netta and Betsy finish eating.

"Mama, do we have to go? It is a little dark. The fireworks will start at dark," Betsy asks.

Carmen and Collin are worried about fog on the road.

"No, we had better be on our way," Collin says. They have decided to leave early. As they drive away, Mary says, "You can see the fireworks from the house." Collin helps the family with unloading their truck. Everyone says their goodbyes.

On the ride home, the day becomes night. Netta thanks Carmen and Collin for the best day of her life. Netta sits back in her seat and hugs the blue bear, reliving her day and feeling freer and more of the age she claims to be.

Today Netta realizes she is a thinker and a leader. She feels powerful in her own world. She feels she can make her own way in life. *If Mama sends for me, I will go home. If she doesn't send for me, then she doesn't love me. It does not matter anymore. I can have a day like this one any day I want if I am here*, she thinks. Netta dozes off to sleep all the way home.

It is late when they reach home. "Thank God the fog did not come," Carmen says, shaking Netta on the knee. Netta shakes her head and wipes the sleep from her eyes. Everyone is fatigued. Netta goes to Martha's cottage to wash and goes to bed. Netta places the small bear on her bed next to her pillow. She kneels to say her prayers, thanking God for a wonderful day.

Chapter 25

Next morning, Martha knocks on the door for Netta. "Carmen asked if you like to go to church this morning?" she says. In spite of how sleepy Netta is, she springs up to get ready for church.

"Please tell her yes!" Netta yells through the door.

Netta comes speeding through the room.

"Did you have a good time yesterday?" Martha asks.

"I had the best time of my life," Netta says as she moves briskly through the room toward the door.

"I won't be here when you come back here, so stay close to the house," Martha instructs.

Netta says "okay" and walks out of the door.

In the kitchen, Carmen, Collin, and Sissy are having breakfast.

"Good morning," Netta says as she enters the kitchen.

"Morning, Netta," Carmen and Collin say. Sissy never speaks. With that statement, Carmen starts to clear the used plates from the table. Carmen starts humming church songs; Netta joins in. Sissy is becoming upset. She feels Netta has formed a kinship with Carmen. Collin leaves the table to go to the garage.

"Sissy, you still have time to come with us," Carmen says.

"No, I am going into town with Ms. Loretta," Sissy says.

The weather is cold with the wind rushing off the bay. Soon the drive to church is over. Carmen leads Netta and Collin to her favorite pew. Halfway down the aisle, Betsy beckons for Netta to sit with her. Netta enters the pew next to Betsy. Netta slides in the pew past Betsy. As the singing begins, BoHeim and Elmo join Netta and Betsy. Netta blushes, standing next to BoHeim. During church, they manage to touch hands several times.

Fellowship after church helps bring Netta closer to BoHeim. This time, she saves a place for him. Betsy teases the two at the table, but on the other hand, she is glad her brother is interested in someone she likes, can do things with, and likes the same things she does. Netta manages to eat fast so she and Betsy can go out front of the church before the adults come out from the fellowship hall. BoHeim and Elmo follow close behind. BoHeim slowly manages to separate Netta form Betsy. His conversation is mostly flattering things about Netta.

Soon the churchyard is becoming crowded with more people. Netta knows Carmen and Collin will be coming soon. Netta is smiling and enjoying talking with BoHeim. He is so easy for her to relate to.

"There you are. I was looking for you," Carmen says. Netta says goodbye to BoHeim and Betsy and walks to the car. On the ride home, Netta feels a newfound self-esteem at the way others see her in their eyes.

A few days later, Netta's letter reaches home. Paul comes into the house with the mail in hand. He kisses Dean on the lips just before he is stampeded by the twins and Anna Belle.

"Here is a letter for you," Paul says. Dean places the letter in her apron pocket, assuming it is from Martha. She continues to prepare a plate of food for Paul.

Paul sits at the table, listening to the twins tell him of their adventures of the day.

"You kids go back in the room so your daddy can eat in peace," Dean instructs. Dean sits down across the table from Paul.

"How was your day?" Dean asks. Paul nods okay.

Dean takes the letter from her pocket; when she unfolds the letter, ten dollars falls onto the table. Paul stops chewing in mid-bite.

"From whom is that?" Paul says. Dean looks through the pages for the signature.

"Netta!" she replies. "Let me see what she has to say." Dean slowly reads every line with attention.

"Well, what does it say?" Paul asks with concern.

"She is fine. She wants me to talk to Lucille about her coming home. She is washing sheets for Ms. Helen. She wants me to give her Mama five dollars and keep five dollars for myself," Dean explains.

A short time later Lucille comes into the house from work.

"How is everybody?" Lucille says, greeting Paul and Dean. Lucille sits down at the table. "Where is my baby? Anna Belle!" she calls.

"Anna Belle is taking a bath with the girls. Paul will dry them. She will be here in a minute," Dean says. As Paul leaves the room, in the background you can hear Anna Belle answer to Lucille's call. "Mama, Mama!" she yells.

Dean gives Lucille the letter and five dollars.

"What is this?" Lucille asks.

"Read the letter," Dean answers. Lucille reads the letter quickly. She hangs on every word, sometimes stopping to reread a line. She picks up the five dollars and looks at it. Dean is waiting for her to say something or to show a reaction. At that very minute Anna Belle comes in, she runs and jumps into Lucille's arms. "Mama, Mama," Anna Belle says, hugging Lucille.

Dean is still waiting for Lucille to say something about the letter. Lucille gathers up the five dollars and Anna Belle, and as she walks out of the door, she says "good night" to Dean and the girls.

Paul enters the kitchen. "What did she say?" he asks.

"Nothing," Dean replies, looking out of the window.

When Lucille opens the door to her house, she can hear Walter working in his workshop. Anna Belle runs to her room. Lucille goes to her bedroom. In her hand is the five dollars, she looks at it. Sadness fills her heart. She feels Netta should have written to her. *Netta should have sent the letter to me*, she thinks.

Her sadness turns to anger, somehow Lucille feels betrayed. She feels the first letter from Netta should have come to her, not to Dean.

It is early in the morning, Netta is sitting in the kitchen when she first sees Mr. Washington come into the garden with digging tools in a wheelbarrow.

"There is Mr. Washington," Netta says to Carmen. Carmen looks out of the window.

"So it is, he will start digging today," Carmen replies.

"He is by himself," Netta notice.

"Go see if he wants some coffee before he starts," Carmen says.

Netta eagerly walks to the center of the garden.

"Good morning, Mr. Washington." Netta says.

"Morning, Netta," he replies.

"Carmen wants to know if you want some coffee or something before you start digging," Netta says.

"No, tell her thank you. BoHeim will be bringing my thermos when he comes in a while. I had coffee before I left home. Tell her thanks anyway," Mr. Washington answers as he pulls a pick from the wheelbarrow.

Netta walks back to the house. She gives Carmen the message, and then she goes to the basement. In the basement, Sissy is placing dirty sheets in the basket.

"Good morning," Netta says. Sissy answers with "Um, morning."

For the next few hours, Netta washes sheets. When she emerges from the basement, the sun is high. Her thoughts are focused on hanging the sheets and going to her room to write. Netta never notices BoHeim, who has entered the garden. As Netta walks toward the clothesline, a whistle catches her ear. She turns in the direction of the sound. There she sees BoHeim coming toward her, smiling.

"Hi, Netta," BoHeim says, coming toward her smile.

"Hi yourself," Netta answers.

"Betsy told me to tell you to call her." He reaches into his overalls to give her a piece of paper from his pocket. As Netta reaches for the paper, she can hear Mr. Washington yell, "BoHeim, come on. I need your help!" BoHeim smiles and waves as he runs off to help his father.

Netta finishes hanging the sheets. She goes upstairs to the kitchen. When she comes into the kitchen, Carmen is talking on the telephone to Mrs. Washington, telling her how Mr. Washington is digging and the progress he and BoHeim are making in building the gazebo for Ms. Helen.

"Carmen, will you let me talk with Betsy, please, before you let the call go? BoHeim says she wants to talk with me," Netta interrupts. Carmen acknowledges her request and continues the talk with Mrs. Washington. Netta starts to prepare the lunch she occasionally looks out the window into the garden.

The telephone conversations soon drift to Netta and Betsy. Carmen hands the phone to Netta.

"Hi, Netta," the small, eager voice calls from the inside of the wire that connects them. "Can you come over on Thursday for Thanksgiving?" Betsy asks.

"I guess so!" Netta responds.

"Okay, BoHeim and I will pick you up," Betsy says.

"That's okay, I can ride with Carmen and Collin," Netta replies.

"They are not coming this time," Betsy answers.

Netta has never left the estate alone. She has accepted the invitation before she knows she will be leaving the estate by herself. She turns toward Carmen who is sitting at the small table.

"Carmen, you are not going to Mrs. Washington for Thanksgiving?" Netta questions.

"No, Ms. Helen is having guests, and she wants a full dinner this year," Carmen answers. Netta knows she cannot turn down the invitation now that she has accepted the offer. She will not turn back now. She and Betsy carry on a short conversation and disconnect.

Once Netta is sitting across the table from Carmen, she continues to talk to Netta about Thanksgiving.

"Collin and I will stay here this time. You go on. Mary Washington is a good cook. She always cooks duck for Thanksgiving," Carmen says. The next few days move fast for Netta.

On this Thursday morning, Netta is excited and frightened at the same time.

"How do I look?" Netta asks Martha.

"You look just fine," Martha responds.

As Netta walks toward the door, Martha reinforces the rules. "Netta, remember what I say about what goes on here. Do not talk about Ms. Helen, you understand?" she says. Netta nods okay. In her mind, she thinks, *Doesn't everyone know what goes on here at Ms. Helen's?* She walks out of the cottage door. By the time she reaches the front of the main house, there are BoHeim and Betsy.

"I am sorry I am late," Netta responds to them.

"We just get here!" Betsy says. Netta climbs into the small cab. She is sitting next to the door. BoHeim leans forward, looking past Betsy's shoulder to say, "Hello, Netta." Netta gives a baby-like wave of her hand with a smile, never speaking a word.

The ride is filled with Betsy's chatter and occasionally a glance between Netta and BoHeim. Soon the ride is over. Netta can smell the sweet smell of Thanksgiving dinner as she and Betsy approach the front door.

"Good morning, Mrs. Washington and Mr. Washington. Thank you for inviting me here for Thanksgiving. Carmen told me to tell you she wishes she was here," Netta says, greeting the couple.

"We are glad to have you, Netta," Mrs. Washington responds.

"Come on, Netta, let's go to my room," Betsy says as she grabs Netta by the wrist. As they walk down the hall you can hear Mary say, "You have get to help in the kitchen, young lady, so come when I call for you."

"Yes, Mama," Betsy answers as she enters her room with Netta in tow. Betsy walks to her closet. "Look what I made for you, Netta. I hope it fits," Betsy says as she holds a skirt in front of herself. "I hope you like it. I made one for myself but in a different color," Betsy adds.

"Betsy, I need your help," Mary calls from the kitchen. Both Netta and Betsy go to the kitchen.

"I want to help too," Netta says. "I always help my Mama and aunt Dean to cook on Thanksgiving," Netta explains.

"Oh, you don't say, sure you can," Mary responds. "You must really miss them at this time of the year?"

"Yes, ma'am, but I write home all the time," Netta says with a hint of sadness.

"Netta, do you have any brothers and sisters back home?" Mr. Washington asks as he walks toward the back door. Netta's first reaction is to say "no," but suddenly Anna Belle's face appears in her mind's eye.

"I have a little sister. She is three years old," Netta answers in a fading voice. "Bet you miss her." He steps outside the door. Netta would not answer; she became entranced, placing herself inside Dean's kitchen.

At that very moment Dean, Lucille, and the family were finishing saying Thanksgiving blessings. Dean ended the prayer by saying, "God, please bless and keep Netta well. Amen."

Netta stands for a short time looking out of the door until her thoughts are interrupted by Mary Washington's voice.

"Okay, let's get the duck out of the oven. Yes, she looks good enough to eat." Mary picks up the pan with the duck in it and inhales the fumes that steam from the perfectly roasted duck.

"You ladies can start to set the table. Get the good dishes out of the china cabinet. Then I need you, Betsy, to go out to your father's workshop and get the small bench," Mary orders. The girls prepare the table in record time.

"Come with me, Netta, to get the bench. We can sit on it together," Betsy says.

In the workshop, they find that BoHeim and Elmo occupy the small bench.

"Get up, Mama wants me to bring that bench into the house," Betsy says with a demand in her voice. "Get up, or I will tell Mama, you and Elmo are smoking!" Betsy says with determination.

"Do you see me smoking?" BoHeim responds, upset.

"No, but Elmo is and you do everything he does," Betsy answers in haste. "You want to have a smoke?" Elmo ask.

"No, I don't smoke," Betsy answers.

"I am not talking to you. I am talking to Netta," Elmo answers.

"No, thanks," Netta replies.

"You don't have to be afraid," Elmo says.

"I am not afraid. I do not like the way I feel when I smoke. I have smoked cigarettes before. I did not like them then, and I know I will not like them now," Netta answers with authority.

"Now she told you," Betsy says sticking her tongue out through her lips and laughing.

"Okay, okay, Betsy. That is enough. Tell Mama, we will bring the bench in. It will be just a minute." BoHeim is speaking as the mediator. As Betsy and Netta turn to walk out of the door, BoHeim calls to Netta.

"Netta, wait a minute. I want to tell you something." Both girls stop. "Betsy, go in the house and tell Mama what I say about the bench," BoHeim orders. BoHeim gives the bench to Elmo and then gives him a sign to take the bench into the house. Elmo slowly pushes Betsy out of the workshop door with the bench in hand, saying to Betsy, "Come on, Betsy, let's leave them alone." Betsy reluctantly moves. She leaves the workshop, protesting all the way to the back door.

"What do you have to tell me, BoHeim?" Netta asks. BoHeim's tongue is all tied up. He is trying to say, "You look pretty today."

"Thank you," she replies. They look at each other, and time seems to stand still.

"Netta!" It is Betsy calling from the back stairs. "Mama says come eat." Netta yells to answer, but her words are cancelled by a kiss on the lips. She stands there in surprise. She places her fingers to her lips as though she is sealing the kiss and holding it forever. No one says a word. She smiles and turns her face toward the door as she slowly walks out of the workshop. Netta keeps her eyes down; she feels shame and excitement at the same time. One thing she knows is that she likes being kissed by BoHeim.

BoHeim scats himself next to Netta on the small bench. During dinner, he holds her hand every time she rests it on her leg. Netta never pulls away or resists.

The conversation around the table was joyful. A lady, whom Netta has seen before at church, asks Netta about Carmen.

"I guess Carmen is at Ms. Helen's, cooking, huh, Netta?" he asks.

"Yes, ma'am. She started cooking last night," Netta answers in a small voice.

Netta is hoping that the question will stop there.

"What do you do up there, Netta?" the woman continues.

"I just wash for Ms. Helen. That's all," Netta responds.

"How do you like living in that big house?" the woman asks.

"I live in one of the cottages with my cousin," Netta explains. Netta can hear Martha's voice ringing in her ears. *Remember, do not tell anyone about what goes on at Ms. Helen's.* Netta tries hard to change the subject.

"Mrs. Washington, Carmen says you are a good cook, and she is right."

"Wait until you taste the pies," Betsy says, licking her lips.

"Speaking of pies, let me go and get the sweet potato pies."

"I will help you, Mama." Betsy volunteers.

"Me too," Netta says, seeing a way out of being questioned anymore by the strange but familiar lady.

Betsy and Netta stands in the doorway of the kitchen. Mary hands two sweet potato pies to Betsy then she hands Netta two pecan pies. Mary slowly pushes Netta with a large cake in her hands. Netta stands still, holding the pies until Mary turns to remove them from her hand. As she takes the pies from Netta, she is handing Netta serving dishes from the dining table. Netta glances over at BoHeim. He winks at her; she blushes. Netta retakes her seat next to BoHeim. He grabs her hand as she sits down.

Soon the men retire to the backyard and the workshop. The woman are cleaning and placing dishes back in their original places. Netta and Betsy return to Betsy's room. Betsy makes several trips to get extra pieces of pie. Soon she is complaining of a stomachache. By the time Netta wants to go home, Betsy is lying on the bed with a cool towel across her forehead. Netta tells Betsy that she is ready to leave, but Betsy just moans, holds her stomach, and turns over.

Netta goes to the front of the house where Mary and her company are located. "Mrs. Washington, I have enjoyed my day with you and your family. Thank you so much for a wonderful dinner and for having me for Thanksgiving," Netta says.

"You are more than welcome any time you want to come here. Betsy, BoHeim!" Mary calls.

"Betsy is in her room on her bed. She is not feeling well," Netta explains. By the time she is finishing her explanation about Betsy's stomachache, BoHeim appears in the doorway.

"Oh, there you are. Netta is ready to go home, and your sister has eaten herself sick with pie, so you will have to take Netta home alone," Mary explains. BoHeim can hardly restrain himself about the changes in the passengers.

This time when Netta gets into the truck, BoHeim rushes to open the door for her. Their eyes meet, but no words are said; only smiles are exchanged. Netta waves goodbye to everyone as the two drive away. A short way down the road, BoHeim reaches out his arm and pulls Netta near to him on the seat. She does not resist; she presses down on the leather seat and glides over as close as possible to BoHeim. BoHeim secures her by anchoring his hand on her arm. Netta is fiddling with her fingers, looking down as she does when she is blushing.

At the bottom of the large hill leading to Ms. Helen's house, BoHeim decides to detour and to show Netta a hidden cove where he and his friend Elmo come sometimes to swim. Netta feels completely safe with him leading her to an unknown place she has never seen. Once the two reach the large rock, Netta pulls back on BoHeim's hands, not because she is afraid but because she is cold from the breeze coming off the water. He looks to see why she stops so suddenly. He sees her fold her arms around her body. Without saying a word, he understands her body language.

BoHeim turns to Netta. In a continuing motion, he embraces her in his arms. This time, the kiss is one of passion, firmly on the mouth. He stops to see if she will pull away, but she does not. Netta places her hands on his face, this time she pulls him to her. With the water crashing against the rocks, Netta feels what a woman can feel when she is young and falling in love.

"Can we go back to your truck? I am cold," Netta says in a voice she hardly knows. It is like a panting whisper spoken out loud. Hand in hand, the two run to the truck. They share one more kiss, and they drive on.

BoHeim takes a really long look at Netta in the full moonlight, reflecting from the sky and ocean. He never says a word. He starts the truck and drives. Netta places her arm on BoHeim's arm; she rides with a smile.

"Did you have a good time today?" BoHeim asks.

"Yes, your family is so nice, and everybody is so happy," she replies.

"Netta, can I come to see you?" BoHeim asks. Netta hesitates.

"No, I don't think that that would be a good thing."

"Why, don't you like me?"

"Yes, I like you, I like you very much. I have thought about you from the first day I saw you, but this is not my house, and I cannot say yes or no about inviting you to keep company with me. I will have to get the okay from Martha," she says.

As they enter the large gate, they can see several cars are parked along the side path. It is clear that Ms. Helen is still entertaining guests. There are a woman and a man embracing on the front porch.

"Stop here, I can go through here to get to Martha's house," Netta says, pointing to a path off to the side. BoHeim pulls alongside a black car that is parked along the side of the walkway.

Netta exits the truck and starts to walk. BoHeim calls to her to come to the driver's side window. He leans his head and one hand out of the window and pulls Netta's face to his lips. Netta smiles. She stands for a minute, watching BoHeim as he drives away.

Netta turns with a smile, thinking about all the events that have taken place this Thanksgiving Day.

Chapter 26

On the sidewalk that leads to the path that will take her to Martha's cottage, Netta sees Sissy emerging from one of the cars parked along the side of the walkway. She is adjusting her dress. A man who has exited the car behind her appears to be in a chauffeur's uniform. Sissy never looks up as he counts out dollar bills for his pleasure. A driver from another car whistles at Netta. This caught Sissy's attention. Sissy is shocked to see Netta. It angers her. She thinks Netta has seen more that Sissy cares for. Sissy turns to prevent Netta from passing. Netta pushes past Sissy and the man. Sissy grabs her by the wrist.

Netta is surprised; she pulls away. Sissy moves close to Netta's face.

"You had better not tell. If you do, even your cousin cannot save you." Netta knows this can happen one day. Sissy was always on the edge of an altercation. It's all about Sissy being jealous about Netta, who is no threat to Sissy.

But this was not the time or the place for Sissy to try and take away Netta's joy, nor to threaten her family. Someone had done that once, but this time, Netta knows how to protect herself and the ones she love. This time, she will not allow anyone to gain control over her fear.

Netta raises her face and rolls her eyes; her fists is posed in a curve.

"You cannot tell me what to do. If I want to tell Ms. Helen about what you do out here, you cannot stop me," Netta replies. Without saying a word, Sissy slaps Netta across the face, causing Netta to stumble backward and fall.

Sissy jumps on top of Netta. The drivers gather around. Netta manages to gain advantage and rolls Sissy over to gain the upper position in the fight. Netta grabs Sissy by the hair and starts to pound and pound Sissy's head against the cold ground.

Netta stands over Sissy. She grabs a nearby branch. "Don't get up. If you do, I will hit you with this stick," Netta says, breathing fast. Sissy stays poised on her elbows.

"You think you are something. You are nothing, and your cousin ain't nothing. Just because she has Ms. Helen's blood don't mean anything. Ms. Helen still treats Martha like her house girl. By the way, did you sleep with BoHeim yet? Because I did."

Netta's heart breaks. Without thinking, Netta swings the stick, striking Sissy in the temple. Sissy grabs her head. She bleeds; she looks at the blood on her hand.

Netta drops the branch. She sees the crowd of drivers, and she turns and runs away. As she passes the window, she can hear the music. It seems so foreign to her with the feeling of heartache, anger, and confusion after a fight not of her making.

Netta runs into the cottage. Martha is not home. *Good*, she thinks. Netta sits on the side of the bed. All the emotion spills out. As she sees the blue bear, she cries out. She yells out loud until she is out of breath. She falls backward onto her bed. Netta composes herself. She quickly washes and tends to her wounds. She changes her clothes and prays to give her strength and to remove the pain from her heart. As Netta crawls into bed, she puzzles about the things Sissy says about Martha and Ms. Helen.

Netta recalls a conversation she had with Carmen months ago about Carmen knowing Martha's mother.

Netta is fatigued. Soon she is asleep, but her sleep is uneasy and full of dreams. Netta dreams of walking to a train. Halfway there, her aunt Dean suddenly appears with open arms. Dean's lips are moving, but Netta cannot hear her words. Instead of Netta hearing Dean, she hears BoHeim's voice saying, "Look for me. I will be there."

In the dream, Netta turns her eyes away from Dean. In the distance, she can see BoHeim running toward her. He is only running, but he is not moving. Netta turns back to look at Dean, but Dean is no longer there. The train is buzzing like a loud mill saw. Netta walks onto the train. She sits in the middle of the car. She is looking out of the window when it starts to bleed red with blood.

At the same time, Dean and Lucille are experiencing similar disturbing dreams.

Dean dreams that she finds herself at a train station, waiting for a train. She is dressed all in black with black lace over her face. She hears a loud buzzing noise. It starts to rain. Soon the water turns into blood raining down, but she is dry.

Lucille dreams of Netta when she was a young girl, playing in an open field. Netta is running toward a white fence where Walter is standing in a hazy fog. Lucille yells for Netta, "You need to come now to help me!" Netta runs to Lucille with open arms. Netta asks, "Mama, where is Anna Belle?" Lucille slowly reaches behind her and hands Netta her doll named Anna Belle. Netta squeezes the baby doll and grabs hold of Lucille's hand. Lucille turns to call for Walter to join them, but by now, Walter is on the other side of the white fence. Lucille can hear the loud buzzing noise of a black thing coming toward Walter. She stands looking. As she starts to cry, the tears turn to blood.

"Wake up! Wake up!" Walter is shaking Lucille, "You are crying in your sleep." Lucille is still in a dream state. She opens her eyes to see Walter. She is so relieved. She snuggles under him and returns to sleep.

Since it was near five in the morning, Walter decides to get up from bed to make coffee. He wishes he had today off too, but he only gets Thanksgiving Day off. Today is Friday. One day will not matter; it will be work as usual at the lumber mill.

Walter prepares his lunch of leftovers from Thanksgiving Day. He drinks the coffee that he has made in the pan on the stove. He goes to make the fire higher in the fireplace so Lucille and Anna Belle will be warm when they get out of bed this morning. After Walter is finished with all his preparation of lunch and making the house comfortable, he goes to his bedroom; he kisses Lucille on the forehead and says, "Goodbye, honey."

In Lucille's trance-state of hearing, these words fade into her dream. Lucille can hear Walter saying, "Goodbye, honey" as he steps into a black car that sounds like a loud saw. She yells back, "Love you! Be careful."

Lucille wakes herself as she hears the thump of the back door closing. She stumbles to the kitchen just in time to see Walter as he drives away.

Lucille turns and folds her arms to think about the dream that will not stop.

Last week, she had the same strange dream.

Walter reaches the lumber mill early. He goes over to the fire barrel and starts the fire. Before the fire is blazing high, Mr. Gordon and Adley are coming toward him.

Mr. Gordon tells the two men to come along to his office. He explains the customer's order. He shows the two men the diagram and the angle measurements for the cuts of wood.

"Because of the slant in the cut, we will have to physically move the standing saw and rotate the blade. The safety guard needs to be manned in order to prevent it from shifting," he informs them.

By this time, there are several men standing around the barrel fire. The three men leave the small office to join them. Mr. Gordon goes to the fire barrel where the men are standing to brief them on the task at hand. Walter and Adley go to the standing saw. As the two men start to dismantle the safety guard, Adley makes a small talk with Walter about the crisp cold of the morning and asks if he brought any extra pieces of the sweet potato pie Lucille made for Thanksgiving.

"Yeah, I think she ate too much of her pie. Lucille tossed and turned in her sleep all night long," he replies.

The pie is chilled as Dean takes it out of the ice box to be at room temperature when Paul comes home for lunch. She looks out of the window to see Lucille and Anna Belle coming down the walk.

"Morning," Dean says, standing in the door that she has pulled open.

"I don't know. I did not sleep well last night. I had the strangest dream that continued on and on," Lucille says as she enters the kitchen.

"I had a rough night myself," Dean replies, feeling emotionally in touch with her sister.

"Want some coffee?" Dean continues.

"Please, I have plenty of work to do at home. Can Anna Belle play with the twins? That is all she talked about this morning—coming to see the twins," Lucille answers in a weary voice.

"Anna Belle just doesn't realize that you are off work today. Once she sees you here early in the day, it will get her attention," Dean explains. Dean and Lucille talk for a few minutes before Lucille decides to walk to the door. When Lucille opens the door of Dean's house, Lucille feels a surge of urgency race through her body. She tells Dean, "I just had a chill go through my body."

Dean steps out onto her back porch; she feels the same sensation. Within seconds, the car horns, the emergency whistle signals, and the alarm bells sound.

Lucille runs back into Dean's house and grabs Anna Belle. Dean can feel the urgency but cannot explain it. Dean calls for the twins to come with her. Lucille is reacting strangely.

When Lucille reaches the gate, she goes in the opposite direction away from her house. She is running toward the store where Paul is. Paul is talking with a small crowd of people who have heard the alarms. Lucille runs directly to Paul, begging him to take her to the lumber mill. Paul is puzzled, trying to understand what Lucille is saying. He sees Dean and the twins, "Tell me what Lucille is talking about. She wants me to take her to the lumber mill."

While everyone is standing in the doorway of the small store, a car pulls up and tells the crowd there has been an accident at the sawmill. Dean looks as the tears roll down her sister's face and fall onto Anna Belle's red sweater. This brings the vision of her dream to the surface.

Dean tells Paul, "You must take her, take her now. It's Walter!" Paul tries to ease the women's minds by saying, "It could be anything. What makes you think something has happened to Walter?"

Paul looks into his wife's eyes. Without saying a word he starts to untie the meat apron and walk toward his truck at the same time. Lucille gets in the truck with Anna Belle. Dean pulls Anna Belle out of Lucille's arms.

"Leave Anna Belle with me!" Dean says. The two drive off in a hurry. Dean and the children walk back into the small store with tears and sadness in their hearts.

By the time Paul and Lucille reach the lumber mill, the doctor and other townspeople are there. Lucille jumps from the truck before Paul comes to a complete stop. Adley, who is covered in blood, sees Lucille running down the hill and runs to stop her. She is fighting to get past Adley. Soon Paul is there, helping to restrain her at Adley's request.

"Help me to keep her back. It's Walter. He is hurt, hurt bad! She doesn't need to see," he says, panting for breath.

Lucille falls to her knees and screams out "Walter, Walter!" in hopes that he can hear her and take comfort in knowing she is there. Adley looks at Paul, moving his head from side to side in a slow pitying motion. Paul closes his eyes to fight back the tears. For what seems like hours, they stand still in that one spot, waiting for a word from the men that are crowded around Walter.

Paul notices the large blade lodged in the wall across the saw safety stand. He knows he cannot ask Adley to explain now, but something has gone very wrong.

Mr. Gordon comes to Lucille.

"Come with me, please come with me?" he requests in a soft voice. Lucille cannot move. She falls backward, fainting. When she becomes conscious, the doctor is waving smelling salts under her nose.

"Where is Walter? Where is he?" Lucille demands. Mr. Gordon takes both of Lucille's hands in his. "Walter is gone."

Lucille lets out the wail of a wounded animal. She tries to run out of the room to go to where Walter is lying. All four men are wrestling with her to hold her back. In the struggle, the doctor says, "Hold her arm!" He takes a hypodermic from his bag to inject her.

Lucille is pulling and yelling, "No, don't! I need to see Walter!" Soon her cry fades as the medicine takes control. They lay her on the old leather couch Mr. Gordon has in his office.

Paul beckons to Adley to go outside with him. On their way down the hill to the body, Adley shakes his head in disbelief at what his eyes have witnessed this day.

"What happened?" Paul begs. Adley takes a deep breath as he starts to tell Paul how the accident came to happen.

"We had just finished adjusting the blade. Everything looked safe and secure. I was on the other side of the saw. I remember Walter bending down. He had his back to me. Someone turned the saw on. It starts to shake as the speed increased. Then the blade bounced off, moving forward into Walter, cutting through his arm and face. He stood up when he heard the buzzing, started to say something, raised his arm. The blade was moving so fast, it only stopped when it hit the wall. It all happened so fast. When I reached the other side of the saw, I could see his arm was lying away from his body. There was so much blood. Paul, I know why he was bending over. He was picking up the safety pin that holds the safety guard in place." With saying that, Adley starts to weep like a baby. Paul fines it hard to fight back the tears also.

Paul and Adley walk to where Walter's body is covered with a canvas soaked in blood. Several of the workers are loading Walter's body into the back of a truck with his arm lying wrapped up across his chest. Paul can go no further.

"I am going back to see how Lucille is doing." Adley hears him say, but he cannot speak as he watches the truck with his friend pass by.

Lucille is sleeping. Mr. Gordon helps Paul put her in the truck. In and out of sleep, she calls for Walter all the way home. Paul has tears streaming down his face, thinking of his friend, his brother who waved at him just hours ago as he drove past. Paul stops in front of the gate of his house. He looks at Lucille with her head slumped down in a drugged state, haunted with pain. He goes around to the passenger's side. He puts Lucille's arms around his neck, and he manages to get her to the back stairs.

"Dean, Dean, come help!" Dean opens the door. The light from the kitchen shines upon Paul and Lucille. Dean is crying. She knows already, without anyone saying, that Walter is dead. She walks down the stairs to help her sister. No one says a word. Only the sound of sniffing as the tears are running. They take Lucille to their bedroom, remove her shoes, and lay her down. Dean climbs into bed with her sister, holding her like a small child. Lucille opens her eyes. She tries to speak, but the only word that is clear is "Walter." They cry. Paul gathers the children, who are standing in the doorway. They walk into the kitchen where Paul starts looking for the whiskey.

"What's wrong with Mama and Auntie Cille?" the twins are asking.

"Your aunt Cille is sick," this is the only explanation Paul can give as he pours himself a glass of whiskey.

Chapter 27

The next morning, Netta is up at dawn. She is tired. She found it hard to sleep and sat up most of the night. Her thoughts are on the fight with Sissy and the horrible dreams she has been having—they terrify her.

Netta sits on the side of bed, awaiting daylight. She decides to get dressed earlier than unusual. As she gets dressed, Netta can hear rain falling onto the roof of the house. *This is good*, she thinks. She knows she will only be able to wash a small number of sheets today because one can only hang a few sheets in the basement.

As Netta runs past the half-built gazebo, her heart fills with emotion. In that instant, she pulls herself into a protective combative mode.

Sissy need not mess with me this morning, she thinks.

As Netta opens the kitchen door, she is relieved to see only Carmen and Collin in the kitchen.

"Good morning, Netta, Ms. Helen wants to talk with you in the upstairs parlor," Carmen says as Netta enters the door.

"Good morning, yes, ma'am," Netta replies, trying to hide the surprise in her face.

Netta slowly walks up the back stairs and down the long hallway to the double doors. The doors open into a large sitting room. At first she can only see Ms. Helen standing by the fireplace. As she walks past the large chair, she sees Sissy sitting there. Netta wonders what lies Sissy has told Ms. Helen about last night.

"Carmen says you want to talk with me," Netta says softly.

"Yes, please sit down." Ms. Helen points and directs her to a chair. At first Ms. Helen paces slowly with her finger on her chin.

"Tell me what happened last night near the cars," she says, stopping behind her desk. Nobody answers. She says the same words again. Still no one answers.

"Tell me what the hell happened out there last night!" she said, shouting and banging her hand on the desk. Netta tries to speak out of fear, but Sissy answers first.

"Netta hit me from behind," Sissy says rapidly.

"That's a lie!" Netta reacts with anger. Ms. Helen raises her hand for silence. "I already know the truth," she says, looking at Sissy. She walks from behind the desk, moving closer toward them. She stops in front of Sissy.

"How can you sit here and lie to me after I have been good to you? You tried to take money from me and disrespect my house. We are not prostitutes on the street. We don't lie with men in the back of cars. You have been heading for the door for months. How dare you charge men on my property? Who in the hell do you think you are? Money come through my hands first. I am the only madam here. Now pack up and get out of my house. I can't trust the likes of you!" Ms. Helen scolds.

Sissy tries to plead her case, but it is useless. Netta sits in shock and in fear, not knowing what fate Ms. Helen has in store for her. Once Sissy leaves the room crying, Netta's eyes follow Ms. Helen around the room. Her body is paralyzed. The room goes silent. Ms. Helen returns to her desk and sits in her chair. She exhales loudly.

"I know what happened last night from my guest. Why didn't you tell Martha or me? You never have to be afraid to tell me anything, especially about around here. I am not angry with you. I had my suspicions about Sissy and the drivers for some time now. I just can never catch her in the act. Did she hurt you?" Ms. Helen asks.

"No, ma'am, I just have a few scratches. They will heal. Thank you," Netta answers.

"I had to send Martha into town to keep her from hurting Sissy over you. I cannot let that happen. It would only bring trouble to the house. It's funny, she tries to protect you, and I protect her," Ms. Helen says as she pours whiskey into the coffee that is cooling on her desk.

"You know, you and I have never really talked. You always go away when I come into the room. Are you afraid of me? If you are, don't be. You are just like family," Ms. Helen continues as she sips her whiskey-laced coffee. Every time the coffee cup gets low, she fills it with more whiskey.

"Yes, you look a lot like Annie. I noticed that when I saw you for the first time. It is almost haunting," she says, taking another drink. Netta is surprised she would say that. Only her family ever compares her to Annie. Annie was Martha's mother, who died before Netta was born.

"I knew your grandmother too," she continues. "She was really something to deal with," Ms. Helen tells Netta.

The more she drinks, the more she talks. Soon she is sitting in the chair next to Netta.

"You are strong like your granny, aren't you? What is your story? Why did you run away from home?" Ms. Helen asks. She takes another drink. Her movements become unbalanced as she walks to pour more whiskey into her cup. Ms. Helen becomes fixated on the rain falling against the window. Slowly she speaks, "The last time I saw your grandmother was the worst day of my life." She starts to tell Netta what happened that day.

"Lilly came to the house that day. She came because she wanted Annie to move off the grounds to move back home with her. I wish she had listened. I wish we had all listened that day. Annie and Martha lived in a house a few yards from the main house. She was my cook. Really she ran the whole house."

"Annie came to work for us when she was fifteen years old. Soon she was living in the guesthouse on the grounds. That was the same year my son was sent off to boarding school in England. He was twelve. When he came back home to stay, he was twenty years old."

"My beautiful baby boy, my husband always says I was treating him like a boy and not like a man." Ms. Helen's voice begins to crack and break as she speaks. She picks up a long cigarette holder and lights a match on the top of the cigarette box. She continues to speak as the smoke flows from her lips.

"I should have known all the signs are there. My son and his father always argued about things, but they fought and killed themselves over Annie." Her words echo in Netta's ears.

Ms. Helen walks to the large fireplace. She gazes into the fire in a trance.

Netta waits to be excused. Ms. Helen slowly starts to speak again.

"When Annie became pregnant she would never tell me who the father was. Once Martha was born, I knows the answer, she looked like my own child. After that, I stopped asking. Robert Jr. flirted with other girls. I had hopes he would marry among our social circle."

"By the time Martha was five, Robert and Robert Jr. were enemies, passing each other like strangers in the house. I should have made my baby leave, but I had missed all of his childhood when he went to boarding school. I hated my husband for sending him away, but women were not free to express herself about a man's decisions."

"On that Sunday, your grandmother came to talk to Annie about a dream she had had, but Annie would not listen. Your grandmother leaves with Carmen and Martha to go to church. On that Sunday, Robert was drinking heavily even before the noon races. After the races, Robert and Robert Jr. had words. I was hiding in my bedroom as usual until the shouting stopped. This day was the exception. When I heard the first gunshot, I looked out of the window toward the sky to see if it was thunder. When the second and third gunshots sounded, I felt my heart shatter."

"I heard Collin call for me to come to the barn. He could not explain. He had tears in his eyes, and his shirt was covered with blood."

"We ran to the barn. There in the hay and dirt were my husband, my son, and Annie—all of them—dead. The fighting was about her, you see. My husband had had Annie by lust, and my son had had Annie for love. According to Collin, the fight was about who was Martha's father. It is still the biggest question in my life—is she my stepdaughter, or is she my granddaughter? Because of this, we are bonded for life."

"We moved Annie's body and told the sheriff my husband and son were shot by horse thieves. Collin went to your great-grandmother's house and told them about the horse thieves, but they know it was all a lie. Don't ask me how they knew, but Lilly told me Robert had killed them."

"Now, one thing else. Martha was only a young girl at the time. She only knows her mother died not how she died. I gave your great-grandmother land, supplies, and money. The same lands that Lilly and Boe farmed. Do you know why I told you this?" Ms. Helen asks.

"No, ma'am," Netta answers.

"I will tell you why. Because I know you know the hearts pain. As young as you are, you have a secret too. So I hope you will keep my secret also."

"You know, with all my pain, I fell in love. I love Martha. She is all the bloodline I have in life, and this is all that matters to me. Please don't hurt her with the details," Ms. Helen says as she walks to the door and opens it. Netta never speaks. She walks out of the doors as they close behind her.

Netta silently walks toward the stairs that lead down into the kitchen. She quietly slips down the basement stairs without Carmen ever turning around to see her.

As Netta looks out of the small basement window, she sees the vision of Ms. Helen's intoxicated story in the raindrops. As she hears the thunder, she makes up her mind to keep the secret about Martha.

The day moves into night. Netta keeps to herself. She doesn't care to face Carmen or Collin. She knows if Ms. Helen knows about the fight between her and Sissy, so do they.

As Netta enters the cottage, she is glad the house is empty. She goes to her room and closes the door. The next morning, Martha knocks on Netta's door.

"Morning, can I come in?" Martha asks.

"Yes," Netta says, wiping sleep from her eyes.

"Are you okay? I looked in on you last night, but you were asleep. I am sorry about the mess with Sissy. I know I have not been around much, but I will start staying around more, okay? I will let you get dressed now," Martha says as she walks toward the door. Netta falls backward and exhales. It is like seeing Martha in a different way.

As Netta leaves the cottage, she notices the sky is overcast with the possibility of rain.

Another inside day of drying, she thinks.

Netta sees Carmen standing on the kitchen steps. She senses Carmen is waiting for her. Netta waves as she moves closer. As she gets closer, she sees a strange look on Carmen's face. Carmen holds out both hands in a reaching motion.

"Come inside, baby," Carmen says, putting her arm around Netta shoulders.

"What's the matter?" Netta's asks.

"Just come with me," Carmen pleads.

As they walk through the pantry, she can hear someone crying. As they come out of the pantry door, Netta sees Ms. Helen consoling Martha.

"What's wrong?" Netta asks anxiously. Martha looks up with tears streaming down her face. Martha slowly gets up; she places her hands on Netta's shoulders and says, "It's Walter, he is dead." Martha collapses into the chair, holding the telegram in her hands.

Netta is frozen in time, not understanding, not believing. Then it hits her conscious mind; Netta falls to her knees, screaming in pain.

Their cries echo throughout the house, waking the others. Ms. Helen and Carmen also began to cry to see Netta and Martha so hurt. Ms. Helen goes to the liquor cabinet and pours two shots of whiskey. She gives one to Martha and one to Netta.

"Here drink this," She begs. Martha downs the whiskey, but Netta gags at the taste. Soon the warm whiskey seems to calm her.

Netta stands up. She walks back through the pantry, through the kitchen, and out the door. Netta walks along the side of Martha's cottage, focusing out to where the ocean meets the sky, thinking how parallel the two are but they never touch. Netta says one word, "Mama."

Martha tries hard to compose herself.

Ms. Helen asks her, "When do you two want to leave for the funeral?" She reaches into the cleavage between her breasts and takes out folded money. She hands the money to Martha with these orders, "Buy a two-way ticket for yourself and a one-way ticket for Netta." Martha never speaks. She takes the money and leaves with Collin to purchase the tickets as she was instructed.

When Martha returns, she finds Netta sitting in the dark. As she turns on the light, she tells Netta, "We are leaving on the morning train."

The morning comes quickly. Netta has spent most of the night awake, thinking about Lucille and Anna Belle, and what they must be going through. Ms. Helen and Carmen are watching as Collin places the suitcases in the car.

Carmen gives Netta a big hug and hands Martha a box stuffed with sandwiches and fried chicken for their trip home.

As they drive away, Netta looks out of the back window. The large house seems to shrink the farther away they go. Down the hill, the ocean gleams like glass in the early morning hours. The ride into town is marked by silence.

The train station is like a small city in itself with the whistles, horns, and bells that create a sense of movement. Collin stands on the platform, waving to them, as the train slowly pulls away.

As the train moves down the tracks, the city disappears from view. The rhythm of the train against the tracks makes a soothing, tranquilizing sound for Netta to sleep. During the three-day journey, Netta spends most of her time looking out at the changing landscape.

When the train pulls into the station of their hometown, Netta is surprised that the small town has not changed, but she knows she has. There on the small platform is Paul waiting for them.

Paul can hardly recognize Netta. She has blossomed into a young woman.

They ride down the old streets, bringing back memories of a time gone by.

Soon they pull up in front of Paul's house. It still looks the same. Netta looks down the walk to see if the lights are on in Lucille's house; it is dark and lifeless. Paul notices Netta looking toward Lucille's house.

"Lucille has been staying with us ever since it happened," Paul explains.

Netta runs to the kitchen door. Dean grabs her and embraces her tightly. Netta cries, holding tightly to Dean. The twins and Anna Belle run and hug Netta. It is truly a circle of love. Dean instructs the children to return to the table to finish eating.

"Come with me, Netta," Dean says, leading Netta down the hallway to a bedroom. Dean opens the door to the bedroom. Inside it is dark. Dean pulls the curtains back to bring in the sunlight. In the light, Netta sees Lucille. She looks ill; her eyes are swollen.

"Cille, look who's here," Dean says.

Slowly Lucille turns over her sight blurred eyes. She blinks to adjust.

"Netta, Netta, Walter's dead," Lucille mourns. Netta sits on the bed to hold her mother. Lucille is sobbing from the heart.

Dean walks out of the room and closes the door behind her. She greets Martha with hugs. Martha can hear Lucille crying from down the hallway. Martha and Dean goes to the front of the house.

"Lucille has not been herself since Walter died. She is grieving so hard, it will destroy her. She will not eat. Paul and I had to make the arrangements for Walter's funeral. Lucille keeps asking, 'Is he home yet?' I brought her over here to stay with us. I was afraid she might hurt herself or Anna Belle. The doctor gave her something, but now all she does is sleep and stay in bed," Dean explains.

By lunchtime, Netta emerges from Lucille's room. The house is quiet; everyone is gone. She goes to the kitchen. Looking out of the window, she sees the children in Lucille's yard. Netta walks out of the door and down the walk to the house she once calls home. Dean and Martha are cleaning the house to bring Lucille home. Now that Netta is home with Martha, everybody will need more space to sleep. They are also cleaning because the funeral is tomorrow, and there will be many people visiting the house.

"Aunt Dean, I am here. Let me help," Netta says, entering the house. Dean is washing dishes. Martha is sitting at the table, drinking coffee.

"Netta, you have turned out to be a beautiful young lady. You look so grown-up," Dean compliments her.

"What happened to Walter, Aunt Dean?" Netta asks. Dean stops washing dishes. She picks up two cups and pours coffee into them, and the three women sit and go through the story of what happened to Walter that fateful day. Dean concludes her story by saying, "Lucille left mentally that same day. I am afraid she will die of grief."

The women finish cleaning and make ready for the wake for Walter this night. That evening, Netta and Dean dress Lucille and sit her in a chair until everyone is ready to leave. Soon the family is ready in a chaotic kind of way.

At the funeral home, Lucille sits in the front row, rocking and swaying, with some occasional moans. She never speaks. No one can tell if she is staring at Walter in his coffin or if she is really there at all.

The next day, Lucille is twice as lost at the funeral until they loaded the coffin. She yells with such pain that most of the guests start to cry.

In the days that follow, Netta can see that Lucille is like a child. She has become a shell of her former self.

By the time Martha is ready to leave, Netta knows that she has only one place to be and that place is here with Lucille and Anna Belle. She thinks how funny, *sometimes life can drive you away, but death will always bring you home*. Living the experience of the past few months in Ms. Helen's house has prepared and educated her for what she must now face.

It will be months before Lucille can function. Within those months, Netta converts Walter's workshop into a fully operating laundry. She is making money and taking care of her mother and sister.

Now that the winter has gone and the sunshine's bright, Netta takes great pride in her cleaning and hanging of the laundry, especially the white sheets.

THE END